Kasmira Mira Marie

Jesse P. Ward

authorHOUSE®

AuthorHouse™
1663 Liberty Drive
Bloomington, IN 47403
www.authorhouse.com
Phone: 1 (800) 839-8640

Published by AuthorHouse   06/13/2018

ISBN: 978-1-5462-4678-7 (sc)
ISBN: 978-1-5462-4677-0 (hc)
ISBN: 978-1-5462-4676-3 (e)

Library of Congress Control Number: 2018906975

Print information available on the last page.

Prologue

Magic is sometimes real, and sometimes what is real is magic

"Well he lasted longer than most. When we get to Aquas Negras we will replace him." The tall dark-skinned sailor took his keys and unlocked the chain which bound the half dead man to his oar. "Grab his arms, and let's get him to the deck."

When the two sailors got the oarsman to the deck, they laid him out and the shorter one said, "You know he is not dead. It won't take long to get to Aquas Negras. We can leave him there and find a replacement."

As the two men pondered what to do, the captain of the trading vessel came up and looked down at the dying man. "He is an evil man and throwing him to the sea is too good for him, but that is what we are going to do. If your conscience bothers you, think of it this way. We are only about a half mile off the coast of Kaspar. We are giving him a chance for life." The taller sailor laughed. "Some chance."

As the half-dead man hit the water, he was shocked into consciousness. Looking up, he could see three men standing on the deck as the ship moved away. He did not have the strength to move, but by instinct his legs began to tread, and he was able to keep his head above water. *Maybe I should let myself drown. I don't have any right to live.* He could remember one of the men saying he was an evil man and the sea was too good for him. *I won't have to worry about it long. The sea is going to make the choice for me.* It seemed like a lifetime, but the sea did make the choice for him. The tide carried him to Kaspar and washed him ashore. Lying on the sand, he did not have the strength to move. With each wave pushing him further up the beach, he thought of his sister and began to cry.

Further up the beach, two men were walking toward the dying man. When they spotted him, they ran and pulled him to dry sand. He was in rags and had deep infected scars around his left ankle. "He has been chained to an oar," one of the men said.

"That means nothing," the other said. "Many poor men have been shanghaied and die this way. There is a healer at Anemoi. Let's take him there."

Giving him water and making a stretcher that they could drag behind a horse, they started the trip to Anemoi.

Hana was standing near the large oasis when a young boy came up and told her she was needed. She quickly returned to the village to see two of the men she knew mounted on their horses with a man dressed in rags lying on a stretcher behind one of the horses. "Your healing skills are needed," one of the men said.

"Yes, bring him inside the tent. How was he injured?"

"We don't know. We found him this way on the beach. We really didn't think he would make it here."

Once the man was inside, Hana told the others to leave and let her work. He was about thirty years old. His shaggy hair was cold black, and he had dark discolored skin. With her head on his chest she listened to his heart. It was weak and unless she used her magic she felt he was going to die.

She reached deep down inside herself and placed her hands on his chest to let the magic flow from her to him. Nothing happened. She tried again and again, but still nothing happened. Looking at him she could see the discolored skin on his chest was glowing. *This man has magic, and someone has placed a powerful spell on him to prevent him from using his magic or anyone else from removing the spell. This is powerful magic. I have never seen magic this strong.*

"I don't know your name, but if you are going to get better, you are going to have to do it without the help of my magic." Hana went to her chest and got two bottles of medicine. One contained medicine to increase his appetite and the other medicine was to give him strength. After she was sure he had swallowed the medicine she gave him a couple of sips of goat's milk. "I guess the next twenty-four hours should tell us your fate."

Leaving her tent, Hana walked to the center of the village and talked to the village leader. "I have done all that I can do. Send two men to my tent to take him down by the oasis. What he needs now is fresh air and water. I will stop by every two hours and give him medicine and food. Food must be administered a little at a time. If he lives for twenty-four to forty-eight hours he may have a chance."

Later that day, Hana stopped by and gave medicine and food until it was late into the night. The next morning when she stopped to check on her patient, he had been set up by a man staying with him. "He is doing somewhat better. Are you going to be here a while? I need a break."

Hana looked at the stranger sitting in front of her. "Yes, take as long as you need. I will stay until you return." Hana noticed that the man staying with him had cleaned him up and put clean clothing on him. "Well, you look much better this morning. I have brought you some dried fish mixed with coconut milk. It will not taste very good, but it will give you some strength." As she gave him the medicine and fed him a spoonful, he looked at her and said, "This is very good."

She smiled. "How could dried fish mixed up in coconut milk taste good?"

He said nothing but thought to himself. *When you have had nothing but rice and sometimes slop made from the crew's left-overs anything would taste good.* While she talked to him as she fed him, he said nothing else. In fact, he said nothing as two weeks passed. He was getting stronger and was feeding himself but could not walk. Two weeks later he was walking with the aid of a crutch.

One morning when Hana got up, she decided to go visit her strange patient. As she walked out of her tent he was standing there on his crutch.

At first, she was scared, then she thought. *I have my power, and he does not have his. I am in no danger.* "Please sit," she said. "Do you want to talk to me?"

"I do." His voice was dry, and it barely came out. He cleared his throat. "I do." He sat down in a chair she had placed outside her tent.

She looked at him. He was now clean shaven, and his hair had been cut.

She pulled a second chair from the tent and sat down opposite him. "My name is Hana. What is your name?"

"My name is Piper. You should have not saved me. You should have let me die."

At first Hana said nothing. Looking into his dark eyes she said, "Why should I have let you die?"

"Because I am an evil man. I was on a ship chained to an oar. I was there to be punished. I have done evil things. Please believe me. I don't want to get better. I want to die. I want you to help me do this."

Hana leaned back in her chair. "Perhaps you have done evil things, and maybe you do deserve to die, but I am not going to help you do that. I don't think in your state of mind you are ready to make that decision. I will help you get well and then you can leave this place and do what you want with your life. You are not going to make a killer out of me. I save lives; I do not take them."

Piper did not say anything. He got up out of his chair and limped back to his camp on the bank of the oasis.

As the days passed, Hana would see Piper twice a day, and as he got better she started coming to see him only once a day but staying longer. Often, they would talk, and he never mentioned wanting to kill himself again. One afternoon she stopped by his camp and found him standing waist deep in the water. Smiling, she said, "What are you doing?"

Turning to face her, he answered, "This makes my leg feel much better. I think in a couple days I might be able to leave."

After coming out of the water, he sat on the ground and leaned against a tree. Hana could see he had gained some weight and was rather good looking. "Where will you go?"

"I think I might go home. I have not been home for many years."

"How long were you on that ship?"

"Two years, four months, and twenty-three days."

"You know exactly?"

"When you are on a ship chained to an oar, you don't have anything to do but count the days. Sometimes you wish for death. You always hope for wind, so the sails can give you rest. I know that you don't have to see me anymore because I am getting better, but I hope you don't stop coming to see me and hope you will welcome me if I come by to see you."

Hana didn't know why, but she agreed, and the two of them started seeing each other every day and having long conversations.

The days turned into months, and Piper could tell that he was falling in love with Hana, and he knew that she cared about him too. He would have to tell her who he was and what he had done. He had to wait until the right time, knowing that the truth would end their relationship.

One afternoon they were eating on the bank of the oasis. "You told me you were not from Kaspar, but you have never told me where you are from."

"I am from an island off the coast of Greece."

"How is it that you speak Arabic?"

"I speak several languages. Languages come easy for me. I also speak Spanish, Latin, Greek, and English."

Hana took a drink of her wine. "Have you been to Kaspar before?"

"I have been here many times, and I know the country well." Piper reached over and picked up the bottle of wine and refilled his glass. "Have you traveled much?"

Hana looked down and said in a very low voice. "I have never been very far from this village. Tell me about Kaspar."

"Well, let me see. It is a large country with a very diverse population. While the country is mostly Arabic, there are also many people of Spanish and Greek origin here. The country is divided by the Viper River and a large mountain range. Most of the people live to the west of the mountains because to the east is a large desert. There are two large cities. The city of Kaspar is the largest, but at the upper end of the Viper River where the river splits into East and West Viper is the city of Lilly. Kaspar is a trading city and is often at war. North of Kaspar is the island of Tranquillo. Before the wars, Kaspar was the main trading port, but now Tranquillo is, and this has caused some tension between the countries."

At first Hana said nothing. Looking down, she tried to find the words, but she just said it. "I know you are a witch and have magic, or at least you used to have magic."

Piper said nothing but just stared at Hana.

"Someone has cast a powerful spell on you and your magic is locked inside you. What happened to you?"

"Do you remember when I told you I wanted to die? It was not because I had lost my power. It was what I did while I had it. You are right. A witch more powerful than myself cast a spell on me and took my magic away. She is why I was on that ship. She either sold me or gave me to that ship."

"Why would she do such a thing? You both had power. Why would she take yours away?"

"Because I tried to kill her. She was not evil. She had much more power than I had. She was a student of the great wizard Epson. He was the greatest of all wizards. He had magic inside himself, but he could also pull magic from the earth. I think when he died he gave his magic to Para, and she is now the most powerful of them all." He stopped talking for a moment and looked deep into her eyes. "The only way you could know that I am a witch is if you are one yourself. You have been wise to hide your power and present yourself as a healer. I will not tell anyone, and when I leave your secret will remain safe."

"You are right. I am a witch, but I don't want you to leave. Who is this Para, and why did you try to kill her?"

"You said you did not want me to leave. You will when I tell you the rest of the story." Piper looked at Hana with tears in his eyes. "As I told you, I lived on an island in a small village. My parents were killed in a mountain landslide. I had a sister who was less than two years younger than me. We were close. She baked bread, and I forged iron. My sister's name was Nyla. One day while I was in a mine digging for iron, five men came to our village, killed our village leader, and took my sister. I had magic; my sister did not. Up to that time I used my magic very little. I was content and saw no reason for it. When I returned to the village and learned about my sister, I turned to my magic to find her. I did find her several miles from the village. She had been violated and murdered. I took her back to the village and after she was buried, I again turned to my magic to find the five men who did this. I was consumed with revenge. I found each man and killed him. It was more than just killing them because with each man's death I found pleasure, and with each death my magic grew stronger. I enjoyed killing them, and with each death, killing became easier. I never returned to my village. I turned my new-found talent into a business and became an assassin. I didn't care who I killed as long as I was paid. I don't know, I may have been willing to kill without being paid. I took a job to kill a queen. I poisoned her, but I did not know she was under the protection of the great wizard Epson. He saved her, and she had more power than myself. You know the rest of the story. I am glad she took my magic away. It has lifted a heavy burden from me. I can never be forgiven for what I have done."

Hana took Piper by the hand. "I think the man who existed before your sister's death has been restored. I will not judge you. You can make a life in this village. We need a man who can work with iron. Stay here. Please stay here."

During the next year, Piper forged iron for the village. He and Hana fell in love and were married. They had one daughter, who they named after Piper's sister.

The Storm

Kasmira could see the reflection of the sea as the light danced high upon her bedroom wall. *Am I asleep, or am I awake? I must be awake,* she thought to herself. The sun was coming up and she had seen the ghostly reflections dance on her wall many times. But something was different this time. She had the strange feeling that she was floating high above her bed. *I must not move. I must close my eyes.* She stayed very still, and in a few minutes, she opened her eyes. It was only a dream, and she felt relieved. She turned to the side of her bed, swung her feet to the floor and sat on the edge of her bed. *This is going to be a great day. Time to get dressed.*

Kaspar was on the sea, and the castle was surrounded by high walls with the west wall going down to the water. It was a very large castle which housed the royal family and several hundred others, who all lived inside the walls. Not far from the castle was a large market with many shops making up the center of the town.

Kasmira was the daughter of Davos. Living inside the walls of the castle, Davos and his family were in a position of importance. Kasmira, her mother, and her father lived just down the hall from the royal residence. Her mother, Ana, was from Valencia, and Davos was Greek. She had been educated with several children of the castle, which included Shakir and his twin sister Shakira. She was also educated by her mother and father. Davos, the royal physician, taught her Greek, and her mother taught her Spanish. The main language of Kaspar was Arabic.

Shakir was next in line to be the king of Kaspar. Shakir, Shakira, and Kasmira were all fifteen years old. They had grown very close and saw each other every day. Shakira and Kasmira stayed together every day, while Shakir would only spend the morning with them. In the afternoon, he received instructions in combat.

Today was a special day. Their education was over. The two girls were having lunch atop the west wall, looking out over the water. Kasmira was looking toward the west. "I have a feeling there is going to be a storm. Look how dark it is over the water." Shakira leaned over and gave Kasmira a hug. "It does look dark, but don't worry about the weather. Today is a great day. What are you going to do now that we are educated women?" Shakira said this with a smile.

"I am not sure. I can't be a physician like my father, because this is not allowed for a woman. I find it strange that a woman can't be a physician in the castle but can be a healer in the villages scattered throughout the land. I could use my skills in language and work at the docks, but I don't want to work outside the castle. I guess I will work with my mother in the library."

Shakira was smiling even more. "You know Shakir is in love with you. You two could get married and you would be a princess, and truly become my sister."

"I know he likes me, and I am very fond of him. Do you really think he is in love with me? Do you think fifteen is too young to get married?"

"Mother got married when she was only fourteen. You are an old lady."

"Just wait, he is going to talk to Father, and then your Father, and within a month we will have a royal wedding."

Kasmira scoffed. "I really don't think Shakir has marriage on his mind. All he wants to talk about is how good he is becoming with a sword."

The two girls stayed atop the west wall, talking and planning what they were going to do next. They had paid little attention to the weather until there was a flash of lightning nearby and drops of rain began to fall.

"I love this kind of weather. I love to hear rain falling. I am going back to my room and read and let the rain put me back to sleep." Kasmira said this as she grabbed up her things and ran from the falling rain.

Shakira had just gotten back to her room when she heard footsteps coming down the hall. She ran to the door. "That must be Barak. It is time for his daily meeting with Father. Sometimes I wonder who is running this kingdom, Barak or Father."

Barak was not from Kaspar. In fact, no one was sure where he was from. He had come to the kingdom about twenty years ago, he was married, and had a daughter. Her name was Jada. She was about the same age as Kasmira, but she was educated by her mother and tutors. Shakira and Kasmira saw very little of her.

Barak had started as a clerk on the docks, and within a short time was working inside the castle. Within five years he had moved up the ladder and was now the second most powerful man in the kingdom.

That morning before he left his room he had talked to his wife. "I am going to put my plan in motion today. There are rumors that young Shakir is going to ask for the hand of the physician's daughter in marriage. If things go according to plan, the entire family will be dead by the end of the week."

His wife with a weak smile on her face simply said, "Be careful." She knew that her husband had plans to gain even more power, but she did not want to see anybody killed. She was afraid of Barak and loved her daughter, so she said nothing and always went along with him.

During his meeting with Kadar, Davos came into the room carrying a pot of tea. Davos poured a cup of tea for the king and left the room. While he was not looking, Barak placed a small amount of powder that he had stored in his ring into the king's tea. After he was sure the king had drunk the tea he left and went about his daily routine.

During the day, the king did not get sick but did get extremely tired. He decided to go to his chambers and go to bed early.

That night as Kasmira lay in her bed, she had a funny feeling. She had to close the window because of the blowing rain. She was hot. She threw the cover back. A burning candle gave just enough light for her to see. She looked down at her feet and her body seemed to disappear. She had the feeling that she was floating above her bed. She looked to her right at the large mirror in her room and she could see she was not there. She became frightened, and she drifted back down to her bed. Then she saw her body reappear. She turned and sat on the edge of the bed. "What a nightmare!" she said out loud.

The next morning Kasmira and her mother were eating alone. As her mother started to clean the table, Kasmira said, "Mother, I had a strange dream last night. I dreamed I disappeared and was floating above my bed."

Her mother had her back to Kasmira, and a cold chill went through her body. For a moment, she said nothing. When she regained her composure, she said, "Everybody has strange dreams occasionally. Sometimes I have some that scare me too. It could have been the storm that caused you to have a bad dream. It did not let up during the night. I fear the city is going to have a lot of damage."

Both women finished cleaning up the kitchen table and left for the library. Kasmira stopped to see Shakira. Her mother went to see Davos. When she entered his room, he was sitting at a table mixing liquids together.

"What brings you here this morning? Did you stop at the library?"

"I need to talk to you. It happened last night. Kasmira told me she dreamed she disappeared and floated above her bed."

"Are you sure it was not just a dream?"

"Yes. She said she dreamed she disappeared and was floating above her bed. You and I both know this was not a dream. I think it is time we told her. She must know what is coming."

"You are right. We will talk to her tonight."

Just as he was about to tell his wife to go back to the library, a young servant came running into the room. "You must come quickly. The king is extremely ill."

When Davos went into the king's chambers, he looked at the king. He was sitting in a chair slumped over on his desk. He knew the king was already dead.

Barak came into the room. Looking at the king, he said, "Is he dead?"

"Yes, and I don't know what has killed him. He was healthy yesterday. We need to find out what he had to eat."

Barak told Davos to leave. He then posted a guard at the door. "Don't let anybody into this room. I am going to see Shakir and Shakira." Shakir and Shakira were in a room just off the library waiting for Kasmira. After he had told them of their father's death, Barak told Shakir to meet with him in the small chamber.

Shakir and Shakira were in shock. They did not know what to do. They hugged each other, and Shakira begin to cry. After a moment, Shakir stepped back from his sister and said, "We must be brave. Go to your room and wait for me. After I meet with Barak, I will come to you and we will make arrangements for Father."

When Barak and Shakir were together, Barak spoke first. "You are now the king, and much will be expected of you. You are young, but I will guide you."

At first Shakir said nothing. He walked over to the window, looked out, and then turned back to Barak. "I know my father trusted you, so I will give you my trust also."

Barak then started to put his plan in motion. "What I am about to tell you will be hard for you to accept. I know who killed your father. It was Davos. I saw him give him tea to drink yesterday. At first, I thought nothing of it. The tea is still on his table. We can test the tea and if it has poison in it, we will know that I am right."

"That does not make any sense. Why would Davos want to kill father?"

"If I am right, he thinks that you want to marry his daughter. If this is true, she would become the queen. Not a princess but a queen. This would put him in a very powerful position."

Shakir thought for a minute. "Have the tea tested. If it contains poison, arrest Davos and his wife."

Barak stepped in front of Shakir. "What about their daughter? We need to arrest her too."

"I don't want to arrest Kasmira. She is my friend. I know she would have nothing to do with this. Why would I arrest her?"

"You cannot show weakness; you must arrest the entire family. The people of Kaspar need a strong leader. If you show weakness, you could lose your kingdom."

Shakir again looked out the window. "I love Kasmira. I am sure she had nothing to do with this."

"Then let a trial decide this. The courts can decide. If they find her innocent, she can still live in the castle and you can continue to be friends. You will not have to bring charges against her. I will do that, and the court can decide the rest."

"Then make it so. Arrest the entire family if the tea has poison in it."

When the tea was tested, it did have poison in it. That night Kasmira and her mother and father were arrested and put in the dungeon. It was dark, and Kasmira was crying when the cell door was closed and locked.

The dungeon cell was dark and cold, and the only comfort was a pile of straw in one corner. The cell had a powerful odor of urine. Kasmira felt sick to her stomach. She controlled her tears and turned to her father. "Why have they done this?"

"They say I have poisoned the king. The witness against me is Barak. He told young Shakir that he saw me give the king tea and that tea was found to have poison in it. It is true that I did give the king tea. This is something I do every day. I fear that this is of Barak's making. For some reason, he wants the king dead and me out of the way. I don't know what his plans are. He is powerful, and if it comes to my word against his, I am afraid we are in trouble."

Kasmira and her mother huddled up together and cried most of the night. The next day they were taken to the court. Shakir and his sister were there. Several other state officials were also there including the twelve council members who would act as the jury.

Just before the beginning of the trial, Barak met with Shakir. "I have checked the law. If Davos is found guilty, he and his entire family are to be put to death."

Shakir had a shocked look on his face. "That can't be true. I have never heard of such a law."

Barak walked over and opened a large book. "Look here. You can see for yourself."

Shakir looked at the book. "Has this law ever been carried out? Maybe we should put this trial off for a few days. I'm not sure I can put an entire family to death."

"To my knowledge we have never had to use this law. It does however serve as a deterrent to protect the royal family. We can't delay the trial. Everyone is already assembled."

Barak looked at the three accused and turned to the twelve council members. "These are the men who will decide your fate. They will hear the evidence and pass judgment." He turned to Shakir. "If they find the accused guilty, it will be your job to invoke the sentence."

Shakir looked at Kasmira. She looked at him, dropped her head and looked at the floor. "Barak, you may present your evidence."

Barak addressed the court. "I saw Davos pour the king a cup of tea.

Later, when we checked the cup, we found poison in it. I don't know why, but for some reason Davos wanted our king dead."

One of the council members addressed Barak, "Could you speculate as to any motive Davos might have to want our king dead?"

"This is only speculation, but I think he wanted his daughter to be queen." He turned to Shakir. "Were you going to ask Kasmira to marry you?"

Shakir's voice was weak. "I was."

Barak turned and faced Davos. "Our king was a young man. Davos would have to wait years before his daughter could become queen."

A second court official addressed Barak. "Did you find the pot the cup of tea was poured from, and did you test it?"

"We did find the pot of tea, it was tested, and we found no poison."

A second council member asked, "If Davos poisoned the king, why did he leave the evidence in the room? Why didn't he just remove it?"

Barak looked at the council member. "I had the room sealed as soon as we discovered the king was dead. He had no time." Barak turned and faced the official and chose his words carefully. This was a question that Barak knew would be asked, and he was ready with an answer. "As I have already stated, we did test the pot and found no evidence that there was poison in the pot. I saw Davos pour the tea and he was the only one that could have put poison into the cup."

Barak then sat down. Davos was not allowed to address the court, but he could tell he was in trouble. He also knew that everything that was said could also apply to Barak.

The twelve members left the chambers and retired to make their decision. They were only gone for about an hour, but it seemed like forever to Kasmira. When they came back, Barak asked for their verdict and it was guilty. The vote had been six for guilty and five saying not guilty. One chose not to vote.

Shakir stood up. He looked over at Barak and knew he had to be strong. "Davos, Ana, Kasmira, you have been found guilty of killing my father." He paused. "You have been found guilty of killing our king. Davos, please step forward. You are to be executed in the morning at dawn. You will be hung."

Kasmira was crying. *How could this be? My father would not harm anyone.* "No, you are wrong. Please, don't do this!"

"Ana, please step forward. You have been found guilty of conspiring to kill my father and our king. You are to be taken back to the dungeon and remain there until you die."

"Kasmira, please step forward." Kasmira was crying so loudly she could barely hear what was being said. Shakir did not want to kill Kasmira or put her in prison. He knew she had nothing to do with his father's death. *I must save her life.* "You have been found guilty of conspiring to kill my father. You are to be taken back to the dungeon, and tomorrow you are to be banished from the kingdom."

Shakir turned to Barak. He could see that he thought all three should be executed. "See that all the sentences are carried out. Find a caravan that is going to cross the desert. Put Kasmira on it and make sure she understands she is never to come back to this kingdom."

Kasmira suddenly stopped crying and her sadness turned to anger. She looked at Shakir and to Barak. "You better hope I die and never come back because if I return I will find you and cut your hearts out."

Now it was Shakir's turn to be angry. He started to speak and tell Kasmira that he could have her executed for making that statement, but he could see the anger in her eyes. He had a feeling of fear, so he said nothing and let her be led from the room.

That night as the three fugitives sat in their cell, Davos said to his daughter, "There is something you need to know. You know I am going to die in the morning. Your mother is going to die in this prison. Your mother and I want you to know that we love you like a daughter, but you are not our daughter."

Kasmira was shocked.   "I thought this day could not get any worse. What do you mean?"

"Your mother was not from Kaspar. She lived west of here in the village of Anemoi. She had magic, powerful magic. Many people would call her a witch, but she was a good lady and used her magic to cure people. I don't know who your father was; she would never tell us."

Kasmira could not believe what she was hearing. "You and Mother are my parents. I don't believe this. This is all just a bad dream."

"For a time, your mother lived in this castle. Her name was Nyla. She too was taken to prison, and there was an attempt on her life while she was there. We think she knew that she was going to be killed and that is why she came to us to adopt you. No one knows that you are not our real daughter, and there is a reason we are telling you this now. Nyla said that someday you might have power, and there is evidence that you do. Your dreams are not dreams. They are signs that you are gaining magic power. We don't know if this is true or not, but you must be ready if it is. We will not be there to help you. Your mother said she would always be close by to help you, but we think she is dead. We don't know, but we have always suspected that Barak had her killed. We have no evidence." Davos reached out and held Kasmira. *There is much more that I could tell you, but I don't think it would serve any purpose at this point.*

That night Shakira decided that she needed to talk to her brother. She found him in the side garden sitting on a bench. When she approached him, he got up and said, "I am so sorry; I should have come to you after the trial. I had too much on my mind."

Ignoring his apology, Shakira blurted out, "What is going on? This is wrong. I know that Davos, Anna and Kasmira did not kill our father. Have you gone mad?"

Without thinking, Shakir raised his hand and smacked Shakira across the face. "Who do you think you are talking to? I am the king of Kaspar." *He knew he should not have struck his sister, but what was done was done. He could not take it back.*

Stepping back from the blow, Shakira stared at her brother and then ran away. Back in her room she decided to try to help Kasmira and her parents escape. She put on a black cape and made her way down to the cells. Her plan didn't go well, and she was discovered just a few yards away from the cell where Kasmira was being held. Being held by guards, she called out for Kasmira, but she was not heard.

She was taken back to her room and locked in. It was not long until her brother was at her door. He unlocked it and walked in.

She thought he would be angry, but he was not.

"I am so sorry that I struck you. I know you are in pain for Kasmira and her family. I am too. What were, you trying to do? Were you trying to see Kasmira one last time or trying to help them? If you were trying to help them escape, that would be treason, and I would have no choice but to have you arrested."

Tears were rolling down Shakira's cheeks. "I don't know what I was doing? I just know you are wrong." She fell across her bed and began sobbing uncontrollably.

Shakir walked to the door, turned and said, "You will be locked in here until this is all over." Leaving Shakira's room, he thought, *Am I doing the right thing?*

The rest of the night Kasmira, Davos and Ana huddled together and just held each other. In the morning, the storm had let up, but it was still raining. Several guards came to the cell, opened the door, and took Kasmira and Davos from the cell. Outside they led Davos away. Once he was out of sight, the men took Kasmira to the edge of the city. There Barak was waiting for her. The leader of the caravan was also waiting.

The leader of the caravan was Omar. Barak pulled him aside. "Here is your cargo. Take her into the desert. I know the weather is bad, but this storm is just about over. When you get to the desert you will wish for this rain. When you are about halfway across the desert, tie her up and leave her. Nature will do the rest."

Several days later Kasmira was tied to the back of a wagon. She had just enough room to walk behind the cart, and she had fallen several times and had been dragged until she could regain her footing. She knew her father was dead, her mother was suffering in a prison cell, and she was about to die. *Barak has done this. He has had my father killed and now is going to have me killed. I think it was me he had to get rid of. He wanted his daughter to be the next queen.*

The caravan had several carts and wagons, and they took the road south which led to the Eastern trade route. About half way, Kasmira's wagon turned east into the desert. Kasmira tried not to think of her mother and father. While several days had passed the trip into the desert seemed like forever.

Kasmira was at the point that she could barely walk when the wagon stopped. Omar came to the back of the wagon and untied her from the cart. "You would bring good money on the slave market, but if Barak found out, I would suffer the same fate as your father." He cut the rope that tied her to the wagon but left her hands bound. He tied her feet and said, "This way you will not be following us." He went to the front of the wagon and came back with a bag of water. "Here, take a good long drink. You will not get another."

Kasmira instantly took a long drink. "If by some miracle I live, I will bring you to this desert and return the favor."

Omar laughed and returned to the front of the wagon. He yelled back at her. "I am going to leave you this bag of water about one hundred feet from you. Barak wanted your death to be slow. Good luck getting to it." As the wagon pulled away it turned south, and Omar threw the bag of water onto the sand.

It was not long until she saw the wagon disappear in the distance. She looked down at the rope that bound her legs. *I am going to die right where I stand.* The sun was hot, and after about an hour she was so weak she passed out and fell into the sand. When she awoke it was dark. It was a clear night and the moon was shining bright. She felt weak, but again looked at the ropes that bound her legs. *If only I could free my legs.* She again looked at the ropes, and they slid off her legs. Quickly she stood up. She looked at the rope that bound her hands. She concentrated but nothing happened. She tried again but got the same results. She quickly started chewing on the rope. She pulled on the knot with her teeth and in a few minutes had her hands free. She started walking in the direction the wagon had left. She quickly found the water and drank down several swallows.

I must save this. I must make it last. Should I follow the wagon or head back toward Kaspar? It really does not matter. I am going to die regardless of which direction I choose. She looked at the night sky. *The caravan is heading south. Kaspar is to the northwest. North is a good direction. If I run into a village I will not be too far from Kaspar, and I can possibly sneak back into the city. I wonder if there are any villages or oases in this desert?* All Kasmira could do was guess the direction she thought was north. She reasoned that Omar's cart had headed south, so north must be the opposite direction.

Kasmira continued to the north until daylight. *I will try to rest during the day.* She looked at the bag of water. It was about three-fourths full. She took another drink, sat down and waited for the heat of the daylight sun. She was thankful she had dark skin. It gave her some protection from the sun's rays. She thought she would never get through the day. By nightfall she started to walk again. Like the day, she thought the night would never end. When light came, she had less than a half bag of water. Daylight did not bring the morning sun. Instead it brought a sand storm. It was no use trying to walk in the blowing sand. She lay down, covered her face with her sleeve, and fell asleep. While she was sleeping, she had a dream. A lady dressed in black was talking to her. She could not see her face but could clearly hear her voice.

"The storm will pass before nightfall. The storm is good. It will protect you from the sun. There is an oasis east of here. You can get there in one half day. You will be safe there. No one knows of this place. While you are there you will have plenty of food and water. You have magic, and while you are there, you can practice your magic. When you want to use your gifts, reach deep inside yourself. The power is there. Use it."

When Kasmira awoke, it was past sunset, but she could see the sun's rays peaking above the horizon. *That is west, I need to go in the opposite direction. The Woman in Black said it was only a half day. What have I got to lose?* She started walking in the direction she thought was east. She was getting weak; her water was almost gone. *This is useless.* She lay down and closed her eyes. She thought of her father and mother and started to cry. She took the last of her water and went to sleep.

When she awoke, she was at the top of a sand dune. She stood up. The air didn't seem as hot. Then she saw it, a pool of water. One end was bordered by a large pile of rocks and all around the water were trees and plants. She made her way down to the water, fell on her stomach and drank. She was surprised that it was cool. She turned over on her back and looked up. She could see the tall trees around the pool of water. *These are fruit trees.* After she walked around the oasis, she found she had figs, plums, grapes and nuts. She also discovered domesticated animals at the far end of the oasis. After she had eaten she felt much better. She wondered about her dream. What she had learned in it was true. *No one knows where this place is.* She took off all her clothes and waded into the water. She found the closer she went to the rocks the cooler the water was, and the further away from the rocks the water was almost hot. She stayed in the water for a long time. It was good to swim, and for a while she forgot about the last couple of days. Being nude in the water made her feel fresh, and it was a new experience for her. She had never been nude in water except while taking a bath. She wanted to stay in the water forever, but she finally gave up the treat and headed for the sandy bank. When she emerged from the water she took her clothes, cleaned them the best she could, and laid them on the rocks to dry. She stretched out on a rock and she also dried in the sun. She could not believe she was lying in the sun nude, and she hoped she was alone. When her clothes were dry, she put them on and started gathering fruits and nuts. When night came, she stretched out under one of the trees.

This place will keep me alive for a while, but how am I going to get back to civilization? She thought of her mother and father and drifted off to sleep. Again, the dream came.

The lady dressed in black began talking to her. *You have made it to the oasis. For the moment, you are safe. In the morning start using your magic. The more success you have the easier it will become. You have already used it once. You freed your legs from the ropes.*

The next morning, she ate and then thought of the dream.

Now to practice my magic. What Davos and Ana had told her must be true, and someone was appearing in a dream to guide her? She picked up a stick and stuck it in the sand. She placed a small rock on top. Stepping back, she thought to herself. *I am going to concentrate and make the rock fall off the stick.* She sat on the ground and looked at the rock. After several attempts, nothing had happened. She got up and walked away and then returned. *If I am going to save myself, I must master this.* She was almost angry. She looked at the rock and this time did not concentrate. She simply looked at the rock and it fell to the ground. She picked up the rock and did it again. She could feel the power inside her was growing, and she continued for several more times. She felt good. It was not a matter of concentration; it was a matter of will.

That night the Woman in Black returned to her dreams. Kasmira wanted to speak and ask questions, but she found she could not.

"*You have mastered simple magic, but there is much more. Keep practicing. I will return in three days. Then you will be ready for your next lesson.*"

The next day Kasmira practiced lifting small rocks off the sand. It was easy. She was able to lift rocks as much as a hundred pounds high in the air. She could tell she was getting stronger. She was walking along the edge of the water, and she thought of her mother in prison. *I can use this magic to help my mother escape.* Without thinking, she saw a rock some fifty feet ahead of her. With just her thoughts, she picked it up and smashed it against the large boulders some two hundred feet away. She fell to her knees and started crying.

Three days later, the Woman in Black again appeared in her dream.

"Magic and anger do not work together. Someone will get hurt, most likely yourself. You must maintain control. You also have the ability to disappear. You have used it before. You thought it was a dream. It will work almost the same way. Remember the first time it happened. See if you can remember the feeling you had when it occurred when you thought it was a dream. When she awoke, she thought of the morning she thought she had disappeared. She remembered the feeling. *How do I create that feeling?* Almost without thinking the feeling returned, and she knew she was disappearing. The sun was coming up, and she turned her back to the sun. She was casting no shadow.

After eating and gathering more fruit, Kasmira lay down under a large tree. She closed her eyes and thought back to her dream that was not a dream. She did have a strange feeling when it occurred. She remembered and found she could bring that feeling back. When she did, she opened her eyes and found she was about ten feet off the ground and could not see her body. At first, she let herself drift, then with just a little effort she could control the direction she was moving. She went across the water to the other side of the oasis. She made the feeling go away and she reappeared.

For the next several days, Kasmira could feel her strength. She had full control of her ability to move objects and could disappear at any time she wanted. Then she began to think of revenge. *I will kill Barak and Shakir. I will banish Shakira to who knows where. I will free my mother from prison. Why would I banish Shakira? She has done none of this. It is Barak and Shakir that have killed my father and tried to kill me.* She looked up at the large tree, made a piece of fruit fall, and caught it with her hand. *Yes, I will get my revenge and save my mother.*

A full month passed. The Woman in Black did not come back to her dreams. She began to feel completely alone. *I need to start thinking about how to get back to Kaspar.* She started making her plans. She would need food and water for ten days. *No, all I need to do is disappear and fly to the north. I can do this in only a day or two or may be even quicker.* The day was hot, but the air coming off the oasis was cool, and it was not long until she was sound asleep.

As she lay dreaming, the Woman in Black spoke, and Kasmira could tell there was both anger and sadness in her voice.

Listen and listen well. You cannot use your power for revenge. It will destroy who you are. You are right, Shakira has done nothing. Shakir did not find your father and mother guilty. He just followed the law. Shakir did not have you put to death. He thought he had made a decision to save your life. It was Barak who had you placed in the desert to die. Now there is some sad news I must share with you. It will make you want revenge even more. You must resist wanting revenge. I have not helped you from the desert for that purpose. The sad news is that your mother has died. There is nothing to go back to. I am so sorry. When you make yourself disappear, you can move through solid objects. Inside the rocks is a cave. In the morning go inside the cave. I will meet you there."

Kasmira could not stop crying. In a month's time, she had lost both her mother and father and was trapped somewhere in the desert. *How could I not want revenge?* The next morning, standing in front of the giant rock, she made herself become invisible. She moved into the rocks. Everything went dark for a moment, and she soon found herself inside the cave. She could see a pool of water to her left. There appeared to be an opening below the waterline to the pool of water outside. The light reflecting into the water was casting a blue neon light throughout the cave. It was like a dream. When she reappeared, her eyes quickly adjusted. She did not see the Woman in Black. The cave to the right seemed to go about two hundred feet, and at the end was a bright light. *This is not possible, and if there was an opening into the cave, why did the Woman in Black not tell me.* Walking toward the light, she heard a voice from behind her.

"Stop. You are not ready to go that way. I must prepare you."

Turning around, Kasmira saw the Woman in Black. At first, she did not say anything. She could not see her face. Walking toward her, she said, "Who are you, and why did you save me?"

"The who is not important, the why might be."

Kasmira struggled to see the face of the Woman in Black. Her face had a veil over it. "Okay, the why. How much did Ana and Davos tell you about yourself?"

"They told me very little. They only gave me the information about my magic the day we were put in the dungeon. They told me that they were not my parents. I think my real mother may have been a wizard or a witch, and she too may have been put to death, possibly by Barak. I was too upset to ask many questions. No, I was not upset. I was scared because I knew my father was going to be executed the next day. I don't care if what they told me was true or not. They were my mother and father."

The Woman in Black walked over and took a seat on a large rock. "What they told you is true. Your mother was a witch. She is dead. She was killed while in prison by someone throwing Greek fire into her cell. It was most likely Barak. You ask about the why. You have enough power to go back to Kaspar and kill Barak, and maybe Shakir, but then what? What happens to you? The why is, I am here to protect you from yourself."

"I don't need protecting. I am going to go back and kill them all. I am going to kill Barak, Shakir, Shakira and even Jada. You can't stop me." Kasmira started to use her power to disappear and leave the cave but found she could not. "What have you done? You gave me power and now you take it away."

"I gave you nothing, and I have taken nothing from you. You still have your power. It has always been with you. When you need it, it will return to you. Right now, there is only one way out of this cave. You will have to go through the light."

"I don't understand. I came into this cave from the oasis. Why can't I leave the same way?"

"You have discovered that you have powerful magic, but you are not ready to use it. I am not going to let you leave and go back to Kaspar with a weapon you are not ready to use. I am going to send you through the light. On the other side of the light you will not have your magic."

"Where does it lead?" Kasmira was starting to become afraid.

"It leads to somewhere in the future and to another place. Many years into the future to a world that is like this one but is not this one. I do know that if you need your power, it will protect you. When I feel you are ready I will send for you, and you can make things right here. When you go through the cave to another world, time will pass here at the same rate it is passing on the other world at the end of this portal. If you spend five years in this future world, five years will also pass here."

Kasmira looked at the Woman in Black. "I am scared. You are sending me into the future to a strange place, and you say even you don't know where I am going. You said five years. Am I going to be gone for five years?"

"When you get to the other side of the portal it will close. It will open when you are ready. It could be days or even years. You must learn to trust your feelings, and you must trust me. I don't know how, but I know you will be safe."

"Will you be here when I return?"

"I am not sure. Now go into the light."

"I am not going. I am afraid, and I need to know more. I need to know who you are and why you are helping me." Kasmira suddenly became quiet. "Are you really helping me?"

The Woman in Black's voice became soft and she reached out and took Kasmira's hand. "I know I am asking a lot. You really have no reason to trust me other than you have no choice. The why I am helping you is that I knew your mother. She loved you very much and asked me to watch over you. If you don't trust me, trust a mother's love."

Kasmira was afraid, but she started toward the light. She took one step into the bright light, and it went dim. As she disappeared she heard a voice. "Goodbye my child. You will be okay. You will not be able to control your magic, but your magic will protect you and help you in this strange new world. With the magic you have inside, you will be able to learn new things at an accelerated rate."

Kasmira looked around, and she was in another cave with light coming through a small opening. She turned and looked back, but the light was gone, and there was nothing there but a rock wall. She felt the wall, and it was solid. She knew her magic was gone, but she remembered the Woman in Black saying that if she needed it, it would come back. She was afraid to go outside. She remembered the Woman in Black saying that she would be safe. *That was easy for her to say.*

What about the voice? Was the Woman in Black her mother? Kasmira thought for a moment. No, the Woman in Black could not be her mother. She said her mother was dead. Her eyes were now adjusted to the dim light of the cave. It was not a large cave and had nothing in it. She started toward the opening with her heart beating so fast that she felt it might explode.

Shakira and Barak

Barak had put the first part of his plan in motion. Kasmira was now dead, but he had to contend with Shakira. He could tell that she hated him, and she didn't believe that Kasmira was involved in a plot to kill the king. She stood in the way of his daughter, Jada, becoming queen. If something happened to Shakir before Jada became queen and they had produced no heir, Shakira would become queen, and all his work would be for nothing. For the moment, his hands were tied. He had to sway Shakir away from his sister.

The next day while meeting with Shakir, he started the second phase of his plan. Looking at the young king, he said, "Now that you are king, you must be aware of those who would do you harm. There are those who could do you harm and not even mean to do so."

The young king was perplexed. "I don't know of anybody that would do me harm."

Barak walked over to the window. "That is why I am here. I will protect you and council you until you are firmly established as king. Until then, be aware of everything and everybody around you. Don't trust anyone. We don't know if Davos had others helping him in his plot. I would not trust anyone, not even your sister, until we have a stable kingdom."

"Shakira? Shakira would never turn on me or seek to do me harm." Shakir walked over and looked out the window. *She has already turned on me.*

"How much have you talked to her since your father was murdered? She was close to Kasmira, and she may not think you were right in sending Kasmira away. What has she said to you about this?"

Shakir scoffed, "She has not talked to me at all, or rather I have not talked to her. I have been too busy. You may be right. I will see her today. I will explain to her that I loved Kasmira but had to show strength, and that what I did was to save her life. I will also let her know that I could not marry the daughter of a man who killed our father."

The rest of the morning Barak and Shakir discussed the decisions that had to be made about the transfer of power to the young king and how he could help him perform his duty.

"You must give me absolute power to help you run this kingdom until you are settled in as the leader. The people will see you as a boy until you have been king for a while. When you have taken a wife and have an heir, they will see you differently. I will prepare the papers. Meanwhile, see what Shakira is doing. See if she is supporting you as the new king."

In the afternoon, Shakir stopped by to see his sister. She was in the library looking out the window, and when he walked up to her, she turned to face him. She looked different. Her eyes were dark from crying, and he could tell that she was still angry.

"Why have you not come to me sooner? Our father is dead, and yet during the last couple of days you have said nothing to me. Are you coming to me now as King or as my brother?" She turned her back to him and looked out the window.

"Is there a difference? Being a king is part of what I am now. Now I ask you, you could have come to me for comfort. Why didn't you?"

Turning to face her brother a second time she said, "I think everything you did was wrong. Kasmira's parents should not have been put to death. You acted too hastily. Davos and Ana were like second parents. Ana was there for us when our mother died. Kasmira was like my sister, and she may have been your future wife. Why did you send her from this kingdom? That was a sentence of death."

"I am king, I had to show strength. There was no chance for Kasmira and myself to be husband and wife. Barak has informed me if I am to rule, I must be strong."

"You are a fool. Father was a kind man, and the people loved him. He ruled with wisdom."

"He may have been kind but look what happened to him. Barak has told me that there are those that looked to this kingdom with envious eyes. I must protect this kingdom."

"Are you king or is Barak?"

"You have insulted me twice. Don't do it again. I am king, and if you wish to stay in this kingdom, take care of how you talk to me. I am going to make Barak vizier until I am settled and give him the power to make decisions on my behalf. This is the way it is going to be until I feel comfortable being the new leader of Kaspar. Let me warn you again. Be careful of how you talk to me and to him." Shakir then turned and left.

Shakira sat down and began to weep. She had lost Kasmira and now maybe her brother. After a few minutes, she regained her composure and left the library and started back to her quarters. On the way, she met Barak. When their eyes met, he gave her a smile, but she turned her eyes to the floor.

As they passed, Barak thought to himself, *she is going to be a problem. I must get rid of her.*

The next day, Barak and Shakir met. "I think your sister is going to be more of a problem than I thought. She was overheard yesterday being critical about the way we handled Davos and Ana. I know she was close to Kasmira, but she has to be loyal to you as our new king."

Shakir scoffed and turned to face Barak. "She also expressed this to me yesterday. I am not sure what I can do. She is my sister. I don't know of anything I can do. We have to give her time."

Barak walked over and put his hand on Shakir's shoulder. "I agree, but why does she have to be here? Why don't we send her to the island of Tranquillo? I know people there who would watch over her, and when you are firmly established as king, she can come back. She really needs to get away from Kaspar until things settle down here."

"She is only fifteen. Who could take care of her?"

"She has someone now, Ameena, who takes care of her. Send them both. It could be like a vacation. Ameena has no family. Her leaving will be no problem."

"Make the arrangement. I will talk to them tonight."

That night, Shakir met with Shakira and Ameena. After they had finished eating, Shakir looked toward the floor and said, "I am sending you both to the island of Tranquillo."

"You are what!" Shakira screamed as she stood up. "I am not going anywhere."

Shakir stayed calm. "Right now, I am telling you this as your brother. Tomorrow I will be telling you this as your king. You can accept this and be on a boat in two days as a passenger or be on a boat in two days as a prisoner. It is your choice."

Shakira walked over to the window. She could see the harbor. *My brother is no longer in charge of Kaspar. Barak is making all the decisions. If I don't go, he is going to kill me. I have no choice but to leave.*

Ameena came over and gave Shakira a hug. "Don't be afraid. I have heard that Tranquillo is a great place. Look upon this trip as a vacation. We won't be there long, and soon we will be back in Kaspar. Come, we need to make plans."

At first Shakira thought that Barak had talked to Ameena and she was going to be a spy for him. But while they were packing and making plans, Shakira could tell that Ameena didn't like Barak any more than she did.

Shakir did not come to the boat to see Shakira and Ameena off. Barak did come and as they started to board said, "Your brother told me to tell you that he would send for you in sixty days. I hope you have a good trip." He then turned and walked away. *Take a good look at Kaspar as you sail away, because you are never coming back.*

As Shakira and Ameena waited to board the boat, Shakira started to cry. She had never left Kaspar. Ameena took her by the hand and told her that everything was going to be alright. She regained her composure, and later they boarded the boat. Shakira and Ameena were standing looking out to sea when a young man walked up and stood beside them.

"Hello, my name is Joseph."

Shakira looked at him, not saying anything. He was tall and lean. She thought he was very good looking. While she was looking at him, he was staring at her. He thought to himself, *she is so beautiful.* He looked at her long black hair and her smooth complexion, and he wondered how old she was. Was she married, and why was she sailing to Tranquillo?

After a moment, Shakira spoke. "Do you know how long it will take to get to the island?"

"Not long, we should be there just about midnight."

We are leaving early in the morning and it is going to be near midnight when we arrive. I wonder what his definition of not long is. "Have you made this trip before?"

"Yes, many times, and each time the trip seems shorter."

Shakira looked into his eyes. "Are you from Tranquillo?"

"Yes, I am going home to see my father and mother. I have a friend that lives in a village east of Kaspar. The village is in the mountains. We like to hunt and fish and just enjoy being outside. I like to come down and visit a couple of times a year."

"What do your parents do?" Shakira said, not taking her eyes off his face.

Better not tell her too much. "They are traders. The island has a good location for trade. What about your parents?"

She also decided not to tell him too much. "They are both dead. Ameena takes care of me. She is like a mother."

Ameena, who was standing close, smiled with pride. She knew that this was all the information that the young man was going to get from Shakira. The rest of the trip, the three travelers made small talk, and the trip didn't seem so long. When the boat got close to the island, Shakira could see there were very few people on the dock. Joseph told them good-bye, and Shakira watched as he walked away. He was met by five men, and all had swords. They disappeared into the night. Ameena and Shakira had been told that they were to be met and escorted to their new lodging, but no one was there.

Ameena could tell that Shakira was scared. "Don't fret; they will be here. We just have to wait."

As Joseph and the men moved away from the dock, Joseph pulled one man aside and said, "Jon, what is going on? Have you heard anything? Who was that girl on the boat?"

"She is the sister of Shakir, king of Kaspar. We overheard the whole story from a drunk last night. Her brother had her exiled from Kaspar. I think she may be in a lot of trouble."

Shakira and Ameena saw six men coming toward them. "My name is Shakira; are you our escorts?"

One of the men laughed. "I guess you could call us escorts." They walked up and two of the men took Shakira by the arms and started dragging her down the dock. Ameena ran to help her, but she was slapped hard across the face and knocked down.

As the two men continued to drag Shakira off the docks one of them said, "Bring the old lady. We can't leave her here. She knows too much." He looked at Shakira. "I guess you can warm my bed tonight. We can wait a couple of days before we slit your throat."

Suddenly, the men stopped. Standing in front of them were Joseph and two of his men. "You can release her if you please."

This brought a burst of laughter from the six kidnappers. They released Shakira and all six pulled their swords. "Six against three, that does not seem fair." And they laughed again.

Joseph smiled and said, "What makes you think that there are only three of us? Have you not looked to your left?"

Looking to their left, the men saw ten men with bows and arrows drawn and pointed toward them.

"Maybe you should also look to your right."

Doing as they were told, they saw ten more men with bows and arrows drawn.

"Drop your swords, and then drop to your knees." The men did as they were told.

Shakira was trembling, but as soon as the men dropped their swords she ran back to Ameena. The two hugged each other and at that moment knew that their troubles were far greater than what they just faced. They were not just exiled; they had been sentenced to death.

Joseph came to the two women. Shakira was shaking and could hardly talk. Ameena was holding her, and Joseph said, "I have sent for a coach, and I am going to take you to the castle. I will arrange a place for you to stay until we know you are safe."

Shakira was beginning to calm down, and she did nothing but nod in agreement. When the coach arrived, Shakira and Ameena got inside. The ride to the castle was about two miles from the dock. Once inside the castle, Joseph escorted them to their quarters.

"How can you do this? Are you someone of importance?"

"I am captain of the guard." Joseph could tell Shakira was looking at him and knew that he was too young to be captain of the guard, so he said, "I know you think that I am very young to hold such a position. It is honorary, and it is part of my training. Tomorrow all will be explained when you meet the king." He then turned to leave, and Shakira ran to him. She gave him a quick hug and said, "Thank you so much."

As they embraced, Joseph could feel she was still shaking.

Shakira and Ameena had a very restless night. So much had happened, and they were still unsure of their plight. When Shakira went to bed, Ameena lay down beside her. "I know you are scared, but I think things are going to be all right."

Shakira turned and faced Ameena. "I am lucky that you came with me, but I am not so sure things are going to be alright. Those men knew we were coming, and they intended to kill us. Only Barak could have done such a thing. Do you think my brother knew about this?"

"Go to sleep child." *Things are going to get better. They have to get better because they couldn't get much worse.*

The next morning food was brought to their quarters, and later a man knocked on their door. "My name is Phillip, and I am chief advisor to the king. You are going to meet with him this morning. He will decide what to do with you. I would suggest that you ask for asylum."

"Then you know who we are." Shakira was again getting somewhat upset.

"Yes, Joseph found out last night before you were attacked. We have spies in Kaspar and in Tranquillo, and they discovered who you were and that you were to be taken when your boat arrived."

Shakira looked to Ameena and then to Phillip. "Did my brother order this?"

"Maybe not. He has turned over his power to Barak. We don't know why Barak or maybe your brother would want you dead. If you have more questions, save them for the king and court. I am to take you there now." Phillip turned to Ameena. "You are to remain here. When the hearing is over, she will be brought back here."

Ameena scoffed. "If I stay here, you will have to use force. There is no way I am letting this child out of my sight."

Phillip smiled. "Very well, come with me."

Shakira and Ameena were led down a long corridor to a large meeting room. When they went inside, straight ahead were the king and queen seated in large chairs. To the king's right was an empty chair. On his left were several chairs with men and women seated in them. As Shakira approached the king, she felt as if her heart was going to jump out of her chest. When she was just in front of the king, she stopped. To the left, she saw Joseph come through a door behind the king and queen. He walked up and stood beside her. He gave her a big smile, and she felt somewhat better. After she had calmed down a little and she could no longer feel her heart pounding, she said, "I am not sure of the procedures, and I don't want to offend anyone." With that said she curtsied to the king and queen.

"I am King Rhodes, and this is my wife, Queen Valetta. Phillip has told me that you have a request to present to this court."

Shakira looked straight at the king. "My name is Shakira, and this is Ameena. We are from Kaspar."

The king held up his hand and stopped her in mid-sentence. "We know who you are, and we know why you have come. Phillip told us you are going to ask for asylum. Do you know what that entails? What do you have to offer the kingdom of Tranquillo?"

Shakira was caught off guard. "We don't have much to offer at all. We thought everything had been arranged by my brother and Barak. We had no idea we were going to be attacked last night, and if it had not been for your honorary captain of the guard, we might have been killed last night. She turned and gave Joseph a weak smile, and she could feel her heart pounding again.

The king laughed and looked at Joseph. "Is that what my son told you? He is honorary captain of the guard? Joseph, good lord, is that the best you could come up with? Get up here and take your seat and help me decide what to do with this child."

Joseph took the seat on the king's right and then looked at Shakira. She was staring at him with a confused look on her face.

Joseph smiled and shrugged his shoulders, and then turned to his father. "If Shakira is the daughter of a king, I would assume she is educated and would have much to offer our island." He turned and looked back at Shakira. He did not see a child, he saw a beautiful young lady who was scared and needed a home and a friend.

The king looked at Shakira and said, "Where do you plan to live?"

"I don't know."

"What do you plan to do?"

"I don't know."

"Do you have any friends in Tranquillo?"

"I don't know anybody or anything." Shakira looked down at the floor. She watched a tear dropped from her eye and hit the marble.

"Do you have any formal education?"

Shakira fought to hold back the tears. Her situation was coming clear. She was in a great deal of trouble. "Kasmira, my friend who was also exiled, and I had just completed the first phase of our formal education. We were deciding what we should do next when my father was killed. I can read and write, I know a little Spanish, geography, astronomy, and have a good comprehension of mathematics. Ameena has taught me the skill of cooking, and other life skills."

The king leaned over and whispered something into his wife's ear, and Shakira saw her smile. The king turned back to Shakira, "For the time, you and Ameena will live here at the castle in the quarters you were placed in last night. Later today Phillip will meet with you and assign both of you a job or task for you to perform while you are here. We will meet again in a month and decide more at that time. You mentioned someone named Kasmira. Who is Kasmira?"

"Kasmira is my best friend. She was the daughter of Davos and Ana, who were accused of killing the king. She was exiled from Kaspar. I don't know what happened to her."

The king said in a very soft and caring voice, "If your brother and Barak had the same plans for her that they had for you, I would doubt that your friend Kasmira is still alive."

With all that was going on, Shakira had not thought about Kasmira. She fell to her knees and sobbed.

Jada

Jada had always thought it strange that she was not educated with the other children of the castle. They were the same age, yet her father, Barak, chose to keep her away from them. Her mother and private tutors had provided most of her education, and as she reached her fifteenth year she had no idea of what she was going to do. The only other person of her age that she had any contact with, and that was limited, was Shakir. On a few occasions, she was allowed to view court and Shakir would be there. They would speak and make some small talk, and she found she liked him very much.

When the day came that his father had been killed, and the awful trial which had the whole kingdom in an uproar, her father seemed so upset. She thought of Shakir and how terrible it must be to lose your father and take on the responsibility of being a king at such a young age. In the days and weeks that followed, she found she was going to court more and was proud that her father was helping Shakir with running the government. She did not know what had happened to Shakira and Kasmira. They had just disappeared. One afternoon she decided to take a walk in the garden, and to her surprise Shakir was there. She could tell he was upset, and even though he was king, he still was just a boy.

She walked up to him and gave him a quick smile. "Are you okay?"

Turning to face her, he quickly tried to gain his composure. "I am okay. So much has happened, and I sometimes come here where things are peaceful. It helps me accept what has happened."

"Do you want me to leave?"

"No, stay with me, I need someone to talk to. I am lonely. My sister and my friend are gone. I miss them."

Jada thought for a moment and was not sure how to respond. "What happened to them? I used to see them quite often walking and talking to each other in the castle."

"I think you know much of what happened. Kasmira's father killed my father and she was banished from the kingdom. My sister questioned Kasmira's banishment and she was also sent away. I don't know where Kasmira was sent, but my sister was sent to Tranquillo, and when she arrived, she was kidnapped."

"How do you know she was kidnapped?" She could see tears in Shakir's eyes.

Jada took Shakir by the hand and led him over to a bench and said, "Sit. How do you know your sister was kidnapped?"

Shakir released Jada's hand and wiped his eyes. "Barak had men that were to meet Shakira at the dock at Tranquillo. None of them have been heard from. I thought that we might get a ransom demand but have received none."

Jada wanted to say words of comfort to Shakir, but all she could do was sit quietly with him.

During the days and weeks that followed, Jada and Shakir became friends and would often meet in the garden or take rides together. Barak's plan was falling into place. Now all he had to do was let time pass, and his daughter would be queen of the land.

France 1941

Oliver and Luce Lavier left Paris in the spring of 1941. Oliver's family had built a cabin many years ago about forty miles northeast of Lyon. Oliver had two reasons to go to the cabin. He wanted to escape occupied Paris, and the resistance wanted a set of eyes in that area.   Luce wanted to get away from Paris for other reasons. Their daughter, Marie, had been killed when the Germans bombed Paris in June of 1940. The June 3 bombing had killed 254 civilians; many were children. Marie was one of the children killed. She was only thirteen years old.

On the road to Lyon, they had been stopped several times and had to show their papers. Oliver hated the idea that Frenchmen were serving the Nazis. Hidden in his car was a radio he could use to report any movement of the Germans to the underground. Once they got through Lyon, the road narrowed, and there were many turns. The last forty miles took almost two hours, but once they reached the cabin they felt safe.

The cabin was small. It was like a box in a box. When you entered, a bedroom built out of logs was in the center of the cabin. Above the bedroom was a small loft, large enough for a small bed. To the right of the bedroom was a fireplace, and further toward the back of the house was a small kitchen. To the left of the bedroom was a small area set up to be an office. There was another fireplace in this area. In the back was a trapdoor covered by a rug which led to a small basement. It was in the basement that

Oliver set up his radio. Once they had settled into their new home, Oliver contacted the resistance.

Living in the mountains proved to be difficult. Both Oliver and Luce had been teachers at the University of Paris before the war. Luce taught English and French while Oliver was in the business department. They planted a garden, purchased some livestock and made the adjustment to agrarian life. At first the Germans came by often to check them out, but they never discovered the cabin had a basement. The Germans wanted to know everything about them and why they had come to live in the mountains. Oliver told them that they had been living in Paris, and the university had closed. He told them they had very little money, and at the cabin they could raise their own food and have hardly any expenses. They had to tell this story to the Germans quite often, but soon the Germans saw them as a couple who wanted to be left alone and saw them as no threat. In the spring of 1942, things were getting better, but Oliver still had to go about once a month to Lyon to get other supplies. They had much of their savings with them, and Oliver had calculated that they would be okay if the war did not last more than three years. In the summer of 1942, Oliver observed several squadrons of German planes in the area. This he reported to the resistance. The next day while standing on the side of the mountain, he was looking into the sky when he heard a noise behind him. As he turned, he saw a young girl coming out of a small opening in the side of the hill. When she saw him, she froze.

At first, he did not know what to say. He could see she was scared.

"Don't be afraid. I will not harm you. Are you lost?"

Her fear increased. She did not understand anything this stranger was saying.

"I live just down the mountain. My wife is there. We can get you some food and something to drink."

The language was strange. She had never heard it before, but the tone of the man's voice was soft and kind. Her fear lessened. He motioned for her to follow him, and this she understood. The two went down the side of the mountain, and soon in the distance she could see the cabin. This was like no home she had ever seen. When they were about twenty yards from the cabin, the man shouted out, "Luce, I need you."

Luce was standing in the kitchen. At first, she thought that Oliver might be hurt, or the Germans had returned. She quickly went to the front door and opened it. Standing on her porch she could see Oliver coming toward her, followed by a young girl.

"Who do you have with you?"

"She was on the mountain. I could tell she was scared. She must have spent the night in a cave. She has not said anything."

Luce took Kasmira by the arm and led her inside. Oliver retrieved a glass of water and handed it to Kasmira. As she took the glass, her hands were trembling. Luce noticed the strange clothing that this young girl was wearing.

"What is your name?"

The words meant nothing to Kasmira. Then she spoke in Arabic. "My name is Kasmira. I don't know how I got here or where I am."

Luce looked at Oliver. "Do you recognize what language she is speaking?"

"No, but it sounds Arabic."

Luce gave Kasmira a gentle smile. "We can't understand what you are saying." Pointing to herself she said in French, "My name is Luce and this is Oliver."

Kasmira was now much calmer and realized she could not communicate with these two strangers. She spoke again, this time in Greek. (*My name is Kasmira, and I don't know how I got here.*)

Luce turned to Oliver. "That is Greek, isn't it?"

"Yes, it is." He pointed to himself. "Oliver. Oliver."

Kasmira pointed to herself. "Kasmira."

"Kasmira." Oliver repeated her name.

Kasmira made a final attempt to communicate with the two strangers. This time she spoke in Spanish. "Mi nombre es Kasmira."

Luce smiled. "Hola Kasmira. ¿Es usted de España?"

"No. Yo soy de Kaspar."

Luce knew very little Spanish. If they were going to communicate, it would have to be with just a few words. "Hablo español muy poco."

Kasmira smiled. "Entiendo."

During the rest of the day the three strangers were able to communicate with just a few Spanish words and hand gestures. Kasmira ate with Oliver and Luce that night. The food was strange but good. They made a bed for her in the loft. Luce gave Kasmira one of her gowns, and when she was alone she put it on and quickly fell asleep.

As Oliver and Luce lay in their bed, Oliver spoke. "What are we going to do with her? We can't take her to Lyon. There is no telling what would happen to her."

Luce agreed. "Let's just keep her with us and see if anybody comes looking for her."

"I will drive to Lyon tomorrow and get her some clothing. They will have to be used. Our money has to last throughout this war."

The next morning, by again using a few words and gestures, they were able to get through breakfast. Later that morning, Luce and Kasmira were sitting on the porch. Luce decided to teach Kasmira a few words of French while Oliver went to get the car. He kept the car in the barn which was about fifty yards behind the cabin. He looked at his supply of gasoline. He had fifteen ten-gallon cans he had purchased from the black market. He quickly figured that this trip would use about ten gallons. He was glad it was time to make his monthly trip to Lyon. He could not spare gasoline for an extra trip. He started the car, backed out of the barn and pulled to the front of the cabin. When Kasmira saw the car and heard the sound, she panicked. She screamed and grabbed Luce and buried her head into her shoulder.

"My poor child, have you never seen an auto before?" She rubbed her back and said it was okay.

Kasmira could tell by the tone of Luce's voice there was nothing to fear. Luce took Kasmira by the hand and led her to the car. Oliver was still sitting inside the car and got out and laughed. "Did you think that this monster had eaten me?"

Kasmira could not understand what he was saying but knew he must have said something funny.

"Two hours to Lyon. Two hours shopping. Two hours to get back home. I should be back between two and three o'clock." Kissing his wife goodbye, he got into the auto and disappeared down the hill.

Oliver made the trip without incident. He was lucky and found a man selling petrol and was able to buy two cans. He went to the market and picked up supplies and some canned goods. Next, he made his way to a used clothing store. As he stood outside the store trying to decide what to buy and how to ask for it, a lady came up pushing a cart. In the cart, she had three large boxes.

"I have three boxes of women's clothing for sale. If I take it inside, they will give me very little. Would you be interested?"

Oliver looked at the lady. Her face was scarred. He wondered if she had been injured in the war. "What exactly do you have?"

"I see you staring at my scars, and you are wondering if they are a result of the war. They are not. My daughter has left France and has gone to Spain. She is not coming back. She was about twenty years old and was about five feet six inches tall. She weighs about fifty-two kilos. Would you like to see what I have?"

"I am sorry, and I didn't mean to stare." Oliver looked into the boxes. She had everything he needed and more. After a few minutes of talking price, he was placing the boxes in the back seat of his car. His car was getting full, and one box had to be placed in the passenger seat in the front of the auto. He was proud. He had spent only about half of what he intended to spend and had four times the clothing he had expected to buy. *Strange forces are at work,* he thought. He looked at his watch, and it was just a little past twelve. *Time to start back.*

Luce and Kasmira spent most of the morning sitting on the front porch. Their communication was limited. Luce thought to herself, *we might as well get started learning French. It will give us something to do.* She motioned for Kasmira to come back into the cabin with her. She started pointing to things and calling them by name. Kasmira immediately caught on and started repeating what she said. After they named about twenty things Luce started pointing at the objects without saying anything. Kasmira knew them all and could say each one correctly.

At about two-thirty, Luce and Kasmira heard the car coming back up the mountain. Oliver stopped the car in front of the cabin.

Luce with Kasmira behind her went to the front porch. "How did it go?"

"It went extremely well. I got all the supplies on the list. Was able to buy twenty gallons of petrol and ran into a real bargain in clothing."

Oliver started unloading the car. He handed a bag to Luce and when she turned and started into the house, there stood Kasmira waiting to help. He handed her a box of clothing.

"These are yours, you might as well carry them in." Again, she did not know what he was saying, but he was smiling, and she took the box and started inside the cabin. When the car was unloaded, Oliver drove to the barn and was soon back in the cabin. Luce and Kasmira were unpacking the supplies and putting them in the storage closet. Each time Luce picked up an object she would call it by name, and Kasmira would repeat it.

"What are you doing? Did you teach her French in half a day?"

"This girl is amazing. She is extremely intelligent. She seems to pick up the words after me repeating them only one or two times."

When all the supplies were in storage, Luce and Kasmira went around the cabin. Luce would point to something and Kasmira would say the name. Oliver was amazed. Kasmira could not only say the names, she could say the names correctly. Kasmira was proud. She could sense that Oliver was proud too.

"Let's see what we have." Luce started opening the first box of clothing. The clothing not only seemed to be the right sizes, most were like new. Luce picked out a few garments and handed them to Kasmira. She pointed to the loft and gave a motion to put them on. Kasmira took the clothing and climbed the ladder to the loft. She laid the clothing on her bed and came back down the ladder.

Luce was somewhat disappointed that she did not understand that she wanted her to put on the clothing. Kasmira smiled at Luce. She took her hands to her face and gave a washing motion. She did the same on her arms.

Luce turned to Oliver. "She is smarter than we are. She wants a bath before she puts on her new clothing. Go get some water while I pull out the bathtub and start a fire to heat the water." When the bath was made, Luce got a towel and Kasmira climbed the ladder to get her clothes. She went behind the curtain and took a bath. The water felt good even though the tub was quite small. She washed her hair and when she was dry she put on the clothing. When she stepped from behind the curtain, Luce and Oliver were as proud as parents. Her hair was wet and dark, her skin brown.

"This young lady is going to be a heartbreaker. She is absolutely beautiful." Just for a moment he thought of Marie, his daughter. She would be just about Kasmira's age. He had wondered how long she would be able to stay in the mountains while he worked for the resistance. Kasmira's coming to the cabin was a blessing and he secretly hoped that no one would come looking for her.

Life in the Cabin

Six months passed quickly because Kasmira had brought purpose to Luce and Oliver's life. She seemed to fill the void of the loss of their daughter. She was learning French at an incredible rate, and they had no trouble communicating.

As they lay in bed, Luce spoke. "She has now been with us for six months. No one has come looking for her, and she says nothing about where she came from and how she got here. I have asked her several times, and all she says is, 'I don't know.' I don't know if she really does not know or simply will not say. Right now, I hope no one comes looking for her. I want her to stay here. She told me she is fifteen years old and will soon be sixteen."

"We will have to give her a party when she turns sixteen. Can you find out exactly when that will be?"

"I think so. She has been a great help both inside the cabin and helping with the garden. I have an idea. You are a teacher, and I am a teacher. Let's do our thing. Let's give her an education. When the war ends, we want her to go to the university."

"I am not sure we can get her into the university, but I like the idea of the education. You know that my father left several boxes of books in the barn. I will see what is there. She is learning French so quickly you need to start teaching her grammar, and I will teach her math, history, and geography."

Luce turned and put her head onto Oliver's chest. "What if she does not want to be educated?"

"I don't think that will be a problem. She appears to have some education already."

The next day, Oliver went to the barn, found several books that he thought would be okay to start with, and took them to the cabin. "You can start with the reading and grammar. I need to climb the mountain and do what I came here for. I will see you this afternoon."

When Luce explained what she and Oliver were going to do, Kasmira was delighted. Their first lessons went extremely well. Oliver had found some basic reading books and Luce had started Kasmira off at the lowest level, but she quickly moved beyond the basics.

Late that afternoon, Oliver returned from his mission up the mountain. "The weather is starting to get cooler. It won't be long until you will have to give one of your coats to Mira."

"What did you call her?"

"I called her Mira. While I was on the mountain I saw nothing most of the time. Later in the day I counted at least twenty fighters. There must be a base somewhere within fifty to one hundred miles from here. Well, anyway, as I was saying, I had plenty of time to think. There is no record of our daughter's death. Remember, all the Ministry of Education reported was that ten of those killed in the bombing of the school were children, and eighteen children were wounded. It was so confusing that Marie was never officially declared dead. If we start calling Kasmira Mira, when and if we get back to Paris we can pass her as our daughter. We can use Marie's papers and Mira can become a citizen and we could get her into the university."

"I like this idea, but what about the color of her skin? She is much darker than both of us."

"Well, your skin is kind of dark, and I am dark. I don't think anyone would question it."

Kasmira had been out feeding the animals and returned to the cabin about an hour after Oliver. Luce took Kasmira to the kitchen and Oliver went to the basement. "Please sit. There are some things we need to discuss." Luce explained the loss of their child, and that they hoped to go back to Paris when the war ended.

"We want you to become our daughter. To do this, you must let us shorten your name to Mira. That way, if people ask we can say that your name is Marie, but over the years we nicknamed you Mira. We hope, if your education goes well, we can get you into the university, if this war will ever end."

Kasmira and Luce both stood up. Kasmira hugged Luce and said, "My name is Mira. How can I ever repay you for the life you have given me?"

Oliver came up from the basement and found Luce and Mira seated in the front of the cabin. Mira smiled at Oliver and said, "Hello, my name is Mira, and if this is going to work, I need to start calling you Father."

Oliver returned the smile. "I have something for you. Tomorrow I am going to start teaching you geography." He opened a drawer in the table and pulled out a map of Europe. He pointed to Lyon on the map. "We are here. This is the city of Lyon." He took his finger and pointed at Paris. "And this is where we want to go when the war is over. Paris is also a city. It is a very large city." He pointed to Spain. "Spain is a country. There is more I need to do in the basement. Look at the map for a while, and I will answer any question you have tomorrow."

When Oliver came back up from the basement, he was surprised to see that Mira was still looking at the map. He took a seat next to her and watched as she took her finger and traced over the surface of the map and found Spain.

"My mother was from Spain."

"Did you use to live in Spain?"

"No." Her tone was sharp and final.

Oliver could tell she was going to say no more, but he had a little more information about her.

Mira asked, "Where did we live in Paris?"

"We lived on Rue Rosalie. We have a house there. I have a brother living there now, but if this war will ever end, we plan to go back."

Mira was puzzled. "What do you mean, Rue Rosalie?"

"Rue Rosalie is the name of a street, like a road. It helps us locate where people live. You continue to look at the map. I am going to the basement."

While Mira was looking at the map, she thought to herself. *Why does he have to go to the basement so often? Didn't he just come from the basement?*

While Oliver was in the basement, he sent the second part of his message about the German fighters he had seen and the direction they were flying. He could not spend too much time on the wireless because too much time and the Germans would find his location. Each time he pushed a key it made a beeping sound. Mira could hear the sound and could tell he was sending a message. She was beginning to understand the war and that Oliver was helping to defend France.

Mira's education went well. It was not long until she understood the layout of Europe. She learned about the war and how Hitler had taken most of Europe. She now understood about the United States and that they might someday liberate and save France from the Nazis. The weather turned cold at the middle part of October. Then the snow came. There was very little to do except study, and by January of 1943 she had mastered reading and grammar. Her math skills were improving, and Oliver was now teaching her economics.

One day in January, Mira came to Luce. "Can you teach me English? I might like to go to America someday." They started English that very afternoon, and like all languages Mira seemed to have an easy time grasping it. By April, Luce and Mira could have conversations in English, but her English was broken, and she needed more study.

Late in April, Oliver heard a truck coming up the mountain. He could see it was the Germans, and the truck had about ten soldiers in the back and two in the front. He quickly went in the house and told Mira to go to the basement. He threw a rug over the trap door. "Why didn't you just leave her here and present her as our daughter?"

"The papers she needs are back in our house in Paris. They might have arrested her."

It was not long until the Germans were pounding on the door. Oliver and Luce opened the door together. These were not Germans they had seen before. Speaking in French, the German officer asked for their papers. Once he was satisfied, he let two of his men search the cabin. They soon found Mira's clothing and her bed in the loft.

"There appears to be someone else living here. Where are they?"

Oliver took a photo of his daughter from his wallet. "My daughter was living here, but she has returned to Paris."

The German looked at the photo. "She is very pretty." As he was looking at the photograph one of the Germans found the trap door. "What is down here?" he demanded.

"Just where we store things, and sometimes I go there for solitude." Oliver's heart was beating so hard he thought the Germans might hear it.

In the basement, Mira could hear that the basement had been discovered. She knew if they found the radio they would all be in trouble. She grabbed a blanket from the shelf and wrapped the radio. Holding it, she fell into a corner of the room. She was scared. She remembered what the Woman in Black had said. *When you need your magic, it will be there.* She reached deep inside and felt the tingle, and she and the radio disappeared. She could see the boots of the soldiers coming down the steps. Two Germans examined the room, looking behind things and finding nothing. They went back up the stairs where Luce and Oliver were standing.

"There is nothing there. It is just a storage area with canned vegetables and a small table and chair. He told the truth."

The officer turned to Oliver. "We are going to leave now, but we have picked up radio signals coming from somewhere in these mountains. If you see anything, please contact us. We will check back from time to time. We are now stationed in Lyon. My name is Captain Otto Beck. We offer rewards for good information." He instructed his men to load on the truck and left the house. Captain Beck started to get in the truck but had to wait for the men who had searched the barn. One of the men reported, "There is nothing there." They joined the men on the truck, and turning the truck around, they drove down the hill.

Luce and Oliver watched the truck going down the mountain. Once it was out of sight they quickly opened the trap door and Mira came up. "How could they not find you? "Oliver exclaimed.

Mira gave Luce and Oliver a sly grin. "It was magic, just simple magic. I am going to get the map. I want to know all about the countries involved in this war."

Luce and Oliver knew that Mira was not going to say any more about what happened in the basement. Mira went over and took the map and spread it on the table.

Oliver walked over and stood beside Mira. He was so relieved that she and the radio had not been found. When he was able to get his heart slowed down he said, "Let's look at a map of the world. This is a world war. There is fighting everywhere." Oliver spent over two hours explaining the best he could about what was happening in the world, and when he finished Mira was in disbelief. Her world had Barak, and this world had Hitler, Tojo, and Mussolini.

The next day, Oliver went into the basement and retrieved his radio which Mira had left rolled up in the blanket. He decided to move it to the barn. If the Germans discovered it, he could claim that Mira and Luce knew nothing about it, and perhaps they would be safe. He was also glad that he had buried the petrol up in the hay in the barn. If it had been discovered, the Germans would have taken it.

1941 United States

David Wilson Van Meter graduated from high school in late spring of 1941. His parents had money. His father was H.D. Van Meter. The H was for Harold and the D for David. He thought H.D. sounded better, and David didn't like being called David Junior. His mother was June W. Van Meter. Both his mother and father had been born into money, and H.D. had made even more. During the stock market crash of 1929 up until 1939 it looked like they were going to lose their fortune. Things changed when war came to Europe. They owned Van Meter Auto Parts. Their company manufactured lots of parts for autos, trucks, and tractors. Their bestselling parts were ball-bearings. After 1939, the demand for their parts skyrocketed, and all their companies were at full capacity. After the Japanese bombed Pearl Harbor in 1941, Van Meter Corporation started producing parts for the Douglas Aircraft Company.

In the fall of 1941, David started his college education at Berkley. During his spring break in 1942, David and his father visited the Douglas Aircraft Company. David was impressed and decided he would like to learn to fly. That summer he started taking lessons, and by the start of the new semester he was a skilled pilot. He had only been at school for one week when he got a letter from the government. He was being drafted. He immediately went home. His mother was crushed, and his father said he might be able to pull some strings if he would go to work at his office. They could apply for a waiver because the war needed their products. David said no, and it was not long before he was taking his physical along with hundreds of other inductees. At the end of the day he was sitting in front of a sergeant getting ready to sign his papers.

The sergeant looked at his papers and said, "Mr. Van Meter, do you have any skills that we might consider in your placement?"

"No, I am just a school boy." He paused. "I can fly an airplane."

The sergeant looked up. "That is something we can use. Would you like to go into the Army Air Corps?"

Two weeks later, he was at Brooks Field in Texas. He had flown a lot during the summer and had already logged more than the required sixty-five hours for primary training, so he was placed in the basic program. After only one month, he was moved into the advanced training program and by February of 1943 was stationed in England. His first mission was in a P-47. He flew three missions and never saw an enemy airplane.

On his fourth mission, his squad was sent out to protect some bombers returning from a mission. It was his first combat. His squad was able to fight off about a half dozen enemy Focke-Wulf 190's, several Messerschmitt, and David shot down his first German airplane, a Messerschmitt. By the end of the summer he was a skilled pilot and had recorded four more kills. He was known as an ace.

In December of 1943 his squad was having a Christmas party when the squad leader stopped the music and said, "Gentlemen, I have an announcement. We are getting Christmas gifts. We are getting the new P-51 Mustangs. I have been told they can fly all the way to Berlin and back. This time next year we may be going home."

The P-51 Mustang was a flier's dream. It was like it was a part of you, and David was able to increase his number of planes shot down to ten. While most pilots took pride in the kills, David did not. He often wondered about who these pilots were, whether they had families. He often thought they might be just like him, wanting the war to end so they could go home. After a raid on a French railway station his squad was given a weekend pass. He decided to go to see a movie at a local theater. As he approached the theater he noticed a young lady standing just outside the ticket booth as if she were lost.

"Are you okay?"

She looked up and smiled. "Yes, I got the day off and decided to see a movie and got down here and found out I forgot my purse. I don't even have a shilling to get in."

David smiled and said, "You are an American, at first I thought you might be a local girl. I have a shilling; in fact, I have a couple of bucks I could give you."

The young lady smiled and said, "Yes and no. Yes, I am an American, and no I could not let you pay my way into the movies. I thank you all the same. I can see that you are a captain. Did you steal someone's uniform? I don't think you look old enough to be a captain, and I see you are a flier. You can't be old enough for that either."

With a big grin on his face he said, "I was just a boy until I came over here. This war has a way of making you grow up fast. I assume you are a nurse."

"Yes, I am at the hospital just across from the base."

David was staring at her thinking how beautiful she was and without asking her name he said, "What part of the United States are you from?"

Without noticing, they found themselves walking down the street as they talked. "I am from California. We live in a small town you have never heard of by the name of Libby."

"I know where Libby is. It is about fifty to sixty miles from Los Angeles."

She looked surprised. "How could you possibly know that unless you are from California too?"

David laughed. "I grew up in the suburbs of Los Angeles. My family has a factory there. I guess that since we are neighbors we should introduce ourselves. My name is David Van Meter, and you are?"

With a big smile on her face she said, "My name is Alice."

David and Alice started seeing each other each time they could break away from the war. David really liked Alice, and they became good friends. While David thought Alice was good looking, he did not want to become romantically involved with her. As the days became weeks and the weeks became months, David was finding himself being drawn more and more into Alice's world. He knew all about her family, where she went to school. Once after going out to eat, he walked her back to her base, and when he said goodnight he kissed her on the lips. It was not a long kiss, and when the kiss ended they stood very close looking into each other's eyes.

David wrapped his arms around her and held her close. "I don't think

I could have endured the last several months of this war without looking forward to seeing you. You have been such a good friend. Do you have any idea what you are going to do after this war ends?"

Never looking away from David's eyes, Alice in a low voice said, "I do. I want to continue to be a nurse and help people. I want to get married and raise a family. I want to have a house with a flower garden in the front of the house and a vegetable garden in the back. I want to forget the horror of this war and hope we never have to fight another one. What are you going to do when the war ends?"

"Go back home, finish my education, and maybe work for my father."

"You are a good man David. "With that said, she returned his kiss and turned and went inside.

After Alice was in her room she thought about the conversation that she and David had just had. *He thinks of me as a friend, and when I asked him what he wanted to do after the war, he did not say he wanted to get married and have a family. I wonder if he will ever fall in love with me.*

During the next four months, his squad was flying escort for bombers flying to Berlin and other cities deep inside Germany. During this time, he shot down three more enemy airplanes bringing his total to thirteen. After returning from flying an escort mission into the heart of Germany, he went to his barracks to lie down. He was extremely tired, and he thought of his mother and sister. He decided he needed to send a letter home.

Dear Mom and Dad,

Tomorrow my squad is providing escort for our bombers. I can't tell you where I am going, but tomorrow is also my birthday. We are winning the war, and many feel it won't last another year. We have so many men and supplies here in England that many are saying this damn island may sink into the sea. I always look to see where the parts are being made, and I am always proud when I see our trademark. There is talk about an invasion into Europe, but some feel that the bombing alone may end the war. I have met a girl. Her name is Alice. We are just friends, but it is good to have some female company. She is a nurse and I found out she is from a small town not far from where we live. I think you would like her, and maybe when we get home you can meet her. By the way, I am now a captain. They tell me that I am one of the youngest. Hope to see you soon.

After about three days' rest his squad was assigned to fly to Munich. The flight to Munich turned out to be a routine mission. The bombers dropped their bombs, and Germans sent up no planes against them, but flak was heavy. When they returned, they were granted leaves, and David decided to go see Alice. It was a nice day, and they ate outside at a local restaurant.

When they finished their meal, David noticed that Alice was distant and seemed far away. "Penny for your thoughts," he said.

She gave him a half smile. "We have been seeing each other for several months. I like you very much. You see me as a friend and I like that. I hoped it would be more and given time it might have been."

He was caught off guard. Nevertheless, he smiled. "Are you dumping me?"

"No, it is not that. I am going home. I have received word that my father is extremely ill. It must be bad, or they would not release me. I am leaving in the morning. I want you to write to me, and I will write to you. If something happens and my father gets better, I will come back into the service, but they may not send me back here. After the war, maybe we could meet and continue our friendship. Here is my home address."

After the meal, he walked her back to her living quarters and they held hands. He felt good with her. When they reached her living quarters, they turned and faced each other. "I will write and after this is all over we can see each other some more. I promise." He then kissed her and held her tight.

Alice looked up at David and gave him another kiss. "This darn war, it gets in the way of everything."

He laughed. "It didn't get in our way. It brought us together."

"I don't think I will see you again until this war is over. You keep safe. I will write as soon as I am home." She kissed him again and went inside.

As he walked back to the main part of town, he thought to himself, *I really like Alice. She is nice to be with. She would be a good wife.*

Three weeks later he received a letter.

his fighter to the left. Looking at his instrument panel, he could see nothing was working. His aircraft was sluggish, and when he tried to turn to head home, the plane did not respond. Smoke was filling his cockpit. He tried to talk to his squad, but the radio was not working. Again, he pulled back on the stick and was able to get just a little more altitude. At that point, he felt his engine die, and he was now a glider. Working as fast as he could, he grabbed his survival kit, opened the canopy, and bailed out. He watched his plane lose altitude and disappear.

It was not long until he was on the ground. Gathering up the parachute, he hid it in the brush. He took the pistol from the survival kit and strapped it to his side. He was in the mountains but had no idea exactly where he was. He knew he was many miles from the allied front. His heart was beating faster and faster. *Get control of yourself. You can handle this. Find a place to hide and at night start moving west.* His kit had a compass and a map, so he started moving west. Spreading the map on the ground, he was not sure where he was. He found Lyon but wasn't sure if he was east or west of the city. *Mountains, they are the key. I am in the mountains. That will put me east of Lyon. But how far east and how far north or south am I?* When his cockpit filled with smoke, he didn't know which direction he was going and how far he went.

As he started down the mountain, he saw a man sitting on a rock with a pair of binoculars. He took out his gun and approached the stranger. When the man saw him, he let go of the binoculars and let them drop to his chest. He put his hands up and said in French, "I am a friend."

David had very little understanding of French. "I am an American." He didn't know what else to say.

Oliver could tell the young pilot was scared, and he took his hands down. In a calm voice, he said in French, "Come with me." He gave David a motion to follow him, and he turned his back on the young pilot and started down the mountain.

David lowered his gun and put it back in the holster. He understood and followed the man. *He is either going to help me, or he is going to lead me to a nest of Germans.*

When they approached the cabin, Oliver stopped and gave a motion for David to stop. He called out. "Luce, I need you." He repeated several more times, and the door opened and Luce came out of the front of the cabin to see her husband and the young pilot.

"He does not speak French. Tell him we will help him. Tell him I will contact the resistance, and they will help get him back to England."

Luce looked at the pilot but did not see anything but a scared young man. Speaking in English she said, "I am Luce, and this is my husband Oliver. Oliver is a spotter for the resistance. We can help you. Are you hurt in any way?"

David felt better. "I was shot down. I am not hurt, but I have no idea where I am. Any help you can give me will be greatly appreciated."

Oliver spoke again. "Tell him that we don't want any information about him, and we will not give him much information about us. Tell him that we only need his first name. If he gives us too much information, it might be dangerous for both of us." Luce relayed the information.

"I understand. My name is David." He looked down and saw that his last name was on a patch on his uniform. He pulled it off and stuck it in his pocket.

Luce and Oliver took David into the cabin. Oliver got David some water, and they continued their conversation. Suddenly David heard the door open, and he quickly got up and was reaching for his gun. Then he stopped. Mira was coming in. She had been tending the chickens and gathering eggs. She had a blue scarf tied around her head and a light blue dress. She said nothing.

Luce spoke in French. "This is David. His airplane has been shot down. We are going to help him get back to England."

Still Mira said nothing. This was the first person she had seen since she was dropped off in the desert other than the Woman in Black, Luce and Oliver, and a few Germans. She just stared. She took the scarf from her head and let her hair fall, never taking her eyes off the stranger. David was returning her stare. Her hair and skin were dark. Her hair was long but had just a little curl. She was about five-six, maybe a little taller. He thought that she was pretty.

Oliver and David continued their conversation through Luce while Mira prepared some food. They usually drank water with their meal, but Oliver went to the basement and got a bottle of wine. When David tasted the wine, he looked at Oliver and said, "Good."

"I have. You know the U.S. is quite large. There are forty-eight states, and I have been to all of them."

"How could that be? Do your parents not work? Are you rich?"

"Remember, we were told not to tell anything about ourselves. I can tell you about places I have been. What would you want to know about first?"

They started working in the garden again. "I know you have been to New York the state. Have you been to New York, the city?"

"I have been to New York several times. My mother likes to go to the shows. She really likes musicals."

Mira just learned he was not from New York, and his family must be a family of means. "What is a musical?"

"It is a show with lots of singing, dancing, and with an orchestra. Have you never been to see a play?"

"I have never been off this mountain." She thought she was telling him too much. "What is your favorite place?"

"I like San Francisco. There are lots of places to eat. You are not far from some great attractions of nature. It has a wonderful history, going all the way back to the gold rush."

"What is a gold rush?"

David took his time explaining the gold rush to Mira. They worked together all morning, and Mira never stopped asking questions. Every time David would tell her about something in the United States it would generate a host of questions. When they got back to the cabin, Luce had prepared lunch, but Oliver had not come down from the mountain. When lunch was over, Luce and Mira cleaned the table and did the dishes. David took a seat in the living area. He laid his head back and the previous day and night caught up with him. Shortly he was asleep.

Two hours later he was awakened by someone coming through the front door. It was Oliver. He looked around the cabin. Luce was there, but Mira was nowhere to be seen. "Did Mira go back to work in the garden?"

"No, she went up the mountain. Sometimes she just likes to get away." Luce gave Oliver a hug and said something that he could not understand. She turned to David. "There is a small cave up there. She likes to go there when she wants some solitude."

"Mira said she has never been off this mountain. How could that be?"

Luce was surprised that she had told David this bit of information.

"We don't travel very much. You might notice that she is very smart. Oliver and I have educated her here. If this war ever ends, we are going to travel and show Mira the places that she has only read about. Now ask no more questions about us."

David knew that he was not fully understanding what was going on. He was not going to ask any more questions. He knew these were good people, and he did not want to put their lives in danger should he be captured. He decided to go back to the garden and continue to remove weeds.

Mira had gone to the cave. She went inside and looked at the wall and hoped that it would give her some clue as to when she could go home. She was not in any hurry. She loved Luce and Oliver. She wanted to see and know more about the world she was living in. She sat down on a rock and thought about her mother and father. *Who was the Woman in Black,* she wondered? Regardless of what the Woman in Black had said, she could not forgive Shakir. She no longer hated Shakira. *I wonder if Shakira hates me. Does she hold me responsible for the killing of her father?* She would just have to trust the cave. It would let her go back when she was ready.

David had worked about an hour when he heard Mira's voice from behind him. "Looks like you are going to make a good farmer."

"How do you know that I am not a farmer already?"

She laughed. "A man of your age that has been to all forty-eight states is not a farmer." She got her hoe and joined him. They worked the rest of the afternoon saying very little.

That night he lay on the hay thinking of Mira. She was young, but he was not much older. Reaching in his pocket he pulled out his name tag. He found a shovel, dug a small hole, and buried it. His thoughts went back to Mira. Why was she raised on this mountain? She was really pretty. Then his thoughts turned to Alice. She would be somewhere in the Pacific. She was a good person, and he liked her very much. *When I leave here, I will never see Mira again, but Alice will be back home waiting for me when this war ends.* He then fell asleep.

That morning he joined Luce, Oliver, and Mira for breakfast. When the meal was over, Luce looked at David. "This morning I want you to give me your clothes, and I will wash them. I have a robe for you to wear. There are some of Oliver's you can wear once you are clean. Go to the creek that I told you about. You can take a bath there. Mira will go with you and show you a spot that is quite deep. It will make a nice bathtub."

David knew that he might be uncomfortable to be around and agreed. Mira and David acted like two school children, and they joked with each other on the walk to the creek. When Mira showed the deep pool in the creek, she said, "You sure look funny in Oliver's robe. Enjoy your swim-bath. I am going back. Hope you can find your way."

Mira did not go back to the cabin. Instead, she hid where she could watch David. When he stripped and went into the water, Mira said "oh my." *I thought he was thin, but he is lean and has muscles.* She watched as he waded into the water, and then she left and returned to the cabin.

The water was cool and about four feet deep. It felt good. Luce had given him a small piece of soap. Once he had completely washed himself, he just stayed in the water. After about an hour he returned to the cabin.

"I thought that you might have drowned. I was just about to come looking for you," Mira said with a laugh.

"No, just stayed in the creek enjoying the water. I have never taken a bath in a creek."

"Father says as soon as your clothes are dry, you need to put them back on."

He laughed. "He does not want to share his clothes with me, huh."

She became serious. "Father said if you are caught wearing civilian clothing, you will be shot as a spy. He says they will shoot you right in front of us and they may shoot us too. How can people be so cruel?" *Cruelty is in this world, and it is in the world I just came from. People will kill innocent people to get what they want.*

"I don't think I would like that very much. How much longer do you think on the drying?"

"It won't be long. Maybe another hour."

A week passed, and they had heard nothing from the resistance. David was worried, but he liked Mira and her family and enjoyed staying with them. They were so completely different from the people he had grown up with. That night Oliver came back from the barn. "Bad news. I have just learned that a division of Germans are in Lyon. That means they might come here. We must keep an eye out for them."

Luce gave David the information. "Oliver says if Germans come, go to the barn. Take your blankets and cover them with hay. Throw a couple of shovels full of cow dropping on the hay. Then go the creek and wade upstream for as far as you can. You will not be able to go far because of the waterfalls. You can hide under the waterfalls, and don't come out until we come and get you."

David knew the situation was getting serious.

The next day, David and Mira were seated on the porch when they could hear in the distance a truck. Oliver was in the house and came outside when Mira called him. "They are coming. Forget what I said. Mira, take David to the cave. I will take care of things in the barn. Go now."

Mira took David by the hand and the two ran up the mountain trail.

Oliver called to Luce. "Get me anything that David has in the house and bring it to me quickly." She quickly returned with his survival kit. Oliver ran toward the barn while Luce hid anything that might show that Mira was there. When Oliver got to the barn, he quickly covered David's blankets and the survival kit in hay and covered the hay with dung. He started walking calmly back to the cabin just as the truck stopped. The truck had eight men. There were two in the front and six in the back. Suddenly, Oliver's heart skipped. They had two dogs. Oliver recognized the officer as the one who had been there before. The officer spoke first. "We found the wreckage of an American fighter, but there was no sign of the pilot. We are going to search the area again, but this time with our dogs. I hope you don't mind."

Oliver tried to stay calm. "Captain Beck, of course not. Do you want to start in the house?"

"That may not be necessary. Bring the dogs." Captain took a scarf he had found in the plane and let the dogs take a sniff. The dogs began sniffing the ground and barking. They started up the trail that led to the cave, pulling the men holding the leashes with them.

Mira could hear the dogs barking and coming up the trail that led to the cave. Leading David into the cave, she said, "Listen to me. Sit as close to me as you can. If they come into the cave you must hug me very tight. This is important, do you understand?"

"If we are going to pretend we are lovers in this cave it will not work. I have on my uniform."

"It will work; you must trust me."

David knew that if the Germans came into the cave, he was going to be captured, and Mira and her family were going to be arrested. "You hide here; I am going to try to outrun them. If I can get back to the creek, I can lose the dogs."

Mira became angry. "Are you not listening to me? I am going to save us both, so get over here and sit with me. I can't hide by myself. The Germans have no idea that I live with Luce and Oliver. It does not matter if you are here or not. If they find me, I will be arrested."

David now knew he was going to die, but he did what Mira said. The pair sat down in the back of the cave. They could hear the dogs getting closer as they came up the trail. They could also hear the Germans talking. When the dogs were near the cave entrance Mira put her arms around David, and he did the same. *This worked once, and it must work again. The Woman in Black said my magic would be there when I needed it, and I need it now.* David felt a tingle in his body, and looking at Mira, he saw her disappear. He looked down at his body and could see nothing. The soldiers and dogs came into the cave, and the dogs ran around barking. Mira looked at the dogs and concentrated. The dogs stopped barking and laid down.

"There is nothing here." They left the cave and started back down the trail. The dogs remained calm.

Once they could hear no more talking, the spell ended. David was still holding Mira. He could feel her heartbeat and the heat from her body. He kissed her on the forehead. "How did you do that?"

She gave him a smile and a light kiss on his lips. "It's magic, just simple magic. We will not discuss this anymore, and you will say nothing to Luce and Oliver."

David nodded in agreement. He noticed that she did not refer to Luce and Oliver as Mother and Father. He gave her a light kiss on the lips. "Thank you."

They lay against the wall of the cave, with neither wanting to move. It was not long until they heard Oliver calling from the front of the cave. "They are gone. For some reason, the dogs lost the scent. You can come back to the cabin. I see the dogs didn't find you in the cave."

When they came out of the cave, David looked at Mira and then to Oliver. "No, they must have gone on by."

That night after supper, Oliver went to the barn. David and Mira were sitting on the porch talking. Luce could tell they were becoming close and worried about Mira. They would never see each other after David left. She wondered if she should talk to Mira about it.

It was not long until Oliver returned from the barn. He spoke to Luce, and Luce turned to David. "Good news. They are sending a couple of men to get you back to the American lines. They should be here in about three days." This was not good news to Mira. She had fallen in love and did not want to let David leave without knowing if they could ever meet again. They said very little the rest of the night.

In the morning, it was raining. After they had eaten, Luce took Mira aside. "I know that you care a lot about David. We like him too. When he leaves here, he is going to be blindfolded. If he is captured, he will not be able to tell the Germans where we are. He does not know our last names, and when the war ends there will be no way for him to find us. Say your goodbyes and know that we have made him safe and given him comfort during what could have been a terrible time for him."

Mira understood, and she tried not to think about David leaving. She walked over to David. "I am going to clean the barn this morning. Do you want to help?"

"I do. This will be like cleaning my room. My mother would say my room looks like a pig sty," he said with a big smile.

When they left the cabin, it was raining hard. They ran as fast as they could, and when they reached to open the barn door, they were wet and breathing hard. David looked at Mira. Her white blouse was wet and clinging to her, showing the shape of her breasts. *She gets prettier each time I look at her.* "Where do you want to start?"

Mira was still breathing quite hard. "I don't want to clean the barn. I just wanted to spend some time alone with you."

He came over to her and took her in his arms and gave her a light kiss. "I have fallen in love with you. What are we going to do?"

She laid her head over on his chest. "We are going to say goodbye and put our future in the hands of fate. There will be no way we will find each other after this war is over."

He released her, and they sat down on a pile of hay. "Do you have someone special waiting for you when you get back to your home?"

"Yes and no. I met a girl in England. Her name is Alice. She is a nurse. She and I became friends and then somewhat more than friends. She was lonely, and I was lonely. We filled a need that each of us had. We were never lovers, but we were becoming close. She is from a town not far from where I grew up."

"You were not lovers, but will she be waiting for you when you get back to England?"

David lay back on the hay and Mira snuggled up against him. "No, she will not be in England waiting for me. Before I left England, her father became ill. She went back to the United States. While she was there he died. She is not coming back to England. She is now on a hospital ship somewhere in the Pacific."

"Are you in love with her?"

"I am in love with you. I know that we have not known each other very long, but I feel so good with you. I don't know how I can let this end. Anything we could do will put us in danger. You will have to be content knowing I love you very much."

For the rest of the morning they lay in the hay holding each other and giving each other long kisses. Holding Mira close made his body ache. He wanted her so much but knew it would not be good for either of them. Mira cried. She had not cried since her mother and father died. She wanted to tell him about herself, that she was not from this time, and someday she might go back. She wanted to give him information about Oliver and Luce so that after the war he could come back and find her in Paris. She knew she could not betray Oliver and Luce. They had been so kind to her, and she did think of them as mother and father. Suddenly David raised up on one elbow and said, "I am not going to give up. Fate brought us together once, and I think we are meant to be together. When this war is over, don't give up on me. No matter what it takes, I am going to find you."

She gave him a big smile and raised up and kissed him. "I won't. You know, we should clean this barn a little. Oliver will expect to see a clean barn when he comes back in here."

They got up from the hay and spent about an hour cleaning. The rain stopped, and they went back to the cabin.

The next day when Mira came down from the loft, Luce and Oliver were seated at the kitchen table. "Has David not come from the barn yet?"

Luce spoke. "He has. He came and got a towel and some soap. He said he was going to take a bath in the creek."

Oliver echoed Luce's answer. "He is leaving sometime today. He might not have a chance to clean up until he reaches the safety of his lines."

Tears came into Mira's eyes. "I am going to miss him. I care a lot about him. I wish there was a way to let him know where we will be after the war."

"Giving him that information might cause our death and the death of many of our friends and their families. Say your goodbyes today and hope some miracle happens and you see each other again."

When David came back from the creek, he came into the cabin. "Why didn't someone tell me that water would be so cold after a rain. I never will get warm again."

Luce, Mira and Oliver tried to laugh, but they were all caught up in the sadness that he was leaving. After they had eaten, David and Mira sat on the porch. In a few minutes, Oliver came out.

Mira looked toward him. "Do you want me to finish cleaning the barn this morning?"

"You didn't have enough time to get it finished yesterday," he said with a smile. "You two can have the morning to talk and say your goodbyes."

The morning passed far too quickly. It was not long until they heard an auto coming up the hill.

Luce turned to David. "Go inside and stand next to the back door. If I don't come for you in a couple of minutes, go out the back door and head for the creek."

When the car pulled in front of the cabin they could see that there were two men inside. They stopped the car and got out. The taller of the two men said, "We seem to be lost. Is this the way to Palmer?"

"Are you looking for West Palmer or East Palmer?"

"We are looking for South Palmer."

Oliver shook the men's hands and asked them to come inside.

"We would like to, but we don't have much time. Where is our passenger?"

"Mira, go get David."

In a few minutes, David was standing next to the car with the two men. "Do either of you speak English?"

"We both do, but we won't be doing much talking during most of this trip."

"Are you going to blindfold me?"

"No, you are going to be in the trunk of this vehicle." They took him to the back and raised the door to the trunk of the car. "This is going to be your home for about the next two days. Climb in and make yourself comfortable."

Before he climbed into the car, Oliver came up and shook his hand. Luce gave him a hug, and both went back to the porch. Mira came up and gave him a hug but didn't seem to want to let go. She whispered into his ear. "Rue Rosalie, if you ever want to find me, this is the only clue I can give. Repeat it back to me."

"Rue Rosalie." He kissed her lightly and climbed into the trunk.

Back in England

Two weeks later, David was back in England. His base was about forty miles from London. When he picked up his mail, he had a letter from his sister, one from his mother, and two from Alice.

His commander insisted that he not fly any missions and gave him a two-week pass which he decided to spend in London.

The letter from his sister was all about her graduation from high school. She had decided to attend USC. She was dating a local boy from her high school which she went on and on about. The letter from his mother had all the "hope you are okays" and "keep safes" but gave him little information about what was going on back home. It did have a lot of information about how Alice had come to see them and how much they liked her and that she was going to stay in contact. There was also a box of cookies that he knew his mother did not bake. He opened the box, started eating a cookie, and began reading the letter from Alice.

> *My Dear David,*
>
> *I cannot begin to tell you how much I miss you and England. I am on a hospital ship off the coast of a Pacific island. The fighting here is intense. Whoever said war is hell was right. I believe it must be hell times ten. Sometimes at night I go out on deck and I see explosions off in the distance, and I think of the poor soldiers on both sides that are on the island.*

We are sometimes in the O.R. as much as eighteen hours. The doctors are wonderful and go well beyond trying to save as many lives as possible.

I got a letter from your parents. It was so kind of them to write me. Your sister is now out of high school. April did write me once, and in her letter, she only talked about you. You two are very close. I can't wait for this war to be over and for us to be back home. There is not anything else I can tell you because we are told not to use any information about the war in our letters. I hope you are doing well. I have received nothing from you so all I can do is pray you are okay. When we get back home maybe we can really get to know each other.

Love Alice

When David finished reading the second letter he picked up a pen and paper. He started to write but stopped when his thoughts turned to Mira. Would he be able to find her after the war, or would she be OK until the end of the war? *I will write to Alice when I get back from my furlough.*

He put a few clothes in a small bag and hitched a ride to London. He really enjoyed seeing the English city and it sites. Finding a room was difficult. He ended up sharing a room with three other soldiers. He got to know the three roommates over the next few days. They would often eat in a nearby pub and drink ale together. All three had received minor wounds in the D-Day invasion.

One morning he was walking the streets of London and saw a jewelry store. He went in and purchased a bracelet. He had engraved on the top side the words "Rue Rosalie." On the bottom side, he had the name "Mira" engraved. He wondered if he would ever see her again. He knew Rue Rosalie was the name of a street. He knew that the Allies were moving toward Paris, and it would be just a matter of weeks until it would be liberated. Once that happened he would try to get permission to go there and start his search for Rue Rosalie. He knew she would not be there, but he could confirm that the street was there. *What if the Rue Rosalie was not even in Paris? It could be in any city in France.* His thoughts again turned to Alice. Should he tell her that he had met someone else or just leave things alone? He decided that when he got back to the barracks, he would write and tell her about being shot down and how the French family saved his life. Maybe he would tell her about Mira.

His thoughts again turned to Mira. When they were in the cave, Mira saved him, but how? *No one can just disappear. Who is she? What is she?* He remembered her words when he asked her about disappearing. *It is magic, just simple magic.* All he knew was that he loved her.

The two-week pass came to an end too quickly. When he got back to his barracks he found himself on the list to take a squad out the next day. The Eighth Air Force was taking heavy losses, and fighters were assigned to escort bombers to their targets and back. Fighters would break away from the bombers only when they encountered German planes. It was on his first mission back that he saw his first Messerschmitt Me 282. He was glad they were short ranged, and the Germans didn't have very many. They were impressive.

After four missions, he was on an escort flight to go deep into Germany. As he was getting ready, his buddy Mill came running into the barracks. "We have taken Paris. That means the war will be over soon."

David stopped getting ready for his flight, "That is great news. When we get back from this flight, I am going to request permission to go there. Man, what great news. I believe you may be right. The war will be over by Christmas."

David continued to get ready. Suddenly he realized he had not written to Alice. He decided he would write to Alice when he got back. He would have to let her know about Mira and that when the war was over he was going to find her. He looked at his bracelet. *Rue Rosalie*, he repeated to himself. *What if it is not in Paris? What am I going to do?*

The squad was to escort Allied bombers on a bombing run over a German city. Several bombers were lost. He shot down two more German fighters. On the way back to England, he could feel his plane grow sluggish. His oil pressure was dropping. *I hope this machine will hold together long enough to get me home.* He radioed to his squad his situation and told them if he could not make it he would bail out over the channel.

Making it to the coast seemed like forever. He was in sight of the shoreline of England when he felt his engine stop, and the plane started to lose altitude. He could see the coast line, so he decided to glide as close as he could to the shore and ditch into the sea. He could see the channel water

It wasn't long until April was sitting beside David on the couch with a photo album. The two of them went through the book, and April gave the strangers names. He was surprised to see his photo in the book so often. "Did I jump in front of the camera every time we took photos?"

April laughed. "You are very photogenic."

"Could we do this again tomorrow? I can't remember all these people."

"Of course, we will also go driving tomorrow. Can you remember how to drive?'"

"I think so, but I have not driven a car since I was hurt." David found that he felt very comfortable with April. When the doctor came that afternoon, he insisted that she be with him.

Dr. Phelps was not an old doctor. He brought with him x-rays. "These were sent to me by the doctors at Walter Reed. They show no damage to your head that would be corrected with surgery. We will have to just wait and see. David, there is a chance that your memory may never come back. You are young and otherwise healthy. Life will go on, and soon your mother, father, sister and friends will become your mother, father, sister and friends again. I will make an appointment to see you in about a month."

During the next two months, he relearned the town, got to know his family and settled into a routine life. There were times when he became depressed and angry. They seemed to become more and more frequent. It was only April who could break the depression and get him back on track. Even though they were strangers, it was April he felt most at ease with.

His mother told him that she had written to Alice and told her that he had been injured in a crash and had lost his memory. She had written back and said she would come and see him when she returned to the United States.

In May, the war in Europe ended. David visited his father's office, and the two went out to lunch. After they had ordered, David turned to his father. "I want to thank you for what you have done for me. I know this has not been easy for you and Mom. I don't think my memory will ever come back. I think it is time I looked to the future and let the past be."

His father said nothing at first, and then he said, "War is a cruel thing. I guess we are lucky in a way. The war robbed so many of their past and their future. We have a future. Have you made any plans?"

"I have. This is why I came to your office. Before the war I was going to

Berkley. I want to enroll there in the fall. I want to spend the summers with you learning the business. When I graduate, I want to come to work here."

"April is going to USC. Why don't you go there?"

"April needs her life. She has done so much for me. I need to try to be alone. If this does not work, I will join her at USC.

David joined his father's firm and continued to work with him throughout the summer. His father was so proud that David seemed to have a natural ability for the business. They even purchased an airplane and David started flying again. He would take his father on business trips. In the fall, he enrolled at Berkley.

Classes were going well for David. He still had bouts of depression, but he was able to control them by looking at his bracelet or calling his sister. *I wonder where I got this bracelet, and what does Rue Rosalie mean? Did I know someone named Mira?*

Back to Paris

Mira could not stop thinking of David. Would he be able to figure out that Rue Rosalie was the name of the street that Oliver and Luce lived on in Paris? The days and weeks seemed to just crawl by. In September, they got the news that Paris had been liberated. It was then that they started talking about going back to Paris. The snow came early, and by the first of November they were trapped in the mountains. The roads didn't clear until the last days of March.

They learned the war was over in May, and that week Oliver's brother Paul and his wife and daughter came to the cabin. Paul explained that he had to leave Paris because his daughter had dated a German during the occupation, and her life was in danger. "I have been hiding her since the liberation. They are shaming the women who dated Germans during the occupation. They shave their heads and parade them through the streets and call them all sorts of names and throw rocks at them. We had to leave."

"This cabin is small. We can't all live here. We will head back in the morning." Oliver explained Mira to Paul. "When we get back to Paris she is going to become our daughter. They are the same age, and she can use Marie's papers."

Mira like Paul's daughter. Her name was Michelle Lavier. That night they sat together on the porch. "Do you hate me? You know you can't help who you fall in love with. He was nice, and he treated me nice. I found out that he was killed by the resistance as the Germans withdrew from Paris."

"No, I don't hate you. Believe it or not, I understand because I fell in love the same way. We parted, and we may never see each other again. I really understand your pain."

The next day, Oliver, Luce, and Mira packed everything into their car. They had to tie some of the things on top because Oliver wanted to carry extra petrol with them. Mira had never ridden in a car, and she was excited. Soon, they were going down the mountain and into rolling hills. When they passed through Lyon, Mira could not contain her excitement. They drove straight through with Oliver and Luce taking turns driving. The trip did not seem long to Mira because everything was so exciting. When they arrived at their house, Oliver turned to the backseat to face Mira. "We are going to change your name again. I hope you understand. You will truly be our daughter now. Your name will be Marie Annie Lavier. We will call you Marie. I have papers that will identify you, and I think we can build you a life here."

Both women were crying, and all Marie could say was thank you. The inside of the house was large compared to the cabin. It was already furnished. The front door opened into a large living room. You could go from the living room right into a dining room which had a large kitchen off to the left. To the right of the dining room was a hallway which led to three bedrooms. The master bedroom was at the end of the hall on the left. Two smaller bedrooms were on the right. The house had two bathrooms and a small upstairs with one bedroom. Marie could not believe the house. It was nothing like the cabin.

After Oliver and Marie had carried in their belongings, Oliver said to Marie, "This is where we lived before the war. Our daughter's bedroom was the first one on the right. We are going to let you take the second one on the right." He took his seat in the living room. "It is good to be back home."

Luce came in from the kitchen. "There is not any food here. Paul left nothing. How is our money supply?"

"We are okay. Tomorrow we will go out and find the things we need. I am not sure what the supplies are like here in Paris, and I hope we can find what we need. I wonder if that small cafe is still down at the end of the street? Do you want to walk down there?"

After a short walk, the three found themselves seated in a booth in the

Alice in the Pacific

Alice did not like being on a hospital ship. When she was in England, she mostly worked with patients who were recovering. Here on this ship she worked with doctors trying to save lives. Sometimes they were not successful, and this was hard on Alice. Sometimes she would be working for as much as twenty hours without stopping. When she was through, she would go over in her mind the ones they had lost and the ones that might not make it. The Battle of Saipan that started in June of 1944 produced many wounded men. It stretched the limits of the medical corps.

One day when Alice finished her shift, she went on deck and sat down and leaned against the side of the compartment. She was exhausted. She rested her head on her knees and started to cry. She felt so bad for the young boys who were not going to make it. While she was sitting there, she heard the compartment door open. She looked up and a young doctor was taking his seat next to her. "Don't stop crying on my part. In fact, you can cry some for me. I know how you feel, and I wish I could cry."

Alice wiped her eyes and said, "You are Doctor Baylor. We have worked together before. You do good work in there."

"I have only been here two weeks. This is a hell of a way to start a medical practice. Your name is Alice," he said, looking at her name tag. "My name is Michael. Where are you from, Alice?"

"I'm from California."

"Me too. I'm from Bakersfield."

"I'm from a small town. I'm not sure if it is big enough to even be a town. I'm equal distance from San Francisco and San Diego."

"I'm too tired to go to sleep. You want to walk down to the galley and get a cup of coffee?" He got up and extended his hand to her. She took it, and he pulled her to a standing position.

As they talked and drank their coffee, they found that they liked each other very much. In the next shift, they were not working together but met at the galley once the shift ended. The next shift they were working together, and during the next month she found that she looked forward to seeing him when they were apart.

Late in August, they were sitting and eating their meal when the senior surgeon came up to them. "There is a general staff meeting in the conference room at 1800." He quickly walked away to another table.

Michael looked at his watch. "We have an hour. I guess we can finish our meal." They took their time and finished their food. They did not try to speculate about the meeting. When the time came, they took their seats with the rest of the medical staff. The head surgeon came and with a big smile said, "How about some R and R? We are going back to Hawaii for three weeks for a much-needed rest." The staff went wild shouting and hugging each other. Michael turned to Alice. "I want to do just what I do here. I want to spend every free moment with you."

Alice gave Michael a big hug. "I feel the same way."

The next day, they were put aboard another ship, and soon they were in Honolulu. Alice and several of the nurses were given housing in a local motel. The doctors were over on another beach in a boarding house.

The next day, Michael picked up Alice in a jeep. "Where did you find this machine?"

"Gave the C.O. some drugs so he let me use the jeep." He paused. "I'm just kidding. They had several for us to check out. Rank does have some privilege."

"Where are we going?"

"Well, I thought we would spend the day riding around the island."

Alice had a wonderful day, and when they got back to the hotel it was just about sunset. "I will go back over to my hotel, clean up, and in about an hour come back and take you out to eat. How does that sound?"

"Wonderful." She gave Michael a quick kiss, got out of the jeep, and headed inside as he drove away. She had not thought of David the entire day. The weeks passed far too quickly.

She was lying in Michael's arms on the beach when right out of the blue he said, "On our next leave, let's get married. This war won't last forever. The war in Europe is going well, and some say it might be over soon. If that happens, the full weight of America can be placed against Japan. They are already losing. By this time next year, we could be back in California starting a medical practice and a family."

"That's not the most romantic proposal a person could receive. Could you please do better?" She gave a laugh.

"Let me try again. I have had the most wonderful three weeks of my life. I can't imagine my life without you in it. I have loved you since the first day we met on the ship. Would you do me the honor of becoming my wife?" He reached into his pocket and pulled out a ring box. He opened it, took out the ring, and placed it on her finger.

She gave him a hug and whispered in his ear. "Yes." Then for some reason she thought of David. *What has happened to him? Why did he stop writing?*

Two weeks later, they were back on the hospital ship. When Alice got resettled, she saw she had several letters. She quickly shuffled through them and saw there was nothing from David. *Has he forgotten me completely?* She saw a letter from David's mother, and her first thought was that David had been killed.

> *Dear Alice,*
>
> *I hope this letter finds you doing well. We have not heard from David for some time. We are hoping that you have. We have received nothing. We are worried. If you have received a letter and he is okay, please let us know.*
>
> *We did go see your mother. She is doing well. Hope to see you soon. We will write a much longer letter and bring you up-to-date in about a week. Right now, we are so worried about David.*
>
> *June*

Alice felt guilty. There was a chance that David had been killed in the war and that was why he had not contacted her. *I need to sit down and have a long talk with Michael about David.* Then she thought, *it makes no difference if David is dead or alive. I love Michael, and he is the man I am going to spend my life with.* She quickly wrote a letter to David's mother and told her that she had not heard anything from David.

> *Dear June,*
>
> *I have not heard anything from David for several months. I had never thought something might be wrong. I just felt he did not want to continue our relationship. We were never lovers, but good friends. I care a lot about him and got to know you and the rest of the family through him. From what you have told me something must be wrong, and I pray he is okay.*
>
> *While I have been in the Pacific I have met someone else. His name is Michael Baylor. He is a doctor on this ship. Just a few days ago in Hawaii he asked me to marry him, and I said yes. I want you to know that I care about you and your family, and I will keep praying that things are okay.*
>
> > *Alice*

The next two months were brutal. They seemed to be just one eighteen-hour shift right after another. Alice was not sure she could continue the pace. Returning to her room, she found that several other nurses were there and were already asleep. She looked on her bunk and saw a pile of letters. She shuffled through them and one caught her eye. It was from June.

> *Dear Alice,*
>
> *I am sorry I did not write you back. We have been busy, and I kept putting it off, and time slipped away. I have good news and bad news. We received a letter last week from the War Department. David was shot down and crashed his plane on the coast of England. He was not killed but has been in a coma for many weeks. The doctors don't know when he will wake up or if he will ever regain consciousness. I will keep you posted and pass any news I get on to you.*

> *I am so happy you have found someone. Not much good comes out of this war, and that someone has found some happiness is good. If you decide to get married in the United States, please send me an invitation. April and I would love to come.*
>
>

Your friend,
June

>

In January 1945 Alice got the letter that told her that David had regained consciousness on Christmas Day. In her letter, June explained that David had lost his memory due to the plane crash. She now knew she had to explain David to Michael. She and Michael were going back to Hawaii. That night, she and Michael sat together eating. Michael took his last bite and said, "I am so glad we are going back to Oahu. Three weeks in the sun and being married are something to look forward to."

"There is something I need to tell you."

Michael smiled. "You are not going to tell me that you are already married?"

Alice returned his smile. "No, but when I was in England I knew a young pilot. His name was David Van Meter. We had been dating when I left England when my father got sick. I never heard from him again. I thought that he didn't care about me, so I moved on. His mother has written me, and he was shot down and crashed. He has been in a hospital for several months and has awakened with no memory."

"Did you care for him, and you are now telling me that you want to postpone our wedding?"

"No, I am telling you that I love you so much, but I don't want anything between us. David and I are a casualty of war. Our relationship was never a serious one, but I did become friends with his mother. I want to stay friends with her. I don't want you wondering why I am writing to a former boyfriend's mother. I liked David, but we were never that close, just good friends. We were just two lonely people a long way from home."

David took Alice's hands. "We are also two lonely people a long way from home. I hope we are much more than that."

"I can't wait to get married. I love you so much. I want to be called Mrs.

Alice Baylor. I am looking forward to starting a family. I can't wait to hold little Michael. We have so much to look forward to."

Two weeks later Michael and Alice were married in Hawaii. Two weeks after that, Michael was on his way back to the Pacific, and Alice was assigned to a hospital in Hawaii.

Michael was back in Hawaii in March of 1945, but by April he left Alice, who was expecting a child, to return to the war. He was killed in the battle of Okinawa in June 1945. Alice stayed in Hawaii until her daughter was born. In December, she took Michelle home for Christmas and left the military service. Staying with her mother, she started working at a local hospital while her mother took care of Michelle.

Alice and the Van Meters

In the spring of 1949, April and H.D. Van Meter came to see Alice. They met after Alice had completed her shift, and they went to a local restaurant. Alice had continued to write to April after the war was over. She had kept up with David's progress, and she continued to hope that David would get his memory back.

After they had hugged and sat down at the table, April opened the conversation. "How is Michelle?"

"She will soon be four. I am not looking forward for her to start school. She looks a lot like Michael. She has blue eyes and blonde hair. I wish she was here. I would love for you to see her."

H.D. realized that was a good opening. "That may be possible. We have to confess that we wanted to see you, but there is another reason we came."

Alice began to feel a bit uneasy. "Why have you come?"

"There are two reasons. One is we wanted to see you, and regardless of how the rest of the meeting goes, that will remain true. You and April have become close in your letters too, and we need your help. We are going to open an infirmary at the plant. It will be staffed by two nurses. We feel that we can really help our employees by having this type of service at the factory. We will have three doctors working part time who will come in one day a week. This is already set up. We need to hire one more nurse. We want you to be that nurse. I must be completely honest with you. We have checked. You are a great nurse, and we want you for that reason, but we also want you for another reason. David is going to start working at the company full time. He will graduate this spring. He still has no memory of what happened before he crashed. We hope by seeing you it will bring back his memory. It might not work, but all you must do is be a nurse. We may or may not tell him who you are. We will just see what happens."

Alice did not say anything for a few moments. "I have to consider Michelle. Mother keeps her while I work. This will be difficult."

April reached over and took Alice by the hand. "The company has a daycare facility not far from the Infirmary, in fact it is in the same building. You will be closer to your daughter than you are now. We will also provide you with a house. The company has a house that was purchased during the war. It is nice."

H.D. rubbed his chin. "You will also make twice as much money as you make working at the hospital."

The next day, Alice gave the hospital where she worked two weeks' notice and called H.D.

Alice really liked working at the clinic. It was not a hard job, and they were not busy. She could visit Michelle just down the hall in the daycare center. She was surprised that she had been at the clinic for two months and had not seen David. April and June would come by, and they had become very good friends. One Wednesday afternoon she had just finished with a patient when the door opened, and April and David walked in. She was not sure how to react. "Hello, April. Are you ill? Seems there is a lot of flu going around."

"No. David and I came to take you out for lunch. We thought we'd take you over to the Idea Café. We could walk."

Alice grabbed her purse, told the other nurse where she was going, and the three headed out the door. On the walk to the restaurant, Alice thought about how she was going to talk to David. She decided just to follow April's lead. Once they were seated, April looked at Alice and said, "Alice, have you met my brother David?"

Alice was not sure how April wanted her to answer but decided to tell the truth. "Yes, I have."

David seemed surprised. "Did we meet before the war? If we had met after the war, I would remember you. I would not forget someone as pretty as you."

Alice blushed and gave David a smile as she turned toward him. "No, we met during the war. I was a nurse stationed in England. You were a young pilot."

Suddenly a waitress was standing next to the table. Holding a pad in front of her she said, "Are you ready to order?"

David wanted to hear more so he turned to the waitress. "No, come back in just a couple of minutes." Looking at Alice, he strained to try to remember her. He was not sure what to say. "They tell me that I was in England, but I don't remember anything." He needed time to think. "Let us order our food and then we can talk." He motioned for the waitress who was behind the counter, and she quickly returned to the table.

After they had placed their orders and the waitress left the table, David said, "Did you work at the hospital that took care of me after I was injured? Were you a nurse that helped take care of me? I believe that I would remember you if you were."

"No, I had already left England before you were shot down. We met just outside a movie theater and became friends."

David felt just a bit uneasy. He sensed that April and his parents had set up the meeting with Alice in an attempt to help him remember. Nevertheless, he surprised April and Alice. "I don't want to continue talking about England and how we knew each other. I want to save that for another conversation. Tell me about yourself. April told me you have a young daughter." Just for a moment he had the thought that the young daughter might be his. No, that was not possible. Mother and Father would have told him, and a granddaughter would be in and out of the house. There would be no way that his mother would not spoil a grandchild if it were his.

"I was married. My husband was killed in the Pacific."

"I am so sorry."

Just for a moment Alice thought of her husband. "Thank you. Michael and I had just a short time together. Short but wonderful."

David looked at Alice. He wanted to take her by the hand and comfort her. "Would you like to have dinner with me this weekend? I have to get back to work, and I so much want to continue this conversation."

"That would be nice. What day do you have in mind, so I can get a sitter?"

"How about Saturday? I will pick you up at six. I will get your address from personnel."

April knew that David did want to continue the conversation, but without her being there. She quickly entered back into the conversation. "That won't be necessary. Alice lives in the company house."

They got their food and continued only light conversation about work, Alice's daughter and April's love life, or lack of a love life.

When David got back to his office, he felt the depression coming on. His first thoughts were to send for April, but he suppressed the urge. They had just been together, and he had to learn to deal with depression on his own. He sat down at his desk, opened the top drawer, and took out a bottle of pills. *No, I am not going to take one of these. I am just going to sit here and see if it will pass.* After just a few minutes he felt better and continued his day without interruption.

Saturday came quickly, and that afternoon David found himself sitting in Alice's drive. When he knocked on the door, Alice opened it and was dressed in a blue summer dress. He thought to himself that she was a very lovely woman.

"I hope this is not too casual. I was not sure where we were going."

"You look fine. We are going to Anthony's if that is okay?"

"I have never been to Anthony's, but I hear that it is very good."

They said very little on the way to the restaurant. When they took their seats, the waiter came to their table right away. "Can I get you something to drink?"

David turned to Alice. "Would you like to have a glass of wine?"

"Yes, I would." She looked up at the waiter. "What do you recommend?"

David interrupted. "Bring a bottle of the red house wine." He turned to Alice. "It is a sweet wine. I think you will like it. It is from a winery right here in the valley."

After the waiter left, David wasted no time in asking questions to Alice. "You told April that we met in England, but you married a person you met in the Pacific. This must be an interesting story. How did we meet?"

"As I have already mentioned, we met one afternoon in front of a movie theater. I had forgotten my purse and had no money, and you offered to pay my way in. We started talking and never even went to the movies."

David looked down. "Were we lovers?"

"No." Alice was a little shocked that David was so frank. "We were friends. We only kissed a couple of times. We were just two lonely people who became friends."

"Why did we part?"

"My father became ill. I came back to the States to be with him. He died, and I was reassigned to a hospital ship in the Pacific. You told me you would write, but you never did. I wrote you several times but never heard from you. I thought that you had lost interest in me, but I now know you were shot down and injured."

"I am sorry about that. When I woke up in the hospital I never even thought to ask if I had mail. I was in a state of shock that I could not remember anything."

When the meal arrived, they continued with only small talk. David could remember nothing. When they left the restaurant, he took her straight home. Standing at the door, he said. "I have had a good time tonight. I know why we became friends in England. You are nice to be with. Can I take you out again some time? I would like to get to know you all over again. Maybe it will help my memory return." He thought for a moment. *I don't want you to think I am using you. I really don't think my memory will ever return. I really could use a friend.*

"I had a good time tonight. I would love to become your friend. Call me anytime. Stop by the infirmary. We might have lunch together in the park." She slipped her key into the lock of the door and went inside.

April

April was not quite two years younger than David. She had been a beautiful baby and a beautiful child and had become a beautiful young lady. She was tall, about five-seven. She graduated from high school in May of 1944. She had no steady boyfriend, and every boy she dated claimed that he had slept with her, although none had. She had an outgoing personality and could talk to anyone.

She and David were close. She had been devastated when he had gone to war. At first, she wrote him once a week, but he had been extremely busy, and his letters came only about once every two weeks. After about a year, she only wrote about once a month because she felt he was too busy with the war to answer everybody's letters. She spent the summer wondering why the letters from David had stopped. Her mother and dad would not talk about it. Deep in their hearts they all felt that David had been killed. Her mother had told her about Alice, and she and Alice did exchange letters.

In August of 1944 she enrolled at USC. Her parents had money, so she took an apartment off campus. She talked to her mother about once a week, sometimes more. She was not only good looking, she was smart. She did not date much, although she was asked often. Near the end of the first semester, she got word that David was alive but in a hospital. When she came home for Christmas, everyone was in good spirits, and hearing that David had come out of his coma lifted their spirits even more. When April found out about David having no memory, she was crushed. She felt that if your memory is gone, the person that had that memory is gone too. It is like dying. David would be someone else.

When David came home, she tried to put up a good front. That night she had cried most of the night. He had not returned from the war like the brother she loved. After several weeks, she and David were growing close again. She had not gone back to USC but had stayed home to help David. She and David were constant companions during the summer of 1945. David would often have periods of depression. He had medicine for it, but he tried not to take it. In August, David decided to return to Berkley. She insisted that he go to USC with her, but he would not. "You need your own life," he had told her. After they had both started classes they talked on the phone at least three times a week. She was the one constant in his life that kept him stable.

When he graduated and came to work for his father, she was already working there in public relations. She was a natural, and even though her father hired her because she was his daughter, he would now not let her go. In fact, she was offered a good job in Oakland, and he increased her salary to keep her there.

When Alice came to work for the company they became good friends. When she had brought David to meet her, April was disappointed that nothing sparked his memory. During the next three years, she saw a friendship grow between Alice and David. They would go out a couple of times a week, but April could tell that there was really no spark between them. David really liked Alice and seemed to really love her daughter. He would often even babysit while Alice would run errands.

Late in the summer of 1952, David came into her office. "It is time to take a ride. I need to talk."

"Can't we talk here? I was getting ready to go home. I have a date tonight. Got to look my best. It will take hours to perform that task."

David laughed and said, "Does Dad know you come and go as you please? If you don't come with me I am going to tell him. You know that you look beautiful with or without makeup or fancy clothes. I won't keep you long."

Once they were on the road he said, "What if I told you that I might want to marry Alice?"

At first April said nothing. Then she spoke. "I would say you are making a mistake."

"Why would you say that? You know that we have been seeing each other for almost three years. I don't think it is fair to her to continue the way we are. Alice needs someone in her life and I don't want to lead her on. She could be dating other men and finding someone to love and take care of her and Michelle." He said again, "Why do you not want me to marry Alice?"

"You didn't say, 'April, I have fallen in love with Alice and I want to marry her.' You said you might want to ask Alice to marry you. You tell me you want to be fair. So, I tell you, how fair is it to a woman to ask her to marry you because you want to be fair? Do you love her?"

"I am very fond of Alice. I enjoy being with her. I love Michelle. She needs a father, and right now I am filling that role."

"Have you and Alice slept together?"

The car almost went off the road. When David had the car back under control he said, "You think I am going to discuss that with you?"

"No, I don't. But my guess is that you have not. I think that if you were in love you would want to hold her and be near her. You are not in love with Alice. If you think your friendship will develop into love, marry her. If it does not, you are going to destroy both your lives. If you ask Alice to marry you, she will. So, think long and hard before you do."

David did not say anything but turned the car around and headed back to the office. "Thanks for talking to me. I know everything you have said is true. I knew you would be honest with me, and that is why I wanted to talk to you. I have a team coming from France next week to discuss a contract about a merger between their product and ours to be sold in Europe under a new name. When this is over, I am going to talk to Alice. I am either going to ask her to marry me or make it possible for both of us to move on."

Marie and the Van Meters

Marie was sitting at her desk. She had just finished reviewing the contract with the Van Meter company. Her thoughts then turned to Oliver and Luce. She referred to them as Father and Mother. That is what they had become.

For some reason, she thought of the Woman in Black. She had told her that her magic would be there if she ever needed it. Why had this woman saved her? Why would she not let her go back and kill Barak? She felt angry. By not going back and killing Barak, she might have doomed many people, including Shakir and Shakira. She pushed it out of her mind. She would go spend some time with Oliver and Luce before her trip to America. The trip should take no more than a week, two at the most, but she might want to spend some time seeing the western sights.

Just before Marie left to go to the States, she met with her team. "I am hoping we can finish the deal with the Van Meter Company in about a week, and if we are lucky maybe even less. When the contracts are signed, I am going to take a vacation and stay in America for a while. I have a friend there, and I am going to look her up. I have arranged for you to stay in America for ten days if you want. If you don't, you can come back here and spend time with your families and relax."

A week later, she was in a hotel room getting ready to meet the Van Meters and their staff. She chose a business suit. She pulled her long black hair straight back and put it in a bun. She grabbed her briefcase and met the other four members of her team in the lobby. When they arrived at the Van Meter main building, they were met in the lobby and escorted to a conference room on the fourth floor. The room was large and on the meeting table there were ten packets of information. Marie thought to herself, *they will have five and we have five. I hope this goes well.* Soon they were joined by Mr. Van Meter and three others from the company. A secretary took a seat off to the side of the table. *Somebody is missing,* she thought, but said nothing.

After the introductions, Mr. Van Meter started talking. "Our lead on this project is not here. We will start without him." He was worried about David. He had missed the morning staff meeting, and April said he was having a bad day with his depression. *Maybe he will be OK.* "In the packets, you will see that we have gone through and marked areas of concern. Most are minor, and I think we can work them out today."

Just then the door opened, and David came walking in. He looked right at Marie and said nothing. He took his seat and started shuffling through papers.

Marie was in a state of shock. She just stared across the table at David. He glanced up from his papers but said nothing. *He does not know me. Have I changed that much?*

David looked up from his papers. "I am going to save everyone some time. This contract will not work. I sent for a ruling from the State Department, and it violates several trade agreements we have in Europe, especially in France." He looked at Marie. "Miss Lavier, if you had done your homework when you drew up this contract, you would have found this out, and we wouldn't be seated here wasting our time and money." He suddenly became cold and even cruel. He looked right into the eyes of Marie. "I don't mind you wasting your time, but I sure don't like you wasting mine." He picked up his papers, shoved them into his briefcase, and started to walk out of the room.

Marie quickly regained her composure. "Mr., whatever your name is. Have you even read this contract? It appears you have not."

"Miss Lavier, does your company think it can send a pretty woman to our company and present an inferior piece of work?" He then left the room slamming the door behind him.

Marie turned to Mr. Van Meter. Before she could say anything, he said to the secretary, "Go get April. Tell her to drop everything and come here quickly." He turned his attention to the other three men on his staff. "Were you two aware of what was just pointed out by David?"

John Higgens was the senior member of the team. "We were, and we called Ms. Lavier about a week ago to discuss it. She told us it could be worked out but could not make any adjustments until we were face to face."

"Did you inform David that adjustments could be made, and that Miss Lavier was aware of the problems in the contract."

"We were going to do that this morning, but David did not come in until just now."

Van Meter turned and faced Marie. "Ms. Lavier, I am sorry for what just took place. Let me make an apology for my son. He was shot down on the coast of England during the war. When he came back he had lost all memory of what had happened before the crash. Most of the time he deals with it, but every so often he has bouts of depression. You just witnessed one."

The door opened, and April came into the room. "Go find David. Take him for a walk in the park. He is having a bad day." He turned to Marie and her team. "This is April, my daughter. She is the best member of my staff. If you need anything, she will take care of you. I think we can meet again at one o'clock. Is that okay with everyone?"

Marie did not say anything. Tears were rolling down her cheeks. Van Meter patted her on the hand. "It will be okay. He will be completely different after April works her magic."

So, this is why David never came to look for me. The war had claimed two more casualties. Back in her mind she had hoped she might see David again, but not like this. He was a stranger. "Is there any hope for your son to regain his memory? Is there anything that can be done?"

"I don't think so. We have not given up hope. We even brought a friend he had in England to see him, but nothing sparked his memory. Sometimes he is a stranger to me and his mother. He has formed a bond with April and maybe Alice. The doctors have told us to not do anything else but just wait and pray."

Marie got up from the table. "I am going to take a walk. After what has happened I need to think and prepare myself for our afternoon meeting."

She turned to her team. "Get the papers I prepared before we left Paris and see if someone here can make copies."

Marie found an empty office and sat down and cried. *Why am I crying? I gave up on David a long time ago, or did I? I fell in love with David, not that stranger who I just met.*

Later, Marie was walking in the park. She was feeling better and was getting hungry. There was a man selling hot dogs at his stand. She walked up to him. "One hot dog and a Coke." She took her meal over to a park bench and took a seat. She was just about through with her hot dog when she noticed April and David seated on a bench about fifty yards away. She could tell that they were laughing. She finished her last bite of hot dog, threw the paper in a nearby trash can, and walked toward them. When she approached them, it was David who spoke first. "Miss Lavier, I am so sorry for this morning. Please try to forgive me." He stood up and extended his hand.

Marie looked into David's eyes. She took his hand and said, "All is forgiven. We can fix the contract."

April spoke up. "Walk with us. We are going to take a walk around the park. It is only about a mile."

Marie looked at David and smiled. "Okay. We don't have to be back for a while."

David turned to April. "You two ladies take the walk. I need to get back to the office. I need to mend some fences. I will see you at the meeting this afternoon." He turned and quickly walked away.

"Is he going home to work in his yard and fix his fence?'

"No, that is just a saying that he needs to apologize to his coworkers."

"Who was that guy? It was not the same man I met this morning."

"David is a super nice guy. Did Dad tell you about the accident?"

"He did. I am so sorry."

"You should have known David before the war and the accident. He came back from the war different. With me, I am seeing more and more of what he used to be. Don't judge him. Maybe someday we will have him back. Do you mind if I talk to you? I need someone to talk to. I can't talk to anybody I know about this problem."

"I don't know if I can be of any help, but let's talk."

"Dad hired a woman about three years ago that David knew during the war. Her name is Alice, and she is a nurse. When David met her, it did not help with his memory loss. He has gotten to know her well, and he helps her with her child. I know he loves her as a friend but nothing beyond that. I think he may ask her to marry him, but I know he does not love her."

At first, Marie didn't say anything. When they walked by a fountain she dipped her hand into the water and said, "I don't think there is anything you can do. After all, David is twenty-eight years old. He will have to make up his own mind."

"I guess that is true. How did you know he was twenty-eight?"

"Just a guess."

"You know that David was shot down not once but twice in Europe. Dad has gotten a copy of the records. The first time was in France. He was saved by the resistance and a French family. The records show that he did not know who they were. It only says that they were a Frenchman and his wife and daughter."

Looking straight ahead, Marie asked, "Is there nothing else?"

"Just one thing. David wears a bracelet. He will not talk about it. But once he left it lying on the sink. I looked at it. On the top, it says Rue Rosalie, and on the backside, it says Mira. I know that Rue Rosalie is a street. I have no idea who Mira is. Dad once thought he could find that street, but there are many streets in France with the name Rue Rosalie. I believe every city in France has a Rue Rosalie?"

Marie's heart was racing. *David did love her, and even if he had wanted to find her he could not. He did not know that the Rue Rosalie she whispered to him that day was in Paris, and she didn't know that the Rue Rosalie Oliver and Luce lived on was several miles long. It didn't matter. They had lost any chance when David was shot down the second time.*

April looked at her watch. "Where are you staying while you are here?"

"We are at the Silver Star. I am on the tenth floor overlooking downtown. I have a great view. It is a very nice hotel."

"It is the best in the city. I need to get back to the office. It has been great talking to you. Perhaps we can see each other again before you go back to Paris."

At one o'clock the disrupted morning meeting continued. David, standing behind his chair, faced the team from France. "I need to apologize for my conduct this morning. I hope you can forgive me." He looked at

Marie and said, "You said you could fix the problems with U.S. trade regulations. What do you have in mind?"

"While we cannot deal with each other as distributors in France, and most of Western Europe, what we can do is enter into an agreement with a company that can. Kunkel, a company that is located in the American sector of Germany, has these rights. They are willing to be the distributor of our product. I have checked, and the agreement is legal."

"What will they want in return?"

Looking at her papers, Marie answered, "Two percent. I have looked at the figures. With the projected sales, both of our companies will do well."

H.D. Van Meter spoke up. "We need to look at these figures, and that will take all day tomorrow. Let's meet on Friday and see what we have."

The meeting came to an end, and Marie shook hands with Mr. Van Meter and turned to David. She looked into his eyes and smiled. "I will see you in a couple of days."

Marie went back to her hotel and lay on her bed. *What a day. The deal is going well, and I have found out what happened to David.* He was even better looking than when she first met him. *I have found him only to find out that I have lost him. Should I tell him who I am? The woman he is seeing is Alice. Is this the same Alice that he told me about that rainy day in the barn? It does not matter. I am not going to tell him who I am.* She turned her head into the pillow and started to cry. Was there any part of the man she fell in love with during the war left? Should she tell him who she was? Would he even believe her? He was about to ask another woman to marry him. It was pointless to tell him about France. She then drifted off to sleep.

Suddenly, she was awakened by a pounding on her door. She turned over and looked at the clock on the dressing table. It was 6:30. She first thought she had slept all night and it was morning, but she glanced out the window and could see it was in the afternoon. She pulled herself out of bed, turned on the light and made her way to the door. She opened the door and there stood April.

April walked right in. "Put on some comfortable clothes, we're going out."

Marie looked at April and thought, *Is this girl crazy?* "Go out where?"

"We are going to do something fun. I am going to surprise you. It will be a cheap treat."

Marie did not know what to say. She looked at April. She was wearing

Friday. She told the lady at the reception desk she wanted to see April and was shown to a large office on the fourth floor. April was delighted to see her. "I thought that you would sleep in or spend the day sightseeing."

"No, I need to catch up on a few things. Is there a place with a phone I could use?"

"No problem. There just happens to be such an office on this floor." April got up from her desk and showed Marie an office about half the size of hers but somewhat far away from human traffic. "You can work here. If you need anything, press seven on the intercom. Betty will come running. If you want to talk to me, pick up the phone and dial twenty-three. By the way, do you want to have lunch together?" April did not wait for an answer. "Say about eleven thirty."

Marie opened her briefcase and reviewed the contracts with Van Meter. Everything was in order. She placed a phone call to Kunkel Corporation and confirmed that they would be there on Monday. Next, she opened her address book and found a phone number. She got an outside line, and it was not long until a familiar voice was on the other end of the line. "This is Phyllis."

"Phyllis, this is Marie. We have not talked for a while, so I thought I would give you a call. I am in the United States. I am one hundred miles from San Francisco. How are things with you?"

"I am so glad you called. Your timing could not be better. I have called your office several times. They did not tell me you were in the States. I am getting married. His name is Ryan Allen Reynolds the IV. We are getting married this Christmas. You must come and be my maid of honor. I will send you all the details. I am coming to San Francisco next week. Mother was coming, but her back is acting up. I will be there on Wednesday of next week. Please tell me that you will still be there."

"I will. I should finish my business by Tuesday, and I will see you on Wednesday or Thursday. Where will you be staying?

"I will be at the Saint Francis."

"I will see you there."

She hung up the phone and called Western Union. She sent a message to her office that she was extending her stay and taking her two-week vacation.

She looked out the window and thought of David. David would never be the man she fell in love with in France. He was now a business man with no memory of her and the time they spent in the mountains. She wondered if underneath he was still the same person?

She was still looking out the window when she heard April's voice. "Are you ready to go?"

The restaurant was not far. Once they had ordered, Marie turned to April. "This may sound crazy, but I have a friend coming to San Francisco next week. I am going to meet her and spend a couple of days with her. I would like for you to join us."

At first, April did not say anything. "Sounds like fun. I will go under one condition. I get to drive us there in my car."

***

The following Monday, the two teams were meeting with the Kunkel Corporation. They had sent three men. Things seemed to be going well when the three German men started speaking to each other in German. Marie told them she needed a restroom break and left the room. She went to the secretary and told her to go and get David Van Meter but do not say why.

When David arrived, she led him to the side. "Things are going to change in the meeting. They are going to demand four percent."

"How do you know this?"

"I speak German. That was what they were talking about. When we get back to the meeting, I want you to say that you have a contact with the Hinkle Corporation and they may offer a better deal. I will take it from there. I will go back to the meeting first, and you come back in five minutes."

When both David and Marie were back in the meeting and they were going over the contract, David spoke up. "I am not sure that two percent for distribution rights is fair to us. I have talked to the Hinkle Corporation, and they might do better."

Marie took the lead. "Mr. Van Meter. My team has been working with this team from Kunkel for several months. They have been more than fair. It is true that we can get a better deal from Hinkle, but I feel we are better off to spend just a little more with Kunkel. They have stated they will do two percent. If they are willing to sign a contract today, I think we should stay with them."

The team from Kunkel was caught off guard. They were going to ask for four percent and found they were signing a contract for two. When David and Marie were back in Mr. Van Meter's office, David was full of joy. He told his father the story and how Marie had handled the negotiation.

Van Meter was as excited as his son. "I was going to complain that you were taking my daughter away from the company to go with you to San Francisco, but all is forgiven."

David walked over to Marie and said, "Miss Lavier, let's celebrate by going over to Moran's and have a drink. Will you join us, Dad?"

"No, you two go on. I need to finish a few things here, and I am taking your mother out to an early dinner. Again, it has been nice working with you and your team, Miss Lavier. Take care of my daughter in San Francisco."

David drove Marie to Moran's. It was about a twenty-minute drive. They took a booth near the back to avoid the noise. David ordered a rum and Coke, while Marie ordered a glass of white wine.

David was staring at Marie. "Tell me about yourself. I want to know you better."

"Well, I grew up in France. My mother and father are Oliver and Luce Lavier. We live in Paris. We have a cabin in the mountains. We stayed in the cabin during the war." Marie was giving details hoping to stir his memory. "I was educated in Paris and have a degree in law from Harvard." She could tell that he had no memory of ever being in France. "What about you? I understand you were a pilot during the war."

"I was. I was shot down and as a result have no memory of the war or anything else before the crash. Many things are missing in my life. Deep inside I feel I might have lost the best part of me." He seemed to drift away just for a moment.

Marie could see that David was getting lost in his thoughts. "I have become very close to your sister in just these few days. I like her. She told me that you might be getting married."

"Darn her. She has a big mouth. I told her that in confidence. I should be mad, but there is no way you can stay mad at her."

"She cares for you more than you can know. She just needed someone to talk to."

Turning back to Marie he said, "Did you give her advice on how she should advise me?"

"She told me that you met this woman during the war. She now works for your company. You see each other quite often. She says that you care about her and her child. She is concerned that you love this woman, but you are not in love with her."

"That is an interesting way of putting it. I am not sure I will ever love anyone. I can make Alice happy. Her daughter needs a father. I think I could make a life with Alice."

"I don't know what you are going to do. I am not sure even you know. I only hope all works out for both you and Alice."

They made small talk for about an hour and he later drove Marie back to the hotel. They got out of the car and he walked with her to the hotel lobby. "Good night Miss Lavier. I have enjoyed our drinks together. If I don't see you again, have a nice flight back to Paris." He extended his hand to her.

Taking his hand, she said, "Thank you for a nice afternoon. My name is Marie. The next time you see me, please use it. I want to call you David. I am not going back to Paris just yet. April and I are going to San Francisco to see a friend of mine. I hope we see each other again before I leave." She didn't realize she was still holding his hand until she looked down and saw his bracelet. *This is the bracelet that April told me about. Should I ask him about it?* Still holding his hand, she said, "I see you have a bracelet. Some girl in your past?"

David let go of her hand and looked at the bracelet. "This bracelet may be a clue to my past. I need to solve its mystery. I think it holds the secret to what happened to me during the war. Again, I thank you for your work, and I hope I see you when you return to San Francisco." He turned and left the lobby.

For a moment, Marie thought about calling after David and telling him she knew the secret the bracelet held, but she did not. She just stood and watched as he disappeared into the parking lot.

Just Simple Magic

Two days later, Marie and April went to the St. Francis hotel and met Phyllis. For the next three days, they were like three high school girls on spring break. They took in all the sights and restaurants of the city. They went with Phyllis for the fitting of her dress. Both Marie and April fell in love with it.

On the third day of their stay, they went to Chinatown. In one shop, they found a music box that was carved from ivory. It was expensive, about twenty-five dollars. April was about to pay it when Marie stopped her. She turned to the store owner and started speaking in Chinese. Marie and the owner spoke for about five minutes, and then the owner said, "You like. It is yours for five dollars."

Once they were outside, April said, "I am impressed. You speak Chinese. How did that happen?"

"I speak several languages. It is part of my job. Let's eat down on the bay."

The next morning April and Marie took Phyllis to the airport. Phyllis made April promise that she would come to the wedding, and they all had tears in their eyes when she boarded the plane.

On the drive back, April asked Marie, "When are you going back to France?"

"I am not sure. I am going to spend another week of my vacation here. I might take a tour of the wine country, or I might go to Yosemite."

"This Saturday night Dad is throwing one of his formal parties at the house. I want you to come as my guest. It will be quite formal. Dad and Mom like to dress up. It will be fun."

"I would love to come." She thought about David. *I would like to see him one more time before I leave.*

That Saturday, Marie went to a local salon and had the works done. A slight curl was put in her coal black hair. She purchased a red sleeveless evening dress and a pair of black high heel shoes. She looked into the mirror. She barely recognized herself. The last thing she put on was a gold chain with a heart shaped diamond. It hung down almost to her breasts. The phone rang. It was April, and she quickly met her in the lobby. April was wearing a blue and white dress. "Aren't we going to knock them dead tonight? You are stunning."

"So are you. I love the dress."

When the car pulled in front of the Van Meters', a valet parked it for them. Marie looked at the house. "You grew up here?" The house was enormous, at least 30,000 square feet.

"No, Dad built this just after the war. I was in college while this was being built. I have my own room, and I come and go, and Mom and Dad don't even see me. I stay here some, but I still have my own apartment."

H.D. Van Meter and June were at the door greeting the guests. Van Meter introduced Marie to his wife, and April and Marie started to mingle with the guests. All eyes were on Marie. Her dark hair, red dress, and her beauty made her stand out. Marie took a glass of wine and ate a piece of cheese from one of the servers. Then she spotted David. He was talking to a woman. *This must be Alice.* It was not long until David saw her, and he and Alice walked over to her. "Welcome to our family home, I am so glad you came. This is Alice Baylor. She is a nurse at the infirmary."

Marie took Alice's hand. "You look so lovely; I love that dress."

"Nobody is going to notice me. All eyes are going to be on you. I am so jealous."

"Don't be. You are beautiful."

It was not long until men were coming up to Marie and talking to her. She was beginning to enjoy the attention. Just before seven, April came to Marie. "I see you got to meet Alice."

"She seems nice."

"She is. I think she may become part of the family."

"You'll have a sister. What do you think of that?"

"Not much. Wait, that does not sound right. I don't want to give the impression that we don't love Alice. I do, I mean we do. The whole family cares for her. I just don't think she is what David needs. David is not going to be happy until he finds his past. That may never happen, and Alice is going to be hurt. I don't want that for either of them."

Marie looked toward Alice, and David was no longer with her. "I believe that only David can decide what is best for David." She was about to continue her conversation with April when David came up behind her. She turned and faced him, and for a moment he looked like the David she had met in France.

"Miss Lavier, have you noticed that we have an orchestra playing music and people are dancing? Would you do me the honor?"

David led Marie to the dance floor, and he took her into his arms. They were looking into each other's eyes and they both felt the attraction. She wanted to rest her head on his chest and close her eyes and just enjoy the moment. Suddenly the music stopped.

A door opened to the dining room and a servant said, "Dinner is served."

The dining room was huge. There were four rectangular tables which seated eight each and two odd shaped tables which also seated eight. The places to sit were marked, and Marie was at the head table across from Alice. David was next to Alice on her right; April was across from David and next to Marie. Mr. Van Meter was at one end and Mrs. Van Meter was on the other. Soup was served first, and the room got somewhat quiet. Van Meter looked at Marie. "My daughter tells me you speak Chinese, and David told me you speak German. How can one person be so beautiful and so smart at the same time?"

Marie smiled and looked over at David, who was listening to the conversation. "Thank you," she said with a hint of pride.

"How many languages do you speak?"

"Several."

Van Meter was not satisfied with the answer. "Tell us what languages can you speak?"

Suddenly Marie was not liking the attention, but she answered Van Meter's question. "French, English, German, Spanish, Greek, Arabic, and Chinese."

"How can one person learn so many languages?"

"It was magic, just simple magic." She looked at David.

David was turning red, and he had gotten dizzy. He had a vision of his plane striking the water. Then another vision of being in a cave and Germans searching for him. He could feel the arms of a young woman letting him disappear into a wall. He stood up and called out, "Mira!" Then he passed out.

Among the guests were a couple of doctors and Alice, a nurse. Several men carried David to a couch in the front foyer, but no one could get David to wake. An ambulance was called, and David was rushed to a nearby hospital. Van Meter and his wife had the guests return to their meals, and they drove to the hospital.

April turned to Marie and gave her a hug. "I am going to the hospital. Will you be here when I get back?"

Marie was scared for David. Still holding onto April, she said, "May I come with you? I need to be with you."

When they arrived at the hospital, the family was in the waiting room. April took a seat next to her mother to give her comfort. Marie took a seat near the door. Time passed slowly. After about two hours, a doctor called the family together. "He is awake and is strong. He seems somewhat confused. He keeps talking about being in a cave and that someone named Mira saved him. He told me she used magic. I think some of his memory is coming back, but he is one confused young man."

Marie was close enough to hear the conversation. *I wonder if he will remember that girl in the cave was me?*

Members of the family were allowed to go into David's room. Van Meter took his son's hand. "You sure know how to liven up a party, Son. Are you feeling okay?"

"Yes, Dad, I am. I am fine. I can remember some things I could not remember before. I remember trying to get my plane back to England after it was shot up in a raid over Germany. I remember being in a cave, but that must be from when I was shot down the first time. I was in a cave with a young French girl. She hid me from the Germans. I can't remember her face, but I remember what she said when I asked her about how the Germans could not find us. She said, 'It is magic, just simple magic.' The same thing that Marie said tonight."

June sat on the edge of the bed. "We talked to the doctor before we came in. He says your memory might be returning."

April came to the side of the bed. "Welcome back, big brother. I feel things are going to be okay now. Marie came to the hospital with me, so I am going to drive her back to her hotel, but I will be back in the morning."

"Don't come back, I won't be here. They are going to let me go home in about an hour. Tell Marie to come in. I want to see her."

Quickly April was moving down the hospital hallway to get Marie. *I wonder why David is asking for Marie and not Alice?*

When Marie came in, she stood at the foot of David's bed. "Thank you for coming with April. I want to tell you some of my memory came back tonight. I want to thank you. It seems what you said started my memory coming back when you said, 'It is magic, just simple magic.' I remembered those words were spoken to me before. It may take days or weeks or months, but I know it is coming back. I owe so much to two French girls who have saved my life. It really must be magic. Thank you again."

Marie turned to April, "Take your time, I will wait in the hallway."

April spent about ten more minutes with David and then found Marie in the hallway. She was crying, even sobbing. April took her in her arms. "Things are going to be okay. Let's get you back to the hotel." *Why is Marie crying so much about David?*

Back in the hotel, Marie asked April to come to her room. "Stay with me just a while. There are some things I want you to know." Once back inside the room, Marie quickly changed into her pajamas and sat on the edge of the bed. "You have been a good friend, and I need to tell you something, but you can tell no one else. You must promise."

April took Marie by the hand. "I promise."

"You don't understand what I am going to tell you. Your promise must come from your heart. I have never told anyone what I am about to tell you."

She sat down on the edge of the bed next to Marie. Giving Marie a hug she said, "I swear with all my being that what you are about to tell me I will keep safe."

Marie got up from the bed and walked over and poured herself a glass of water. "My name is not Marie. I was not born in France. I was born in Kaspar, which was in North Africa. I was adopted by Davos and Ana. Davos was Greek, and Ana was Spanish. During the war, I was separated from my family. Davos and Ana were killed, and I was taken in by Oliver and Luce Lavier. They had lost their daughter during the war, and I took her name. My real name is Kasmira, Mira for short. It was Oliver and Luce who saved David during the war. I was the young French girl who hid David in that cave."

"David needs to know this! You can't hold me to this promise!"

"Yes, I can. David and I fell in love that summer. He promised to find me at the end of the war. He never came, and now I know why. If he loves me and his memory returns, he will look for me again. This time I will be easy to find. He will know that Marie and Mira are the same. On his bracelet is the name of the street that my French parents live on in Paris, Rue Rosalie. Our love will only exist if he remembers who I am and still feels the same way."

April looked down at the floor. Tears were falling from her eyes. When she got control of her emotions she said, "When did you know David was the pilot you saved?"

"The day he came into the meeting late. Your father explained the loss of his memory, so I said nothing. I am going home. If David regains his memory and still loves me, he will come after me. He must come because he loves me and for no other reason. I trust you will honor your promise. I love you April. You and Phyllis are my only true friends."

April could not find the words for a moment. When she regained her composure she said, "Thank you for saving my brother's life during the war. Thank you for saving my brother's life now. Thank you for becoming my sister during the last several days. There is something I don't understand. If you love David, why won't you stay and help him get his memory back?"

Marie wiped a tear from her cheek. "There is much you don't understand. The time in France that David and I had may be all that we are allowed to have. Trust me, there are forces here that even I don't understand."

April had no idea what Marie was talking about. "When are you leaving?"

"I am going to try to get a plane tomorrow. Remember your promise."

April gave Marie a hug. "I don't understand what forces you are talking about. I know that David is going to remember everything, and I think you should be here when he does."

Marie gave April a hug. "Please trust that I love David, but I need to go back to France. For some reason, I have a feeling that things are going to change in my life."

Dreams

The next day, Marie was on a plane flying back to Paris. She looked at her schedule. She would have a layover in New York and catch a plane five hours later to cross the Atlantic. She would be home by early the next morning. Seated near the front of the plane, the stewardess came back and asked her if she needed anything.

"If you could bring me a blanket, I think I might want to take a nap." Fifteen minutes later, the steady roar of the plane had her in a deep sleep. While she was sleeping, she dreamed of the Woman in Black. She was telling her that it was dangerous to seek revenge. She had magic, and to use it to get revenge would change her and she would become something else, something evil. The plane hit a patch of rough air and the toss of the plane caused Marie to wake up. *I had that conversation before with the Woman in Black. Why am I having it now? I am not seeking revenge. I can't even get back to Kaspar.*

Marie called for the stewardess. "Do you have something to help me get back to sleep? This is a long flight, and I would like to sleep during most of it."

In just a few moments the young stewardess returned with a paper cup with water and two small white pills. "One will put you to sleep and two will put you in a much deeper sleep."

Marie took both the pills from the stewardess. "Let's go for deep."

It was not long until Marie was in a deep sleep, and a second dream came. It was the Woman in Black again. She could see her standing in the cave. "It is time to come home," she said. She turned her back to her and repeated, "You are ready, it is time to come home."

Marie woke, and her heart was racing. She had not ever had a dream about Kaspar while she was living in the present world. Now she had had two in less than a couple of hours. She often thought about Kaspar, but never in a dream. She pushed the button for the stewardess.

"May I help you?"

"I need something to drink. What do you have?"

Marie looked down at her watch, and to her surprise she had been asleep for two hours.

Looking down at her, the stewardess said, "What would you like?"

"Bring me a rum and Coke. Make it more rum than Coke."

Before they landed in New York, Marie had three rum and Cokes. When the plane did land, she was just a little unsteady when she departed the plane. After a meal at the airport, she bought a magazine and spent time reading waiting for the next flight across the Atlantic.

Later she was back on the plane, and she had not thought anymore about her dream. She was tired, and she closed her eyes and drifted off to sleep again. This time the dream came again, and the Woman in Black was again standing in the cave. "It is time to come home."

Suddenly, Marie could feel her body tingle, and she opened her eyes from the dream and saw her body disappear and then reappear. She quickly looked around to see if anybody was looking at her, but nobody had seen what had happened. She looked to her right, and the woman seated next to her was asleep and had seen nothing. Getting up quickly, she made her way to the restroom, and locking the door she splashed water on her face. She felt different. Looking into the mirror, she could see she also looked different. Her eyes seemed darker and had a shine to them. Then she heard a voice. "You have your power back. Use it to come home."

When she landed in Paris, she went to her apartment, called her parents and told them that she needed to see them as quickly as possible. She called a taxi, and a few minutes later she was seated in front of them telling them the story of how she came to be in that cave where Oliver had found her.

Oliver and Luce were in disbelief.

Luce took Marie by the hand and said in a very gentle voice, "What happened in America?"

Marie looked at Luce and then to Oliver. "You don't believe me, you think something happened in America that has upset me and that I am confused. Something did happen while I was there. I met David. His name is David Van Meter. The reason he did not try to find me was that he had been injured and lost his memory after he left us. At first, he did not know me, but while I was there he was starting to regain his memory. I think by now he may know who I am, but this has nothing to do with why I am going home. I was sent here by the Woman in Black and she has told me to return. I think I may be a witch. No, I am a witch. I had magic before I came to this world and it has returned. I fear I am needed."

Oliver stood up. "Let me get something to calm you down, and I will call a doctor."

Marie stood up and walked over to the wall. "Do you remember when the Germans could not find me in the basement of the cabin? While I was there I could hear the Germans had found the trap door. I grabbed the radio, wrapped it in a blanket, and leaned against the wall and disappeared inside the wall." Leaning against the wall, she disappeared into the wall. Seconds later she reappeared. Oliver and Luce could not believe their eyes. Marie smiled and said, "It is just magic, simple magic. Sit down and let me tell you everything that has happened and what I must do."

Shakir

Shakir had never asked what had happened to Kasmira after she was banished from Kaspar. He wanted to, but he was afraid the news would be worse than he wanted to hear. He had no idea that Barak had ordered her killed. His first thoughts of his sister had been that she had been kidnapped, but he never received a ransom demand or heard anything from Barak about the men who were supposed to meet her, so he assumed that she was dead.

About two weeks after his sister had disappeared he was with Jada. "Did you know Kasmira?"

"No, I only met her a few times. For some reason, Father did not let me mingle with you, Shakira, or Kasmira. It is strange, because now he seems to encourage it. He wants me spending time with you. I hope you don't mind."

Shakir did not answer Jada. "What do you think happened to Kasmira?"

"You liked her a lot, didn't you? I can tell. You were close. Some people thought that she would be the next queen of Kaspar."

Shakir took Jada by the hands. "That is not an answer to my question. What do you think has happened to her? Has your father ever said anything?"

"He has not. He does not talk to me about what goes on in the castle. I get more information from you than him. I did talk to one of the council members. He says that she was put on a caravan heading east, and he thinks that by now she has been sold into slavery."

Shakir looked away from Jada so she could not see the tears in his eyes.

After a moment, he regained his composure and said, "I hope not. I hope something good happened to her. If I had it to do over, I would have put her in prison and after a short time I would have granted her a pardon. After I have thought about it, I would not have let your father make that decision. I am grateful for what he has done for me. I am going to let Barak run things until I am sure I can be a good king. He is much wiser than I."

Jada smiled and said, "My father is good at what he does. Your kingdom is in good hands. Meanwhile, would you like to take a walk down by the sea? It will get your mind off your sister and Kasmira."

Shakir did not have any idea that Kasmira was still alive and that his sister was living in the palace at Tranquillo. She had been granted asylum, and she and Ameena were hidden from nearly everyone except those in the castle.

Shakira

Shakira's room was large, even larger than the one she had in Kaspar. Ameena's room joined Shakira's, and for the first few weeks they stayed mostly in their rooms and only came out to take their meals. During this time, Joseph would come by and see them but not very often. At first, he would not stay very long. After several weeks passed, his visits were more frequent and his stays much longer. Around that time Shakira started leaving the room more and started doing her assigned duties and taking walks with Joseph.

After several weeks had passed, Joseph was called to the king's chambers. "I called you here as both king and father," Rhodes told his son. "It has been brought to my attention that you are seeing quite a lot of Shakira. She is young and beautiful, but we must consider more. You are eighteen, and she is fifteen. She is from Kaspar, and there lies the greater problem. Reports from Kaspar are that King Shakir is increasing his army and building more ships. I don't think the young king is doing this. I believe it is Barak. He is the one in charge, but Shakir has given him free reign. It is my belief that he wants our island, and if he can't have it, he will try to destroy it so that Kaspar will become the main trading port in this area. Do we know how Shakira will react if we go to war with her country? If conditions start to become hostile will she become a spy against us? I appointed you to the council, against Phillip's advice. Twice you have brought Shakira to meetings. We must be careful. You must be careful."

At first, Joseph didn't say anything. He walked over to the window and gazed out. "I am not too serious about Shakira. I like being with her, and I am learning a lot about Kaspar. I am also learning a lot about her brother and Barak. I will not bring her to meetings anymore, and I will see her less. I do think I need to continue to see her to find out as much as I can and to help determine if she will support us should war come."

Rhodes walked over and put his arm around Joseph. "If I were your age, I don't think falling in love with Shakira would be out of the question. She is going to get even more beautiful than she is now. Go slowly."

Joseph decided not to see Shakira for a couple of weeks. He even left the castle and went on an inspection of the northern port. He was gone for ten days, and each day Shakira was on his mind. When he returned to the castle, he sent word to her to meet him in the garden. She was there before he was. As he approached, he stopped behind some vines and with his hand parted them to see her. How could she become any more beautiful than she already was? He stood there for a few moments and then approached her. "Did you miss me?"

"Of course not," she said with a flirt in her tone.

"I did not miss you either, but here we are," he said as he took her hand, and they sat on a white bench that was surrounded by flowers. "My father knows just about everything that is going on. Barak is now ruling Kaspar. What more can you tell me about him?"

"Is that why you asked me here?" She pulled her hand away from his. "I thought you wanted to see me, not push me for information about Barak and Kaspar?"

Joseph could see the flush in Shakira's face. She was only fifteen, but she was going to speak her mind even if she was a guest in his country and an exile from hers. "I am sorry." He decided to test her. "Shakir and Barak do not know what has happened to you. If they think we are holding you against your will, this would be an act of war. I was only thinking of you and your future here on this island."

Her tone softened. "I am sorry. I forget my place. I know that I am a guest of your kingdom, but it is more than that. I want to make this my home, and I want you to be my friend. If Barak and my brother discover that I am here, I will make it clear that this is my home and I do not wish to return to Kaspar."

He smiled and took her hand again. "There is another reason I asked you to meet me here. I wanted to talk in private. I am leaving for a long trip. It might take several months. Before I leave, I want to make sure you have everything you need. Father and Mother will take care of you. They know that you are my friend and that I care for you."

Shakira was in shock. She had only been there for a short time, and she was losing her main support at the castle. She tried to conceal her concern. "Can I ask where you are going?"

"It is not a secret. I am taking several ships to Greece. It involves our trade agreements, and we must fulfill them. We have several cities that we trade with in that area."

"Is that going to take several months?"

"Well, it involves more than just taking several ships to trade goods. I will also serve as ambassador and be there setting future agreements and treaties. We also want to expand our trade throughout the east. I really don't know how long it will take. Stay my friend while I am gone."

Shakira didn't understand what stay my friend meant. Was he saying he liked her more than a friend and that she should not see any other men while he was gone? "I will always be your friend. I owe you my life, and what future I may have belongs to you. It is only because of you that I have a future. Let me say it again. I will always be your friend."

Pulling her just a little closer, he said, "I wish I could take you with me or I wish I didn't have to be gone so long."

To his surprise, she gave him a hug. "Me too. I will be here when you return. Please come back quickly. Next month is my birthday. I was hoping you and I could celebrate together, but it looks like it will just be me and Ameena."

He kissed her on the top of the head and said, "I am sorry I will not be here, but I will be here for another two weeks."

Joseph and Shakira spent as much time as they could with each other, and the two weeks passed too quickly. It was not long until they were standing on the dock saying their goodbyes. Facing her, he said, "I hope the time passes quickly. Think of me on your birthday because I will be thinking of you. I am sorry I will not be there." He kissed her on the top of her head and turned and boarded the boat.

As Shakira watched the boats sail out of sight, she began to cry. *I wonder if he loves me as much as I love him.*

Rue Rosalie

Alice rode in the ambulance with David to the hospital. The paramedic took off David's watch and bracelet and wallet and put them in a bag and gave them to Alice. "See that his family gets these when they get to the hospital." While in the emergency room, David regained consciousness. He did not see Alice in the room. He kept saying to the doctor, "I was in a cave and the Germans came in. Mira saved me. She used magic."

Alice and the doctor stepped into the hallway. "I think his memory is coming back. He is confused, but he is remembering something. I am going to give him a shot to calm him down. His heart needs to slow down. Go see the family and tell them I will be up shortly. Don't tell them anything until I get him calmed down."

Alice realized that she had the bag that contained David's personal items. The bag was a clear plastic, and she could see the bracelet and could read the inscription on the back. Mira, she thought. This was what he called out at the dinner party. *Who is Mira?*

***

It was well past midnight when David got back to his parents' house. They had insisted that he spend the night with them. When he finally got to bed, he found sleep came very easily. In his dreams, he saw the cabin and two people but could not make out their faces. The next morning, he ate breakfast with his parents. They were asking so many questions that he could not answer. He was glad when breakfast was over, and he was back in the bedroom. Van Meter told him not to come to work, but he decided he needed to talk to April. Picking up the phone he called his sister. When she answered, he said, "Have lunch with me today. I need to talk."

***

Once they had taken their seats and ordered their food, David turned to April and said, "I have been a lot of trouble. I don't know how I could ever thank you enough."

"Good grief, David. We are family. You have always been there for me. How are things going today?"

"I feel good. I have two solid memories that I didn't have before. I remember coming back from Germany and crashing my plane. I also remember being in a cave and the Germans searching for me. This is the strange part. I remember this young girl taking me in her arms, and it was like we disappeared into the cave wall. When it was over, and the Germans had left, I asked her how she did that, and she said, 'It was magic, just simple magic.' That is what Marie said last night. I would like to talk to her again. Do you have her room number? I will give her a call and see if she would like to have dinner."

"You can't. She left this morning going back to Paris. Do you have any memories of the young girl? Do you know what she looked like?" April so much wanted David to remember that the young girl was Marie. The secret that Marie had told her was a heavy burden to bear.

"No. In my memory of the cave I can't remember her face. I remember that voice." David paused for a moment. "You know, she may have sounded like Marie. It must be that French accent."

Just then the waitress brought the food and placed it on the table. Once she had left, April said, "I have an idea. When the contracts are ready to be signed, why don't you take them to Paris yourself? You could go to England first and visit where you were stationed. It may help bring your memory back."

David didn't say anything but began to salt his food. He looked across the table at April. "I don't think that will help, but I will give it a try."

Two weeks later, the contracts were ready. Van Meter and David signed, and April drove with David to the airport.

April took David by the hand. "I am glad you are letting me fly to New York with you. I am going to spend several days in New York."

"I know you are going to spend some time in New York. Who is this person you are going to meet?"

"Her name is Phyllis Brooks. She is a friend of Marie's. I met her in San Francisco."

David gave April a big smile. "I had hoped that you were meeting a young good-looking man. You know you can't be an old maid for the rest of your life."

Later, as they sat together on the plane, David had another memory. It was when they were very young, and they were playing together. He looked at her and realized that she was not only his sister. She was his best friend.

That night, David, April, and Phyllis had dinner together. David looked at Phyllis. She was a beautiful woman in her own right. "How is it that you know Marie?"

"Marie and I went to Harvard together. We shared the same dorm room. I got to know her very well and really not at all. She talked very little about her family. She had a boyfriend when she came to America, but they broke up while she was here. I don't think there has ever been anyone she was serious about. Maybe there is hope for you two. You both are unmarried." Looking down at his water glass, David drifted away in thought. He first thought of Alice, and then he thought about what Phyllis had just said.

Snapping out of his daze he said, "That is not the purpose of this trip. Has April told you about my problem?"

"She has. I hope this trip helps you." She turned to April. "I am so glad you came, because I have a question. I want you to be one of my bridesmaids. Please say yes. I know we have only known each other a short time, but I feel that we have been friends forever. There will be five bridesmaids if you agree."

"I do agree, and I can't thank you enough for asking me."

For the rest of the meal, the two women turned into two schoolgirls and talked continuously about the wedding. When the meal was over, David told them goodbye and went back to his room. That night as he lay in bed, he had another vision and a memory. The young faceless girl was whispering in his ear. She was saying "Rue Rosalie." She was telling him where she would be after the war, but she did not tell him which city.

The next day on the flight to London, he dozed off in his seat. He dreamed about the war, and when he awoke he had a strong memory of being at the base in England. He remembered being there with Alice. He could remember his parents and bits and pieces of his memory going to Berkley. For some reason, he could not remember being shot down the first time. He knew a French family had saved him but nothing else, no faces, nothing except being in a cave with a young French girl.

When he got to England he visited the old base where he had been stationed. It was closed, and much of it was gone, but his memory was getting stronger. As he walked out on the old unused runway, he could see weeds growing in the cracks of the pavement. He decided not to spend any more time at the base. He needed to find Rue Rosalie.

The next day, he flew to Paris. He decided not to call and tell Marie he was coming. He would just drop in. When he arrived, he walked up to the receptionist and said, "David Van Meter to see Marie Lavier."

"Do you have an appointment?"

"No, I worked with her on some contracts, and I have brought the completed documents for her to look over and sign."

"She is not here, but I will get her assistant. His name is Paul, and he is free. His office is just down this hall, the first one on the left."

He knocked on the door, which was ajar.

"Mr. Van Meter, please come in. I'm Paul. We met while working on the contracts."

"Paul, yes I have the completed contracts. I was hoping to see Miss Lavier, but the receptionist said she was not in. Will she be in later today?"

"I am afraid not. When she came back from America, she took a leave of absence. She said she had some personal matters to work out. She still may be in Paris. Would you like her number? I am sure she would like to see you."

"I would, and her address too, please."

Paul quickly pulled out one of her cards. "This has the office phone, and I will write her home phone as well as her address on the back. I will also write her parents' address on the back. I don't have their number, but she may be with them. They are very close, and she stays with them from time to time."

David took the card and put it in his pocket. "Thank you so much. Please look over the contracts. I am staying at the Golden Paris Hotel. Call me there if you have any questions."

When David got back to his room, he took out the card and called Marie's number. No answer. He looked at the back of the card. When he saw the address of Marie's parents, he lay back on the bed. *This can't be. Oliver Lavier, 1006 Rue Rosalie.* He still had not made the connection that Marie was Mira. He quickly left the hotel and got a taxi. It took about twenty minutes to reach the address.

"Please wait," he told the taxi driver. "They might not be home." He knocked on the door, and it was opened by Luce. "David," she said with a shocked look on her face.

Suddenly, his memory of her and Oliver came back. He felt like he was going to pass out and lost his balance and fell against the wall.

"Oliver, come here! I need you."

In just a moment, Oliver was standing beside David and helping him to the couch. "Get some water. No, make that a brandy."

Luce went to the street and paid for the taxi and soon came back with the brandy. David sipped a small drink. "I am okay now. Where is Marie?"

"She told us that she had found you. She told us you had lost your memory, but there was hope you might get it back. It seems your memory has returned."

David lay back on the couch. *Marie and Mira are the same person. I fell in love on that mountain with a young French girl. Marie is that girl.* His memory was now completely clear. The love he had for Mira returned, and he knew he now had to find her more than ever. "It has, where is she?"

"She is not here. She is not even in Paris. She told us the most remarkable story. If I had not seen what she can do, I would think she was insane. I am not going to tell you her story, but I will tell you where she is. She has gone back to the cabin where we lived during the war. I will also tell you this. She said she was going home, and that cabin is not her home."

"Where is her home? I thought she was from Paris."

"You are not going to believe this. She said her home was Kaspar. I have tried to find Kaspar on a map, but I don't think it exists. Marie is not our daughter. We found her wandering in the mountains. We never knew very much about her. We grew to love her as Mira, but she took the name of our daughter who was killed in the war when we came back to Paris."

"How do I get to your cabin? I must find her before she can leave." Then it hit him. "Oliver, you are speaking English."

"I found that after the war it was necessary. It took some time and a good teacher, but I am getting better each day."

Oliver left the room and came back with a map. He drew out the directions, and David gave Luce a hug, shook hands with Oliver and quickly left.

David rented a car and was on the way to the cabin. The drive seemed to take forever. Finally, he was driving up the mountain that led to the cabin. When he came in sight of the log structure, he could see a woman standing on the front porch dressed in Arabian clothing. It was Marie. Stopping the car, he ran and took her in his arms.

"You can't go," he said. "I just found you, I can't lose you again."

After a long embrace and a few kisses, Marie spoke. "I am leaving; I don't have any choice, but if I can I will come back."

"There is always a choice. You can stay with me."

She looked into his eyes and could see the love he had for her. "Did Father and Mother tell you how I came to be here, and how Barak had my real parents killed?"

David had no idea what she was talking about. "I don't know anything about you or where you are from. Wherever you are going, let me go with you."

"You can't. I am going to tell you this, and you will not believe me. I am not from this time. My parents were killed, and an evil man took over the kingdom of Kaspar."

Suddenly, David felt guilty. "You are confused. Oliver said something about Kaspar. The stress of the last few days has been too much for both of us. It will pass. I have my memory back and we are together. That is all that matters."

"You don't understand, and you can't. A woman of magic sent me here to protect me from the evil that was in Kaspar and to prepare me for what I must do. I am going back to seek justice for my family."

David had no idea what to say. He was becoming more confused. "You told Oliver that you were from Kaspar. Where is Kaspar?"

Marie took a deep breath. "It is not a place as much as it is a time. I had no idea that I would be here this long, and I don't have any idea why I am being called back at this time. I just know I have no choice. It seems neither of us has any say in what happens to us. I didn't know that I would fall in love while I was here. I just know I will do what I must do to get back to you, Luce and Oliver and all the people I care about. I am not going to leave until tomorrow. Just spend time with me and trust me. I am not confused, and I am not crazy. Let's not talk about it anymore."

David did not believe what Marie was telling him but thought it best to not say anything else.

Marie took David by the hand and said, "I brought food, would you like to eat?"

David gave a weak smile. "Why not, do you have any wine or something stronger?"

"Oliver and Luce had a place where they hid wine from the Germans. After the war, Oliver's brother turned it into a wine cellar. I am sure there is some there."

A few minutes later, Marie had found some wine and they were eating cold sandwiches.

David looked around the cabin. "It does not look the same. I don't remember it this way."

"It is not the same. Oliver's brother came to live here after the war to protect his daughter. She had dated a German during the occupation of Paris. They lived here for several years and made some much-needed improvements. It is larger now and has a bathroom. You no longer have that long walk to the creek or have to heat water for a tub. They still use it as a vacation home."

"Where do they live now?"

"Oh, they are back in Paris, but their daughter now lives in Canada. She is married and has a couple of kids. She is doing well."

David and Marie continued to make small talk late into the night. Neither wanted to face saying goodbye. That night, they lay down on the bed together. Holding her in his arms, he could smell her sweetness and was amazed how soft she felt. He kissed her several times as they talked, and both confessed their love to each other, but they did not make love. Sometime during the night, Marie fell asleep in David's arms. *Have I done this to Mira? I told her that I would find her after the war. When she came to California, I treated her badly and did not recognize her. What could she be thinking, working with me and me not remembering her? No wonder she is confused.* As David held her, he watched the steady rise and fall of her breast. The rhythm of her breathing and pressures of the day brought sleep.

The next morning David awoke, and Marie was gone. He called out her name several times and realized she had left. His heart was racing, and many terrible thoughts ran through his mind. *No telling what she would do in her state of mind.* As he looked out a window, he caught a glimpse of her going up the hill that led to the cave. He ran after her, and when he was near the cave, he saw her go inside.

Once Marie was inside the cave, she looked at the wall. She knew the wall would let her return to Kaspar. She took a letter she had written and placed it on the floor of the cave and faced the wall and walked through it.

David came running into the cave just after she had disappeared. He looked for her, but she was nowhere to be found. He saw the letter lying on the floor of the cave. He took the letter outside and sat on a large rock and begin to read.

> *Dear David,*
>
> *I can't tell you how much I love you and what you mean to me. I am sorry I left you this morning without saying goodbye. It was just too hard. I can't believe that in just a short period of time I really became part of your family. I love your mother and father, and April became like a sister. I told you that I would try to come back. I now know that I have powerful magic, but that magic was not needed here. This place is magic. You have machines that fly, images that can be seen on movies and television. I don't think the people who live here know how much magic there is here. The real magic is the magic of love. I hope that magic will bring me back. If it does not, find someone to love that will also love you. My time with you was more than simple magic, it was simply magical.*
>
> *Kasmira Mira Marie*

121

David did not know what to do. He felt like crying, and he had a feeling that he might never see Marie again. He again read the letter. He wiped his eyes, stood up, and walked back down the hill toward the cabin. He noticed the keys to the cabin door were still in the lock. He went inside, gathered up his things, locked the door, and returned to his rented car. When he got to Lyon, he called Oliver and Luce.

Luce answered the phone.

David took a long breath. "I am in Lyon. I did get to see Marie before she left. I don't understand what happened. I saw her go into the cave, and when I followed her, she was not there."

David could hear Luce take a deep breath on the other end of the phone. "We will have to trust that she will come back to us. Will you come back to Paris for a visit?"

"I will be there late tonight or tomorrow."

The next day, David was knocking on the door of Oliver and Luce's home. Oliver came to the door, and when he saw it was David he gave him a hug. "I am glad you came by. There is much we need to talk about. Luce said you got to see Marie."

"I did." Just about that time Luce came into the room.

Luce sat on the couch, and Oliver and David sat in the living room chairs. "We are lucky it is Saturday. Otherwise, we would be at the university. Do you want something to drink, coffee or perhaps tea?"

"Yes, coffee will be fine."

Once the coffee was made, they moved to the kitchen and sat around a table. David told his story of seeing Marie only to lose her in the cave.

Oliver did not seem surprised. "It is hard to believe, but I think that our Marie is an enchantress from another world. She saved our lives more than once during the war and saved you in the cave. She had to have magic to do that. Now, for some reason, she has gone back to her world. Did she leave you any message about coming back?"

David showed the letter to Luce and Oliver. "If it takes a lifetime, I am going to wait for her. Today I am going by her office to finish the contracts, and tomorrow I am flying back to California. If she comes back, contact me. I will drop everything I am doing and fly back."

Oliver and Luce looked at the letter. After they had read it, Luce looked at David. "She signed the letter Kasmira/Mira/Marie. She came to us as Kasmira, she loved you as Mira, and she became our daughter as Marie."

***

That afternoon David finished his business with Marie's company. Talking to the secretary he said, "I know that Miss Lavier took a leave. Did she indicate how long she would be gone?"

"No, she said she was not sure. She is the only person in the company who could do that. She has so many skills and is so important that she can do just about anything she wants."

On the flight, David could not get Marie out of his mind. *When I get back, I can't tell anyone because they will think I am crazy. I do have to talk to Alice. I can't keep stringing her along.*

When the plane landed, it was about noon. He went straight to the factory and stopped by the infirmary. Alice was just about to leave to go to lunch, so David drove her to a nearby café. When they finished their meal, David took Alice by the hands. "I have something I must tell you. I have my memory back. I was shot down twice in the war. The first time, I was saved by the French Resistance. I stayed with a married couple, Oliver and Luce, and they had a daughter, and I fell in love with her. You have seen my bracelet. On one side, it has her name, Mira, and on the other the street she lives on in Paris, Rue Rosalie. While I was in France I found her. I am still in love with her."

At first, Alice did not say anything. "You need to relax. I knew you were never going to commit yourself to me. I think this Mira was always hidden deep in your heart. When can I meet her?"

"You have met her already. Here comes the strange part of this story. The person you know as Marie is Mira. I had no memory of her, and for some reason she did not let me know who she was. I think she thought I would never get my memory back and that I had moved on with my life. My memory of her came back while I was in Paris. She did not come back with me, and there are some problems that may prevent us from ever being together."

Alice again seemed baffled. "I don't understand. Is she married to someone else?"

"No, and I can't tell you any more other than I am going to wait for her, no matter how long it takes. I wanted you to know because you have been such a good friend."

As they drove back to the infirmary, they said very little. When David stopped the car, Alice bent toward him and kissed him on the cheek. "Don't worry about me. You and I are always going to be good friends."

David drove the car around front and immediately went to April's office. Walking in, he said to April, "Get your purse, we are going for a drive."

"Great to see you too, big brother. I am glad you are back. Did you find Marie? Can you remember more things about your past now?"

"Slow down, you are talking a mile a minute. Stop talking and come with me." When they were alone, he said, "Marie is Mira, the same French girl who saved me during the war. I have seen her, and that is why I need to talk to you, and only you, about her."

They drove to the park and stopped the car overlooking a lake. Shifting his body to face April, David started talking. "It was Marie that brought my memory back. When she said, 'It is magic, just simple magic,' that was the same thing she said to me in a cave back in France when German soldiers were about to find us, and they did not."

April shifted nervously in her seat. "Marie told me it was her family that saved you during the war, before she left for Paris. She made me swear not to tell you. I am so sorry. Where is she now? Are you going to be together?"

David took April by the hands and said, "You are the only person I am going to tell this story to. You are not only my sister; you are my closest friend." David then told the incredible story about Mira. When he finished, April looked at him and said, "Wow!"

Nyla

Nyla lived in a small village called Anemoi and never thought of going anywhere else. Her mother was a healer and had taught her the art. Her mother also had a special talent. She knew much about the art of healing but also had magic. Her mother had taught her all the skills of healing and had told her that one day magic would come to her.

"Keep your magic a secret and use it only to heal. Good people will fear things they don't understand and try to destroy the gifts that you have. The more you use magic the stronger it becomes. If you use it unwisely, it will take you over, and you will become evil." Her mother would tell her this over and over. Hana knew what had happened to Piper, and though she never told Nyla the story, she would make sure that Nyla understood that magic was both a blessing and a curse.

Nyla's magic came when she was about fourteen years of age, and she quickly found she had far more magic than her mother. Her mother died when she was sixteen, and she replaced her as the village shaman. After the death of her mother her father sat down with her and again warned her about her magic. He told her his story of how he once had magic and how it became locked inside him. He made her promise to never use her magic in anger, or revenge, or pleasure.

When Nyla turned eighteen her father died. He had just lost the will to live after the death of Hana. Standing at the grave of her father, Nyla again promised she would use her magic for healing people. Using her healing skill along with her magic, she had become well known, and people often would travel great distances to seek her and her cures. Nyla always did as her mother had asked. She not only kept her magic a secret, she would not use it unless it was a matter of life or death. She feared her magic and knew the more she used it the more powerful it would become and the more she would be tempted to use it for something evil. It was just after her father died that everything changed. Two kingdoms had gone to war, and the reports that came into the village were that fighting was everywhere. It seemed that two great religions had gone to war, and a lot of the people who were fighting were just following their leaders and really didn't know why they were fighting. One morning, she heard shouting in the village. The fighting was now just north of Anemoi. Nyla thought some of the wounded might be brought to Anemoi, but this did not happen.

One afternoon, she was standing outside her tent, and she saw dust rising on the horizon. *Soldiers are coming*, she thought, and she watched as the dust turned into five soldiers who came straight into their camp. She watched as one of the men dismounted from his horse and called for the leader of the village. The two men talked, and the village leader turned and pointed to her. The man quickly approached her and said, "You are Nyla, the village healer. We have heard much about you. We have a wounded man with us. All I can tell you is that he is important. He cannot be allowed to die."

Nyla watched as the other soldiers carried the wounded man toward her. "Take him into my tent," and she pointed to the large red tent in front of them. Once they were inside and he was lying on a mat, she looked down at him. *He is barely a man. He can't be over nineteen or twenty years of age.* She quickly kneeled and removed the bandage and saw he had a wound to the left side of his chest.

"What happened," she asked.

Raja, a tall soldier, spoke. "He was struck by an arrow about a week ago. We removed it, but he is getting worse. Our healers say that he will be dead in less than a day. What do you think?"

Nyla looked at his wound. It was about one inch wide, and the skin was dark red about six inches around it. Turning him to his side, she saw that the arrow had come out on his back side, and he had a similar wound on his back. There was white pus coming out of both wounds. He was burning up with fever. Looking up, she said, "Your healers are right. He won't be alive this time tomorrow."

Raja said, "This can't happen. Everyone, leave the room and let me be alone with the healer." When they were alone, Raja looked at Nyla and said, "This is no ordinary man. His name is Jaul. He is the king of Kaspar and my friend. He has no heir. If he dies his brother will become king, but he is not the leader that Jaul is. All that we have fought for will be lost. I am going to take my men back to our camp. Do what you can to keep him alive until we leave tomorrow. I will tell the men there is hope, and we will leave. We must not let the news of his death reach our enemy. They will see our weakness and exploit it. Our men will scatter, and Kaspar will be undefended. We must keep who he is and that he is severely wounded a secret."

"I will try to keep him alive until you leave. I will promise no more." She watched as Raja left the tent, and she turned to the man on the mat. She quickly removed his clothing and took them outside and threw them on the fire. Returning, she quickly cleaned his wounds and covered them with clean bandages. She dressed him in a white gown. Then she really looked at him. He was tall and dark. He had a short beard and a small scar on his left cheek. He was slender and muscular. *I bet he was a great fighter.* On his lower left arm, he had a birth mark. It was in the shape of a crescent moon with what looked like a star above it.

When she finished her examination, she said to herself, "I am going to do more than just keep you alive until tomorrow. I can heal you, but it must be over several weeks. My magic must remain my secret." She took out a small bottle and said a few words and placed some on his lips.

Placing the bottle aside, she put her hand on the wound and concentrated to bring her magic forward. She got a second mat, lay down beside him, and went to sleep.

The next morning, she brought some broth and opened Jaul's mouth and fed him some. She could tell he had not had anything to eat for several days so she also gave him some goat's milk. While she was letting him taste and swallow the milk, he opened his eyes and looked up at her. *I am with an angel,* he thought to himself, and quickly went back to sleep.

When Raja returned with his men, he feared the worst. When he approached Nyla's tent, he could see her seated outside eating bread and cheese. She rose to her feet and greeted them. The village leader was also with them.

Staring at her, Raja said, "What type of night did he have?"

"Better than expected," she said. "He had a good night."

Raja thought to himself, *she is playing the role perfectly. My men won't expect anything.* "Good, we will leave him in your hands and return to our camp. May I see him before we go?"

"Yes, but bring in a couple of men with you. I need to turn him over for a while."

Raja was caught off guard. He did not know what to say. He simply pointed to a second man, and they all went into the tent. Raja looked at Jaul lying on the mat. She had propped him up just a little, and he knelt and took his hand. "We are leaving now, and I will return in two weeks to see how you are doing." To his surprise, Jaul opened his eyes and seemed to smile, and then drifted off to sleep. Under Nyla's guidance, the two men removed his pillow which propped up his head and gently turned him over.

Outside the tent, Raja turned to Nyla. "What have you done? He is getting better."

"It was magic, just simple magic," she said with a smile, knowing you can hide the truth within the truth. "Cleaning the wound, and a special ointment that I have, and forcing some liquid down him has started him toward recovery. His wound is still bad. We made some gains during the night. He still needs a lot of care, and I don't know if he will continue to get better, but he is better off than he was yesterday."

Nyla continued for several days to let Jaul's wounds heal on their own. During this time Jaul would go in and out of consciousness. On the fifth day, Nyla was lying on her mat next to Jaul when he turned toward her and weakly said, "Where am I?"

She quickly stood up and looked at him for a few moments. He just stared at her and said again, "Where am I?"

"You are in the village of Anemoi about twenty miles south of your camp. You were wounded, and your men brought you here to see if you could be saved. Don't say anymore, and I will get you something to eat and drink. You have had only liquids for several days. It was all I could get you to swallow. It is time we got you something a little more solid."

While Nyla prepared the food, Jaul watched her through the opening in the tent.

Jaul was given milk, bread, and soup. The soup contained just a little meat, and Jaul ate well, but Nyla didn't let him eat too much.

"I would like some wine."

"Not yet, maybe in a couple of days. Let's see how this does, and we will go from there."

"Why did my men bring me here? We have healers in our camp."

"You were brought here because your healers had given you up to die. Raja had heard of me and thought that I might give you a chance at life, so here we are. Your wounds are severe. The arrow went all the way through to your back. Over several days your wounds began to fester, you lost consciousness, and your wounds became more severe. It responded well to a healing salve I have, and you have been slowly getting better. Don't plan on going off to war anytime soon. It is going to take time. What do you remember?"

Trying to move, Jaul wrenched in pain. "Very little. I remember being hit with the arrow. It took me off my horse. Raja came to me and broke the arrow and pulled it through from the back. When he got me back to camp, I was already getting sick. After that, everything is hazy. I have some memory but not a lot. I remember someone saying I was going to die, I think, but here I am."

Nyla opened his gown and took the bandage from the wound. "It is looking better every day. I am going to give you something to help you sleep. I think you will sleep anyway, but I don't want you to move very much. You have already felt what any movement will do. If things go well, we will let you sit up tomorrow, but there will be some pain."

Jaul gave a weak smile. "Don't give me anything just yet. We need to talk. Do you know who I am?"

"Yes, I do. Raja told me."

"How many in this village know who I am?"

"Just me. I was told it must be kept a secret. You can trust me. I will get you well and back to the battle before our enemy knows what has happened."

Nyla went to her supply shelf and got a potion to help Jaul sleep. Returning to him, she said, "Take this, and when you open your eyes, you will be much better. I promise."

Nyla lay down on her mat and waited until she heard the deep breathing of Jaul. Getting up, she walked over to him and placed her hands on his wounds. Concentrating, she called on her magic again, and then she too went to sleep.

The next morning, Jaul awoke feeling much better. He was awake even before Nyla. He shifted his body, so he could see her, and she was right. There was a lot of pain. He looked at her and watched her sleep. Her breathing was even, and he watched her chest rise and fall with each breath. Her dark skin was smooth, and she was a beautiful young woman. *How could she know a lifetime of medicine at such a young age? She can't be more than eighteen or nineteen.* As he watched her, she began to wake up.

"What is your name?" he said when she appeared to be awake.

"Nyla. I have lived in this village my entire life. I became a healer when my mother died."

"What about your father?"

"He died shortly after my mother's death." Nyla got to her feet and grabbed several more pillows. She helped him raise up and used the pillows to keep him upright. She could see the pain in his face. "I could give you something that will help with that pain, but if you can stand it, it is better that I don't. It may put you back to sleep, and I want you to stay awake for a while. A little movement will help the pain go away quicker."

Jaul smiled and said, "I think you just want to punish me for being so much trouble."

Nyla returned his smile. "I am going to fix you a more traditional breakfast this morning. Today you are going to have some dates, a couple of eggs, and some dried meat. Don't ask what kind."

He spoke in a serious tone. "We need to give me a new name. I will give you the honor of the name, and I will create the man behind the name."

She smiled and thought for a moment. "How about Mazin? That is a good name."

Returning her smile, he said, "No, I don't like that name. It is an old name, try something else."

"So much for giving me the choice of name."

"Alright, give it one more try, and whatever you come up with I will accept."

Taking her finger to the side of her face, she smiled, "I have the name. It will be Jabir. It is a good name. What do you think?"

"Jabir, it is. I will create a story to go with the name. Do you have that breakfast ready? I am starving."

The next day, the village leader, Fadi, came to visit Jabir. He was even stronger than the day before, and Fadi didn't miss a chance to brag on his healer. "She is the best around. Why did your men bring you here? What about your healers, are you someone of importance?"

Jabir had anticipated the question. "They thought that I might die, and they need information that I have. I am a scout. I was sent to measure the strength of our enemy and their location. I was not able to give them that information before I passed out. I am sure they will be here any day to retrieve what I know."

Fadi looked at Jabir with a smile. "I know who you are. I have been to Kaspar and have witnessed the court proceeding. I understand that you must keep who you are a secret. Does Nyla know who you are?"

"She does. I am trusting my life to you two."

Jabir and Fadi talked for a long time before Nyla came in and said, "I know you two want to know everything about each other, but Jabir needs rest. Why don't you continue this conversation tomorrow?"

A few days later Raja and two men came back to the village and went directly to Nyla's tent. They were greeted by Jabir sitting in a chair and Nyla working over an open fire. Jabir tried to get up but could not. "Have you talked to anyone in the village on your arrival?"

"No," Raja answered, and the other two men shook their heads in agreement.

"Good, right now my name is Jabir. I am a scout for the army. They think that you brought me here because you needed my scouting information. Does anyone suspect that I might be dead?"

"There is some talk, but we can put that to rest when we get back. There is no fighting, and both sides are taking a break to take care of the wounded and dead. There might not be any more fighting until you have returned. When do you think that might be?"

Both men turned and looked at Nyla. "I am not sure. His wounds were severe. I would say at least three weeks and maybe four or five. If I send him back too early, all of this will be for naught. You saw how bad the wounds were. It is strange, the front side of the wound is looking better than the backside. He is lucky he can sit up. In the next couple of days, I hope you can walk, and in about two weeks we will see if he can sit a horse. That is the best I can give you, and that is just a guess."

Neither of the two men said anything, but just stared at Nyla, with each waiting for her to say more. She did not, but thought to herself, *I don't want him to return to the fight where there is a chance he may be killed. I enjoy him being here, and I like taking care of him. I enjoy the conversations that we have been having.*

Raja and his companions spent a day and night at the village. They had the dinner meal with Fadi, and the next morning they said their goodbyes to Jabir and the camp and rode back north.

In the next couple of days, Jabir began to walk with the help of a large stick he used to keep his balance. His strength was coming back quickly, and two days later he tossed the stick aside. It was that night that Fadi came to visit Jabir. "We are going to move you to another tent. Your health is improving more each day. I will have a young boy stay with you, and you will be free to move about the village. You will see that it is quite large, and we have an oasis on the southern end of the village. There is a private area where men can bathe. You can see why you must move. Nyla is a young unmarried woman, and she must be protected from words that might do her harm."

"I understand. Where is my new residence?"

"Not far. Only about 200 feet away. You can still come for your treatment, and you and Nyla can visit during the day. She seems to enjoy your company."

"I owe her more than I ever can pay. I don't have much to move. Nyla got me some clothes to wear. I guess that is fair because when I asked what happened to mine, she said she burned them."

Fadi smiled. "My son is about your age. I am sure we can get you more clothes and that way you can keep clean. I must go."

Jabir moved out of Nyla's tent and each day would walk back to her tent for her to dress his wound. Each day when she looked at the wound she was so pleased with the progress that she decided she would let nature finish the job. She encouraged him to take longer and longer walks, and she was surprised when one day he called her out of her tent to see him sitting on a horse smiling.

"What are you doing? Has your healer okayed this?"

"That's what I am here for. I have talked to Fadi, and he has loaned me a couple of horses. I need to see if I can ride, and I need you to fix me if I fall off," he said with a big smile.

Nyla scoffed. "If you could get on that horse, I don't think you are going to fall off." She walked by him and took the second horse by the reigns. "Where are we going?"

Jabir glanced up at the sun. "Fadi told me that there is a small cool oasis to the west of here. He said it is about two miles. That will test my wound and give me a place to rest before we start back. Do you know the place in case we get lost?"

"I do, but don't you think we need somebody to go with us? Just in case you do fall off. I could never get you back on your horse."

Jabir scoffed and smiled. "Have faith, woman. Let's go."

Watching Jabir ride in front of her, Nyla could tell he was very at home riding a horse. She thought to herself that he must be a great warrior, and she also sensed that he must also be a good king. She pulled her horse alongside his. "Why are you, or I mean why are we fighting this war? Several of the young men of the village have joined the fight and none have returned. What is this sacrifice for?"

His tone became very serious. "We have tried to spread our way of life far beyond our borders. I am not sure this is something that we should have done. We are overextended, and our united front has started to lose ground. Several kings have taken their armies home, and we are weak. The fighting is getting closer and closer to Kaspar. If we don't stop the enemy, they will take Kaspar, and no one to the east will be safe."

"Is there not some way you can make peace?"

"We need a great victory. If we can do this, I think they will talk peace. Enough talk of war and armies. How far is it to the oasis?"

"Not far. We are almost there."

When they arrived at the oasis, Nyla was surprised that no one was there. It was a little out of the way, and most only visited it if they wanted to get away from the village, but there were always one or two people there. It was not large and consisted of a small pool of blue water surrounded by several large palm trees. The trees produced ample shade, and the water bubbling from the ground cooled the air. Just outside the line of trees was tall, brown grass which hid the water.

Jabir got off his horse slowly and turned and faced Nyla. "I think I will rest for a while before we start back. This was a bit harder than I thought. On the back of your horse you will find a couple of blankets. If you will get those I can lie down for a while. There is also some food wrapped up with the blankets. I went to that small market and got a bottle of wine. Wine here is like gold."

When the blankets were spread, and they were stretched out on the sand very close to the water, Jabir spoke very seriously and in a low tone. "When I go back to the camp, why don't you come with me? We could use a healer of your skill, and you could take care of me."

At first, she thought he was joking, but seeing his face she could tell he was serious. "I don't think you know what you are asking. I know you are grateful for me helping to heal your wounds, but I am the healer of my village. They need me here."

"I have been here several weeks, and if it were not for me, you would not have had anything to do. But that is not what I am asking." He turned on his blanket and moved close to her. He gently kissed her, first on the forehead and then on the mouth.

Her head was spinning. She had never had a man in her life. Most of the time in a village marriage was arranged, but healers were exceptions. Her mother had found love and marriage, but she had told Nyla that was often not true of female healers. For a moment, she said nothing, and the warmth of the kiss spread throughout her body. She did not move away and stayed close to him. "What are you asking?"

"I am asking you to come with me. I am in love with you."

She moved away. "You are the king of Kaspar. There can be no life for us. The only life for me is to become your camp lover. If you really love me, you will not ask this of me."

"I am asking much more. If I can end this war, I am sure I can make a life for us as king and queen of Kaspar."

Nyla was more and more confused. "Do you not have somebody waiting for you back at Kaspar?"

He first started to lie and say no, but he decided he would be honest. "I do, but I don't love her, and I have never loved her. I think she would want out of our betrothal as much as I do. Our union was arranged."

"So, you are telling me that your coming marriage is arranged by law."

"It is, but I am king, and kings can change the law. All I need is to know that you love me too."

"This is crazy. I can't tell what I am going to do, but I can tell you I am not going to leave the village to go to the camp. It won't be long until you return north. Go end this war and then come and see me." She then moved back close and returned his kiss. "I have never been kissed before. I like it."

They spent about an hour resting on the blanket holding each other close, and then he got up and walked over to the edge of the water. Nyla had put the bottle of wine into the water, and he felt of it. "I hope this stayed cool this close to the water." He reached into the bags and pulled out the dried meat, bread, and cheese. Nyla had never tasted food so good, even though it was just plain bread and cheese from her village. She had never felt so good and alive. *Is this love?*

She and Jabir spent lots of time together during the coming week, and at the end of the week Raja returned to the village. That night Jabir and Raja sat near the fire and Jabir spoke. "If something happens to me in the coming weeks, if I am struck down in battle or captured, this village will be destroyed if our army cannot defeat the enemy. If it looks like defeat is going to occur, I want you to come back to this village and get Nyla and take her to Kaspar where she will be safe, or at least safe for a while."

"What are you telling me?"

"I am telling you that I love this woman, and if I can end this war, she is going to be my queen. If I can't, I want her safe. Do you understand?"

"I do. Don't worry, we will win and end this war. I am going to sleep now. I suggest you do the same. We have a long ride tomorrow."

"Wait, I want you to go to the tent of Fadi and wait for me there. He is expecting us."

After he was alone, Jabir left his tent and walked to Nyla's tent. Once outside, he gently called her name and went inside. "I want you to come with me to the tent of Fadi. I have asked him to marry us. Maybe I should do this first." He stood in front of Nyla and said, "The life you saved is no longer my own. It belongs to you, and I want you to become my wife and queen.

I am going back to my camp, but I want to know that you are here waiting for me when I return. I am going to do as much as possible to end this war."

When Jabir and Nyla came to Fadi's tent, Fadi and Raja were both waiting.

Fadi was dressed in a long blue robe, and candles lit up the tent. "I am going to say the words that will make you man and wife. You must profess your love in front of me and this witness, and we will sign this book. Jabir, you must sign your real name. This book is a record of all the marriages of this village."

When the ceremony was over, Nyla and Jaul returned to Nyla's tent. A small candle gave just enough light to let him see her lying on her mat. He thought to himself, *she looks so beautiful*. He lay down beside her and took her in his arms. They spent the rest of the night making love and holding each other.

Jaul was holding Nyla in his arms when she reached out and touched the birthmark on his arm. "I can tell that this is a birthmark, but it looks more like a tattoo."

"I have kept it hidden while I have been here, because it might have given me away. All the kings of Kaspar have had this birthmark. If we have a son, he too will have this birthmark."

The next morning, he kissed her and said, "I will come back for you. I love you so much, and you are now and forever my queen."

Jaul had been gone for about four weeks when the signs of her pregnancy began to appear. She wasn't sure what she should do. She and Fadi had kept the marriage a secret to protect Jaul. With her power, she could hide her pregnancy. But what about a child? Once the child was born, what would she do? When Jaul came back, how would he explain her to the people of Kaspar?

Jaul had been back at the front for only a week when the fighting resumed. He found that his army was now fighting a defensive war. The enemy army was stronger than his. For about five weeks his army was able to hold its own against this superior force, but the last battle came. Both sides threw everything into the encounter. The losses on both sides were great, but in the end the enemy force won. They had won the battle but lost maybe the war. They had destroyed most of Kaspar's army, and taken many prisoners, but in doing so had made their army weak and ineffective.

Lucas, leader of the enemy army, called his advisors together. "We are weak, and I am not sure we can take Kaspar. What do our spies tell us? Do they have any army to defend their castle?"

"Jaul left a moderate force to defend the castle. I am not sure we can take it with the force we have left after our last battle. Our men are weak and tired. It would be a great risk to attack a castle."

Lucas walked to the front of the large tent and turned and faced his men. "We will rest for another week, and then go south. There is a village there. We will take it and resupply our army. By this time, they will know the fate of their army and be willing to talk peace."

One of the men asked, "What do we want?"

"We need to stop the fighting, so we will have time to rebuild our army. I am willing to give up some of the land we have gained and move back across the sea. I think Kaspar will agree with this. We will be dealing with Kadar, Jaul's brother. His name means powerful, but he is not. He will want a quick peace, and I don't think he will rebuild his army. We just must make peace and wait. It may take years, but we will be back."

Nyla and Raja

Nyla was in the middle of the village when Raja came riding in. He went directly to the village leader. "We have lost the battle, and the enemy is coming this way. I suggest you move as much as you can toward the castle at Kaspar. No defense stands between you and Lucas's army."

Fadi did not hesitate. He called together all the leaders of the village, gave the news, and told them to prepare to move east.

Later that day Raja came to Nyla. "I don't know the fate of Jaul. I fear he could be dead or at best captured. He told me that if this happens, I am to take you to Kaspar for safety."

Nyla did not answer. She passed out and fell to the ground. When she awoke, she was in a cart, covered with a blanket. Raja was sitting with her. "Where am I?" she asked.

"About halfway to Kaspar castle. We will be there sometime tomorrow. I am carrying out Jaul's wishes."

Nyla had the power to know where people who were close to her were. She could not sense Jaul. Looking at Raja she said, "I fear Jaul is dead."

"I did not see him fall. He ordered a retreat, and when what was left of us came together at the camp, he was not there. If he had been captured, Lucas would be making a show of him and be demanding a ransom or some concession."

Raja considered for a moment. "By the time we get to Kaspar, Kadar will be king. Your life and the life of your child may be in danger if we present you as queen."

"My child will be a daughter, but you are right. My child and I will not be welcome by Jaul's brother. If we present my child as the heir to the throne, I am sure that the proof they ask for will be destroyed and both my child and I will be killed."

"There is proof that the child is Jaul's. I can testify that Jaul loved you and set me to protect you, but that is all I can do. However, there is something else, and we just have to wait to see if we can use it."

***

When Raja, Kadar, and Nyla did meet, Kadar seemed to accept Nyla and her unborn child. The problem seemed to be with Barak, the minister. Raja and Nyla decided not to make any knowledge that she and Jaul were married known. Raja could see how powerful Barak had become, and he feared for Nyla's safety. Nyla was given a room at the castle. Raja had introduced Nyla as his sister and said that her husband was killed in battle. While she waited for the birth of her child, she found that she was not the only one expecting. Barak's wife was expecting a child, and Kadar's wife was also expecting. Kadar made peace and agreed with the conditions set forth by Lucas. While living at the castle, Nyla made few friends. The only ones to treat her kindly were Ana and Davos. One day Raja came to see her.

"I am leaving; I have given my statement to the council. I am going to go west and see if I can find anything about Jaul. It is probably a fool's mission, but I have not been assigned any duties with the army, and I am useless here. I would watch my back. I don't think Barak can be trusted. He has gained too much power with Kadar. If there is a chance that your child is going to be the new ruler of Kaspar, you are not safe. I do know that the people of your village have gone back to their home at the large oasis. I hope that Fadi protected the village records, and we have proof of the marriage. If you want to return, I will take you there with me."

"Raja, you have been so kind to me, and I can't thank you enough for what you have done for me and my child. The time has come. I need to let the council know that Jaul and I were married. If the council does not believe my story, I will again be an outcast. I want more for my daughter than that."

Zanzura

That night after she had eaten, Nyla began to feel weak. By the time she got back to her room, she could barely keep her eyes open. Her first thoughts were that she might have been poisoned, but she fell asleep before she could take anything to counter it. When she awoke she was alone in a prison cell. The room was small and rather dark. *So, this is what it has come to.* She started to get angry but remembered her mother's warning that she should not use her magic for revenge or in anger. She could almost hear her mother's words. *Once you turn dark, you can never return.*

She had not been awake long before she heard footsteps coming down the steps. The lock made a loud clicking sound, the door opened, and there stood Barak and two other men.

"I could not let you undo everything I have worked for. Look around. This is your new home. Once I have convinced the council and our new king, Kadar, that you went back to your village because we were going to find out you lied, you will be forgotten. Once we have disgraced you with the council, your life, and the life of your child, will come to an end."

"What about Raja? What if he finds records that Jaul and I were married?"

"He won't because he is already dead."

***

Day after day, Nyla sat in her cell and as she did she started to plan her escape. Escape would be easy. She knew she could just walk through the door, and when she needed to, she would do just that.

She got so used to the guards coming that she paid no attention when she heard a guard coming down the corridor toward her cell. Suddenly, there was the sound of something crashing on the dungeon floor, followed by a flash of light. Fire was consuming everything in the cell. Some of the liquid had splashed on her face, and she was on fire. She quickly gained control, ran through the wall and fell about twenty feet into the water below. At first, the water did not put out the fire burning on her face, but she used her power, and it went out. The pain was almost more than she could bear. Swimming to the bank, she caught her breath and checked her baby. It seemed to be okay. Using her power, she turned herself invisible and moved down to the dock. There she slipped aboard a boat that was heading upstream to Lilly. Once she was hidden, she tried to heal her scorched face but found she could not.

When the fire was out, Barak came down the dungeon steps. "Is she dead?"

"This is the first time we have used Greek fire. We did not know it burned so hot. There is nothing left in the cell but ashes. Even some of the rock floor was destroyed by the flames, it burned so hot."

Barak looked inside the cell and started back up the stairs. "Clean it up and get someone to repair that floor. I have a feeling I may need the space."

It took two days to reach Lilly. Nyla did not know what to do next. Hiding in a small abandoned room she found in Lilly, she remembered that her mother once told her about a mythical oasis in the Great Desert called Zanzura. It was supposed to be a paradise in the middle of the sand. The next day she went down to the market and found that there was a caravan going east. Inside the market, she used her power and stole enough money to buy a camel, other supplies and passage east with a caravan. On the third day, she left the caravan and headed east across the desert. As she traveled across the desert, she used her power to locate Zanzura.

Zanzura was everything her mother had told her. It had cool water coming from the rocks. There were a variety of fruits and nuts. She had brought seeds for vegetables, and she planned to start a garden. It was not long until she found that under the rocks was a cave. She went inside and found it had ample light reflecting from the water outside. When she found the cave had a passage leading about one hundred feet deeper into the rocks, she followed it and found that it came to an end but had the feeling it went on forever. Touching the wall, she could feel that it led to a strange and wonderful place. During the next several months she established with her magic that it led to a different world.

Now that Nyla knew where Zanzura was, she made a few trips back to Lilly to get some other things to make her stay comfortable. While living in the cave, she found she could only use her powers in limited ways. Zanzura was a magical place on its own, and she could not be sure if Zanzura was controlling her power or her fear of her magic was not allowing her to use all the power she had. She could only feel the presence of people she wanted to contact if she was about fifty miles from them. She tried many times to heal her face but for some reason could not. She was able to establish that if she needed to send her daughter into the other world, she could, and that she would be safe.

Nyla liked living at the oasis. When her daughter was born, she thought about just raising her there. *No, this is not where Kasmira needs to grow up. There were two people living at Kaspar that were good people. When Kasmira is one-year old I will take her to them and ask them to raise her.*

***

When Ana and Davos had finished eating their evening meal they saw a woman dressed in black standing in the middle of their room. She threw back her hood and revealed that she was Nyla. At first, they did not recognize her because of her scarred face.

"Don't be afraid, you know who I am, and everything I have told you is true. I need your help. I need to protect my child. Are you willing to listen to my plan?"

Ana and Davos agreed, and Nyla told them of her plans. "I want you to leave and go to Lilly. If I am not there, wait for me; I will come. My child is back at a hidden oasis. She is safe. I have cast a spell that will protect her until I return. I will bring her to you, and I want you to raise her as your own. If you agree to do this, I will make no contact with you or the child unless the child is in immediate danger. Here is the hardest part. You cannot tell her who her father is or tell her about me. The reason I can come and go as I please unseen is that I have magic. My daughter will also have magic. It will come to her when she is about fourteen years old. You can then tell her about me and why she has power. You cannot tell her about her father. She has the same birthmark as her father. I have hidden it to protect her. Do you understand, and do you agree?"

Ana and Davos agreed and after Nyla left, Davos turned to Ana. "Any doubts we may have had about Nyla's story can be put to rest. She knows about the birth mark."

When Davos and Ana returned to Kaspar Castle with Kasmira, everyone just assumed that they had adopted her.

Jada

Barak was seated on an inset that allowed him to look out the window to see the garden. Below he could see Shakir and Jada sitting on a bench. They were talking and laughing. *Things could not be going better,* he thought to himself. His plan had started when his wife was with child. He had received news that Jaul, who was the king at that time, was missing in battle and was assumed dead. He knew that Kadar would become king. Kadar was a kind but weak man. He would rely on him to run the government. It was Barak who received the message that Jaul was captured and that Lucas was holding him for ransom. He did not share this news with Kadar. He simply took some men he trusted and took the ransom to meet with Lucas.

Lucas was surprised by Barak's request. He did not want Jaul returned. He told Lucas he would pay the ransom if he agreed to put Jaul to death. Lucas, who needed money to help rebuild his army, agreed. When Lucas rode away from the meeting he thought to himself, *it might be better to keep Jaul alive.* He could be the source of more money or leverage in a treaty. He would send him to the prison at Isla de la Muerte. He would keep him alive. Lucas only lived two more years. Jaul was forgotten and left to die in the prison at Isla de la Muerte.

Barak continued to think how his plans were falling into place. His plans changed when Kadar's children were born and a month later his daughter was born. He just had to wait. Someday his daughter would be queen and he could rule Kaspar through her. He had removed Jaul and

Kadar. Shakira and Kasmira were most likely dead, and Shakir and Jada were seeing each other.

Just for a moment he regretted using his daughter to get power. Perhaps he did not have to do anything. If he had let Jada and Shakir grow up together, they might have fallen in love, and he would just have had to wait until the right time to kill Kadar and Shakir.

As Barak watched Shakir and Jada, she got up and went back into the castle. She had no idea that she was being used as a pawn in Barak's deadly game. She was becoming a woman, and as she walked back she began to think how her life had changed. She had not had much opportunity to get to know most of the young people of the castle. She liked visiting with Shakir, but she found him strange. He had given all his power to her father. She understood that he was so young that he needed guidance, but he seemed to have no interest in running Kaspar at all. He liked training and was told he was becoming one of the best with different weapons. While she talked to Shakir in the garden that morning he had told her that he was going to ask Barak to assign him to a garrison. He wanted to patrol for bandits along the southern border. *Why did he have to ask Barak? He could just make it happen,* she thought.

Barak agreed, and for the next four years a pattern developed. Shakir would take his men on a patrol of the southern and sometimes eastern border and be gone sometimes for months. Those months turned into years, and each visit with Jada became more and more important to her. When he was 19 years old he returned from a patrol and sent for Jada to meet him in the garden. When she got there, she saw that he had a table sitting below a large palm tree with flowers all around. He was seated when she came, but he quickly stood up. She came to him and threw her arms around him. "I have missed you so much. Please don't go back so quickly."

He held her for a moment and whispered in her ear, "I am not going back at all, and we are not alone."

She stepped back and standing about fifteen feet away were her mother and father. "What is going on? Is something going on I need to know about?"

"I asked your father for your hand in marriage, and now I am asking you. Will you agree to be my queen? Before you answer, I think you know that your father has agreed, and by law that is all that is required. I will not go by the law. If you say no, our marriage will not happen. If you say you need more time, it will be granted. Please say yes."

Jada looked over at her father, and to her mother, and smiled. She hugged Shakir and whispered into his ear, "How could I say no?"

The engagement lasted a full year, and when the wedding took place they were now twenty years old. Shakir was now king, and Jada was his queen, but he still showed no interest in running the government.

Barak was the true power, and over the next five years he slowly increased the size of the army and started to build a fleet of war ships. He wanted the island of Tranquillo and was going to have it at all cost.

Joseph and Kira

Joseph had been gone for less than a week when Shakira was summoned to appear before the king. She was nervous about the meeting and feared for the worst. Now she was standing in the king's chamber, and to her surprise there was only the king and queen there. Valetta could tell that the poor child was scared to death, so she gave Shakira a smile.

King Rhodes spoke. "We are glad that you have come to live with us, but now we must do two things. The first is we must hide you from the rest of the world. We don't want your enemies to find you. It would not be good for you and would be even worse for us."

Shakira had relaxed when Valetta had smiled, but now she felt as if she were going to throw up. She thought to herself. *The king is going to put Ameena and me out. We are going to die, and I will never see Joseph again.*

King Rhodes could tell what Shakira was thinking, so he spoke quickly to ease her fear. "You think that we are going to send you away. We are not. We want to protect you, and we can do that best while you are living at the castle. I also don't want to explain to my son why you are not here when he returns." He glanced over at Valetta and smiled. "Joseph thinks very highly of you, and you will be here when he returns, but I am afraid that is going to be in the distant future. What he is doing is very important, and a member of the royal family must be there when the agreements and treaties are made. He is only eighteen, but he is wise beyond his years. I know you have a birthday coming up, but I am afraid you may see another before he returns."

This was news that Shakira did not want to hear. But all she could say was, "I understand."

Rhodes again looked at his wife. "Our plan is simple. We are going to change your name and give you a new life. First your name. We don't want to change it much, so we will shorten it. From this day forward, you will be Kira. You are the daughter of Rebald, a brave man I knew several years ago, from a small kingdom in the northern part of the main peninsula. He really had no children, but now he does. The second part of this deception is that you are going to be chancellor to the queen. You have an education and can read and write. The job will not be demanding. You will meet with the queen in the mornings and stay with her until noon. This task will require you to know Spanish. In the afternoon, you are going to continue to learn to speak and write Spanish. This will not be difficult because you already know some of the language. I hope this meets with your satisfaction."

Shakira, now Kira, started to breathe easier. "I don't know how I can thank you. I will do my best to be a good chancellor to the queen. When do I start?"

Kira started the next day and soon was more like a daughter to the queen than a chancellor. She did not know that one of the reasons she had been assigned a job with the queen was so that Valetta could keep an eye on her. When her birthday came, she received a package from Greece. She knew that it was from Joseph and opened it with excitement. What she found inside was an amazing, wonderful gift. Before her was a beautiful silver Byzantine bracelet. It had twenty-four silver links, and each link had a black ruby in the middle surrounded by a gold set. Her heart was about to jump out of her chest as she put it on. Then she thought, *I can't accept this. This must be worth a fortune.*

Picking up the note that came with the gift she started reading. "Shakira, I think you are saying to yourself that this bracelet is too much, because we have not known each other very long. It is not as much as you think. I made a trip to Egypt and discovered that jewelry is only about a third of the cost you would pay in Tranquillo. Secondly, I paid nothing for it. I won it in a game of chance. Please enjoy this gift, and happy birthday. I wish I were home, but that is not going to be any day soon."

She quickly put the bracelet on and admired it. She got a quill and started writing a letter.

Dear Joseph,

How can I thank you for such a wonderful birthday gift? You were right. I do think it was far too much, and my first thought was to return it to you. Reading about how you got it and that you were thinking of me made me realize that wearing this bracelet will keep a part of you with me. You are the only friend that I have made since coming to Tranquillo, and I treasure that friendship.

I am now working for your mother. I like her very much, and the job is very easy. The job requires that I carry her communications to other parts of the castle, and I am meeting more and more people, but I don't have a best friend. Back in Kaspar, my best friend was Kasmira who is now dead. I hate to put a burden on you, but you now have to be my best friend. Again, thank you for the wonderful gift.

Kira.

When Joseph got the message, he had to read it twice. *Who is Kira?* Then he realized what was going on. His father was protecting her and had changed her name. He sat down and started writing another letter to Kira. They exchanged letters as often as possible, and his job became more and more demanding. He had not only traveled to Greece, he had been to Egypt, India, and southern China where he established trade agreements and trade routes. Before he knew it, two years had passed, and he and Kira had fallen in love by way of their correspondence.

He now was standing on the bow of a ship watching the Island of Tranquillo come into view. While being away, he had gained weight, but in a good way. He was wearing a short beard, but he kept his hair a medium length. He had not told Kira that he was coming home, and he had told his parents not to tell her. He could not wait to see her and the expression on her face as he came into the dining room that night. He had so much he wanted to tell her. He wanted to hold her in his arms and express his love. He knew by her letters that she loved him too.

After the ship had docked, he quickly made his way to the castle and cleaned the salt from the trip from his body. After that, he went to see his mother and father. After hugs and tears, he sat down and gave a full report to the king.

"You have done well my son; you have made a great sacrifice, but it has been worth it. I am not going into it now, but my spies tell me that Kaspar has been building up their army, and they now have a fleet of warships that will rival ours."

"Maybe I should make a trip to Kaspar and see Shakir. After all, he is the king and about my age. I have been making treaties for the last couple of years; perhaps I can make one more."

Rhodes scoffed. "If I thought that would work, I would have you on a ship in the morning, but it won't. Shakir does not want to be king. He has turned everything over to Barak. I fear we are going to have a war. It is not a war that I want, but I want you to go to the northern part of the island and oversee our production of warships. We must keep pace with Kaspar, and we must keep it a secret. We will talk about this tomorrow. We are dining in the small chamber tonight. I take it you will be just a little late, so you can make your grand entrance." He gave a laugh. "You don't want to ask Kira to marry you? Your mother has just about adopted her as a daughter, and we can't let you marry your sister." Then he gave his son a hug as they laughed together.

As Kira came down the long hall which led to the small dining room, she began to think about what was going on. She and Valetta had become very close, and she often had eaten with Valetta, but she had never been invited to eat with Valetta and the king together. The king and queen knew that she had been corresponding with Joseph, and they might just want information. *Joseph. Is he ever going to come home?* When she reached the door of the dining hall she stopped but did not go in. *I don't want to be early,* she thought. She could hear Rhodes and Valetta talking and laughing so she opened the door and entered. When she entered, they both stood up. *This is strange,* she thought, and she went over and took a seat at the table. The table was a small table which could seat about six people. As she sat down she noticed that there were table settings for four people.

"Are we expecting someone else?" She said this with a curious look on her face.

Rhodes looked at her and smiled. "Yes, we are. We know the good work you have been doing, and we are so proud. One thing we have noticed is that you don't seem to have any friends your own age. We have invited a young man to dine with us. He is just a little older than you and like you is of a royal family. He will be here in just a few moments."

Kira was caught off guard. She did not want to meet anyone. She was going to wait for Joseph to return. She decided that she would just go along with Rhodes and Valetta's plan and reject this unknown suitor later.

Valetta was somewhat enjoying seeing how uncomfortable Kira was becoming.

Suddenly, there was the sound of the large door opening and Kira turned to see who this unknown young man was going to be. When the door was fully open, there stood Joseph with a big smile on his face.

Kira could not contain her excitement and got up from the table and ran to him, throwing her arms around him, pressing her face into his chest and sobbing. When she finally got control, she leaned back and looked into his face. He was smiling, but he too had tears in his eyes.

Leaning very close, he whispered, "If mother and father were not here, I would give you a big kiss, maybe two or three."

"If your mother and father were not here I would never let you go." But they did release their embrace and walked over to the table.

"I see you approve of the new suitor," Rhodes said with a grin. "Joseph came in today, and he wanted to surprise you." After they had taken their seats, Rhodes said, "I have good news, bad news, and more good news."

Kira looked at Rhodes with anticipation. She was somewhat concerned about the bad news. Rhodes clapped his hands together, and servants entered the room carrying the first course of food. Wine was poured. Kira could not stand it anymore and said, "Good news, bad news, good news. Which are you going to start with?"

Rhodes looked at his son. "Do you want to tell her, or shall I?"

"I yield to you. You are the king."

Looking at Kira, Rhodes started giving the news. "Joseph has done a great job in the East. He has secured trade agreements with countries as far as India. There are some things we want to explore even further east, but the good news is we are not going to send Joseph to explore these possibilities."

Kira leaned slightly over, gave a friendly bump with her elbow, and looked at Joseph and smiled. She was so happy.

Rhodes continued to talk, "I am sure you will see this as bad news, and I guess it is. Joseph is going to be leaving soon, but he is not leaving the island. We have an outpost in the northern part of the island. It is across the mountains, and he will be there for about a month. He will be here for about two weeks, so you two can catch up."

"Is the good news that he will be here for two weeks? That does not sound like very good news."

Rhodes started to speak but Valetta interrupted. "Why don't you let Joseph give the good news. Joseph, do you want to give the news here or in private?"

Joseph looked at his mother and then his father. "I am with the three people I care the most about. I want to give that news here." He then turned to Kira. "When I return from the northern outpost, I want you to become my wife." He reached into his pocket and pulled out a ring. "If you will wear this ring, I will be honored and be a most happy man."

Kira was speechless, and all she could do was nod her head. Rhodes and Valetta got up and walked around the table and gave a hug to Joseph. Rhodes turned to Kira and said, "Welcome to our family."

The two weeks passed very quickly, and soon Joseph was at the northern outpost seeing that extra warships were being constructed. A month quickly passed, and when he was sure that construction was on schedule, he returned to Kira. Their engagement lasted for three months and then they were married. On their wedding day, Kira said a prayer for Kasmira and her brother and then turned her attention to making a new life for her and Joseph. Joseph and Kira were childless for two years, but when Kira turned nineteen, she found she was expecting a child.

Nyla and Kasmira

When Marie entered the cave wall, she was greeted by a bright light, and then she found herself standing inside the cave at the oasis. She looked around and saw no one, so she started walking toward the front of the cave. She could see the light from the water reflecting off the cavern ceiling. She could feel the power and magic she now had, and she knew that she was very powerful. She took a seat on a stone bench that faced the water. Suddenly, she knew she was not alone. She could feel the Woman in Black standing behind her.

Without turning around, she said, "How long have you lived in this cave?"

The Woman in Black came around and took a seat beside her. "I found this oasis many years ago. I have only left it a few times to get supplies and to check on things."

"When you approached me from behind I felt your presence. I have felt your presence before but never understood that it was you. You have been with me on many occasions. I had the same feeling when I fell off a horse and broke my arm. You were with me when I was extremely ill when I was twelve. You were with me when I was cast into the desert. You have been watching me my entire life. You have also been in this cave for as long as I have been alive." Marie turned and faced the Woman in Black. She reached out and lifted the veil from her face. She saw a face scarred by burns, and tears began to run down her face. "You are my mother. You did not die in the fire. You gave me up, and you came here. Why did you not heal yourself and come and take me away from Kaspar?"

"I could not. I found that I had no power to remove the scars even though I tried several times."

"Why did you not save Davos and Ana from their death?"

Tears were now also streaming down the face of the Woman in Black. "When all this happened, there was a great storm over Zanzura. I only felt your danger when you were left in the desert and only knew of Davos and Ana after their deaths. I have pushed my power away. I am afraid of it. I fear your power and what it may do to you. You are now able to control it. After I found out about what had happened, I wanted to kill Barak, but I fought it because I knew that I could not use my power for revenge and help you at the same time. I am so sorry for Davos and Ana. They were good people, and that is why I chose them for you. I have tried to use my power in very limited ways because I don't know how it affects the future. I was a healer at Anemoi. I saved many that would have died. I hope that was what was supposed to happen."

"How did Ana die?"

"When I found you in the desert, I started guiding you here. I went to the castle to see what had happened. Davos had already been executed, and I found Ana hanging in the cell. I touched her body, and I could sense that she had killed herself the same morning that Davos had been hung. Barak had not killed her, but he had caused her death."

Even though Kasmira knew that Davos and Ana were dead, it was like they had died all over again. She started to cry, and the Woman in Black did not try to stop her. "You need to cry. This has been inside you for a long time." Marie did not say anything, and finally she got control and was able to speak.

"Can you sense people and know where they are? When I came into the cave I could sense your presence."

"I can sense people who are near. I sensed your presence from a long distance. You have never been out of my ability to sense where you are. Even when you went through the portal I could sense where you were. By the way, I know you have been all over your new home. You have traveled thousands of miles."

Marie reached out and gave the Woman in Black a hug. "This is my home." *Is this really my home? David, and many people that I love are not here.*

Nyla could sense what Kasmira was thinking. "That remains to be seen. Back to your question. My mother had the ability to sense people from great distances. Only you will know if you too have that power. When I went to check on Davos and Ana I could sense Shakir and Shakira. When all this happened Shakir was just a boy. Shakira was already becoming a headstrong young woman. Shakir let Barak take his authority away and did not care. I have checked on him from time to time, and he has no desire to be a king. He is now married and has a young child. It is a boy. Now that he is a man, he still has no desire to run the kingdom."

Kasmira could feel her power, and she knew things. "Shakir married Jada. She is now the queen."

"Jada is a good person and has no knowledge of her father's deceit."

"What happened to Shakira? I know she is not in Kaspar, but somewhere to the north on a large island."

"Good, you do have the ability to sense people from a long distance. Your power is much greater than mine. Shakira questioned why you were banished and began to question the justice of Davos and Ana's death. Barak convinced Shakir to banish her. She was to be killed by Barak's men but was saved and is now married and has a child, a young daughter. Enough questions. I must prepare you for what needs to happen."

"Not so fast, I have other questions. I know your name is Nyla. Outside that I have no other knowledge about you. Where are you from? What about my father? I need to know."

Nyla thought carefully before giving her answers. "I am from the village of Anemoi. It is a small village east of the Viper River." She decided not to tell her that her father was the king of Kaspar. She decided to use the name, he used while healing in the village. "Your father's name was Jabir. He was a warrior and fighting for Kaspar. He was wounded so badly that he was going to die. His friend Raja had heard of my success and brought him to me. I used my magic to save his life and start the healing process. We spent several weeks together and during that time we fell in love. When his wounds were healed, he went back to the war and was killed. Raja came back to the village and took me to Kaspar. You know the rest of the story."

"You are wrong. I don't know the rest of the story. Why were you put into prison, and why did Barak try to have you killed? Was it because you and Father were never married?"

"I was accused of being a witch, and Jabir and I were married. We only got to spend one night together."

Oh Mother, just one night with the man you love. How terrible your life has been. Marie knew there had to be more to the story and could sense that Nyla was not telling everything but decided not to question her about it. "How do I develop the power to feel where people are?"

"You already have the power, and you have been using it. You could sense Shakira. You could sense me from behind you and know that I have been with you before. You will not be able to sense just anyone. It must be somebody you have a connection with. The stronger the connection the better. You could feel me and knew that I was walking up behind you. You will not be able to do this with a stranger. When you want to make a connection, you must think of them and you can make a link. You will be able to sense what to do."

"Can they feel the connection?"

"They could if they knew a connection was being made. If they are asleep and your connection is strong you can talk to them, but they will think they are dreaming."

"You talked to me in the desert."

"Yes, I did, and you were able to understand what was going on. You made it to the oasis."

Kasmira thought for a minute then thought of Shakira. She could feel her and sense what was around her. She turned to Nyla. "I thought of Shakira and could sense her. I could almost see her. She is in the north, and she was in a room holding a young child."

"Kasmira, I want you to come with me." Nyla took her by the hand and the two walked through the wall and stopped by the blue pool of water. "You have more power than ever imagined. I can feel your power, and you may be able to transport yourself. If you can, you could go anywhere you wanted to in an instant. I have this power, and I hope you have it too. I want you to think about the palm trees at the end of the pool and imagine that you are there."

Marie did, and in an instant, she was standing next to the trees. Nyla was standing next to a rock about seventy-five yards away. She walked back, and the two women went back inside the cave.

For the next several days, Marie and Nyla got to know each other, and Marie started to think of herself as Kasmira again. She was finding that Nyla was more than her mother. Kasmira could see what Nyla told her was true. She was afraid of her powers. *That is the reason she can't heal herself. She is holding back her power. She might be as powerful as she says I am.*

She was surprised how fast she began to understand her magic. With the help of her mother she grew in confidence, but each time she learned more about her power, Nyla would caution her about keeping her power under control.

On the fifth day, they started talking about what they could do to remove Barak from power in Kaspar.

Kasmira said, "I am going to visit the castle at Kaspar. I want to see what is going on. I don't want them to see me, so I will be careful."

"Kasmira, you need to shake up Shakir. You need to appear to him and let him think you are a ghost and make him feel threatened, but you will also have to protect him. You can't trust what Barak is going to do. Please be careful using your power. Your grandfather used his power to avenge his sister and turned dark. You must promise me that you will not use your power for revenge and will only use it if there is no other choice."

"I promise, and I will be careful, and you don't have to wear that veil. There is just me and you here, and I don't see your scars."

"You don't see them because you care for me. I hope that someday you can see me as your mother." She walked over to the water, removed the veil, and looked into the water. She could see the deep scars that covered her face.

"You are my mother and I wish I could have known my father." Kasmira came up behind Nyla and placed a hand on each shoulder. She turned her, so the two women were face to face. "Mother, I said I don't see any scars." She placed her hands on each side of Nyla's face. "Let me repeat, I don't see any scars."

Nyla turned away from Kasmira and looked back into the water. Her face was now smooth. She turned back to face Nyla. She did not say anything. Kasmira could see a tear rolling down her face. She gave her mother a big hug and said, "One injustice has now been corrected, and I am just getting started."

During the next few days, Kasmira and her mother got to know each other even more. Kasmira discovered her mother was a good woman who cared about people and loved her very much. One day while they were eating fruit and sitting under a tree, Nyla became very serious. "You know I don't like to use magic. I have had magic since I was fourteen, and I know the more I use it the more powerful I become. That power scares me, and I only use it when I have no other means to solve a problem. The more powerful you become, the more you are tempted to use it wrongly. I never want my magic to go dark. You have already let your magic become more powerful than mine. Don't be tempted to use your magic for anything evil."

"Mother, you keep telling me this over and over. I already know that you are reluctant to use your magic and why. I don't understand why getting revenge against a man who tried to kill my mother, killed Davos and Ana, and banished me to die in the desert would be an evil thing. How do I separate revenge and justice? They seem like they are the same thing."

Nyla took a bite of her fruit, and when she finished she said, "There is a big difference between revenge and justice. Getting revenge gives you an evil pleasure; justice gives you a satisfying feeling, but it does not give you pleasure."

Kasmira lay back against the palm tree. "Mother, I have a concern. I am going to do things that could change the future of the people I came to love when I went through the portal. I don't think I can seek justice if I put their future in danger."

Nyla smiled. "You are not using your gifts. Think and feel and tell me what you know is true. I mentioned this to you just before you went into the light at the end of the cave."

After thinking to herself for a moment she said, "I think the world you sent me to is not the same as this one. I can feel that they are somewhat different yet connected. I hope this is true because there are people in the future world I care a great deal for. While I was in the other world, I met a young man and fell in love. That love pulls at me, and it is so powerful I feel I must go back."

"The first time your father kissed me, I had never had such a feeling. It is not magic. It is better than magic."

"Tomorrow I am leaving, and I am going to see what has happened to this world since I left. I don't know how long I will be gone. I know you can contact me and talk to me in a dream, and I can do the same. Only contact me if you need me. Be patient with me. It will be like learning to ride a bike. It will take some time."

"Like a what?" Nyla said.

Kasmira laughed. "Never mind, it is just something from the other world and in the future of this one."

Kasmira thought about how lonely her mother must have been. Having a child without a friend to help. "Was there anyone else besides Davos and Ana who tried to help you after my father was killed?"

"Yes, Fadi the village leader was very kind and helped me go to Kaspar, and there was Raja. He was a good friend to your father and became a good friend to me. After your father was killed he came back to Anemoi and helped me go to Kaspar. We were afraid that Anemoi was going to be overrun by the enemy, and we had to leave."

"What happened to Raja? Do you know?"

Nyla wiped a tear away. "He went to see if he could find out what happened to your father, and Barak had him killed."

Why would Barak have Raja killed? And why would he try to kill Mother? None of this makes any sense. I know why he would want me dead and why he would want Davos blamed for the death of Kadar, but there is no reason to kill Raja and Mother. She decided to let it go. If her mother wanted to tell her, she would.

"Did you know that if Barak had not had my father, I mean Davos, killed and banished me from the kingdom, I might have become queen of Kaspar. I think that Shakir was going to ask me to marry him."

Nyla turned her back to Kasmira. *That is one problem I did not have to solve. I would never allow you to marry your first cousin.* "Were you really in love with Shakir?"

"When I lived in the castle I loved Shakir and Shakira, but it was the love one feels for their family. I fell truly in love on the other side of the portal."

Nyla changed the subject. "I need to see your back. Slide your garment from your shoulder and show me."

"Why do you want me to do this?"

"You have a birthmark. I have hidden it with my magic. I think since you have come back it may have reappeared."

Kasmira did as she was told. "Yes, it is back, I need to hide it again. You must trust me. There may come a time when you need to show that you have this birthmark. It will show that you're the daughter of Jabir."

Kasmira thought that this was strange. *Why not just leave it? Why does Mother want to hide it?*

When Kasmira left the oasis, she used her magic only to get out of the desert. Once she was in Kaspar, she disguised herself and wrapped her head in a light blue kufiya. Touring the markets of the city she began to feel at home. She found this somewhat strange because she also felt that Paris was her home. When night came, she found herself standing outside the castle walls. *Here goes nothing.* Using her magic, she moved through the thick wall and found herself standing in a lower hallway. She remembered playing there as a child with Shakir and Shakira. Using her magic, she was able to avoid any contact with anyone until she was inside the king's meeting chamber. Hearing someone talking while coming down the hall, she quickly moved behind some drapes and waited until she saw Barak and three other men enter the room. There was no sign of Shakir.

Barak began to speak. "Now that our army is strong, and we have a navy, we can expand our kingdom and increase our trade by taking Tranquillo."

The man to the left of Barak spoke. "Tranquillo is strong, and we have no reason to attack them. If we attack them without any reason, we might anger our allies."

Barak walked over close to the curtain and turned and answered the man who just spoke, whose name was Akeem. "We have a small outpost about three days' ride to the west. Take about twenty men, disguise them in uniforms of Tranquillo, and attack the outpost. There are only about eight men stationed there. Do not kill all of them. Let about half escape and come here to tell their story. There will be an outcry among the people for revenge, and we will give them revenge. Get your men ready and send someone to see when our fleet will be ready to sail. Get the soldiers ready. This must be done in a couple of weeks. We will meet here in about five days and be ready to move on Tranquillo as soon as we receive news from the outpost. I think two weeks is a good timeline."

Shortly, there was a knock on the door, and a man entered dressed in a grey robe. He did not say anything.

Barak spoke first. "Plans are going well. It will not be long until we have

Tranquillo, and we can make this a very rich kingdom. I am not too sure of Shakir. He has changed since the birth of his son. He may want to take a more active role in running the kingdom. I think the time has come to make my daughter a widow."

The man in grey gave a rough laugh. "Like father, like son. Should Akeem get more poison ready?"

"No. It was easy to use poison to kill Kadar. We had a scapegoat in Davos. This must be different."

Suddenly Akeem held a finger to his lips. He walked over and quickly pulled the curtains back with a hard jerk. There was no one there. Turning back to Barak, he said, "I swore I could feel the presence of someone here."

Barak scoffed. "You must be losing your power. Am I paying you too much?"

Walking back from the curtain, he said, "What do you want me to do?"

"I want you to plant a seed in Shakir's mind that he needs to inspect the northern outpost. Make sure he only takes two warriors with him. He will need to be there a week from today. This is important. Can you do this?"

"I can. Is there anything else?"

"Yes, tell the men you are sending to attack the northern outpost that Shakir is to be killed. This is important, and the people will be demanding war. Now go. If I need you I will send for you."

All the men left the room and Kasmira reemerged from the wall. *So, someone else has power and can sense my presence. I must be careful, and I must come up with a way to save Shakir. Maybe I should just let him die.* Kasmira was not able to know who the third man was. Only that he was involved in having Davos killed.

Waiting until after midnight, Kasmira moved down the hall and entered the king's room. Standing at the foot of a large bed she could see Shakir and Jada lying together. *That could have been me lying in the bed with Shakir.* She felt the anger starting to consume her body, and then she had the feeling that a union between her and Shakir should never be. There was never any romantic love between her and Shakir. Like she told her mother, he was more like family. Then her thoughts turned to David, her French mother and father, David's family. *I have lost so much, but I have also gained so much. What we need here is justice.* Standing at the foot of Shakir's bed she entered into Shakir's dream and said, "Shakir, why did you send me to my death? You should have known that I would have ended up dead or a slave in some evil person's household. You are evil, and you need to be stopped, and the only way I can stop you is to kill you." She ended the dream, so he would awake. He awoke in a cold sweat and sat up in the bed. Looking toward the foot of the bed, he saw Kasmira. "This is not a dream." She then disappeared.

Shakir was shaking so hard he woke Jada. She finally convinced him it was a bad dream, and he began to feel better. *It really didn't seem like a dream.*

Mira and Jon

The next morning Kasmira decided to find Shakira. Using her power, she concentrated and could sense the Island of Tranquillo. Knowing that Shakira was safe, she decided to catch a boat to the Island and not use her power. On the trip, she relaxed and made her plans. She could find Shakira and let the king of Tranquillo know of Barak's plot.

Once she was on the dock she wrapped her head with her kufiya. She covered her face and made her way up to the castle. It was a brisk walk and uphill. *I know that Mother does not want me to use my power very much, but this would be much easier with a little help from my magic.* When she got to the gate, it was blocked by guards. She decided she needed to be incognito. She needed to use a different name. Walking up to the guard she said, "My name is Mira. I seek an audience with Shakira."

The guard looked puzzled. "I am sorry, but there is no one in the castle by that name. Perhaps you are confused?"

"I am sorry." Mira stepped back away from the guards. Using her powers, she could sense the presence of Shakira inside the walls of the castle. Leaving the castle, she found a market not far away. Stopping at the first vendor she asked, "I am not from here. Who are the king and queen of this land?" The vendor scoffed. "Where could you be from and not know this information?"

"I am from a village on the mainland of the Greek islands."

The shop owner started speaking in Greek. "The king is Rhodes, and his queen is Valetta. They have one son. His name is Joseph."

Mira answered in Greek. "Does Joseph have a wife?"

"He does. Her name is Kira. Does this information help you?"

"It does, thank you very much." Mira could tell that there was a lot of distrust from the man giving her information. As she started walking away he said, "Aren't you going to buy anything?"

She gave him a smile. "I am not, but I am not going to steal anything either."

Returning to the castle gate, she approached the guards. "I am here to seek an audience with Princess Kira."

The guard scoffed. "Just a while ago you wanted to see a person who is not here and has never been here, and now you want to see the princess. Be gone or we will see you as a threat to the princess, and you can see the inside of our dungeon."

Mira looked at the guards and concentrated. Then she asked, "Does the princess ever see anyone?"

"She does, and today she will greet several women from the village. That meeting will take place in just a few moments. Would you like to join them?"

"I would." She walked through the gates and made her way to the area in a garden where Kira was about to talk to a group of women from the village. Her face still covered, she waited for Kira to appear. In just a few moments Kira was standing in front of the small group. Mira was surprised that Shakira still looked much the same but had changed too. She was no longer a little girl but had become a woman.

Kira began to speak. "I want to thank you for coming. I want you to know that we are here to address your concerns from our last meeting. The water draining down from the higher grounds and flooding your shops is being diverted, and you should not have any other problem. Are there any other concerns?"

A large woman came to the front of the group and said, "Just one more thing, and I'm not sure you can do anything about it. The fishing ships that come into the harbor unload there, and the fishermen clean their fish right there on the dock and throw the scraps into the water. There is an odor, and many flies are invading our stores. Could the ships unload on the east harbor further away from the shops? I know this would create more work on the fishermen, but it would make a much cleaner environment where the shops are located."

"I understand your concern, and I will present this to the council at the next meeting. Is there anything else?" Mira, with her face still covered, moved to the front of the group. "Have you forgotten your old friends and become a recluse in this castle? You know your friends still care about you."

Kira looked closer at the woman standing in front of her. Her face was covered, and she had no idea who she was or why she made such a remark. *What kind of question is she asking? Does she know something about my past? Is she here to do me harm? What do I need to do?*

Kira called to a guard who was standing nearby. "Jon, escort this woman to the private meeting chambers. Stay with her until I get there." The guard took Mira by the arm and led her away while Kira finished the meeting.

While Mira waited for Kira, she wandered about the room. She decided to be coy. She would use her magic to see if Kira was the old Shakira she remembered. The guard stayed with her but did not talk to her. She walked over to the window and was looking out toward a garden when she heard Kira enter the room. She kept looking out the window, and Kira dismissed the guard. "You can leave us, but please go get Joseph and tell him to come here."

Mira did not turn and face Kira but remained looking out the window with her face still covered. At first Kira said nothing, and as she started to speak, her voice broke. She cleared her throat and spoke again. "I am sorry, but what you said disturbed me. It has caused me concern, and you heard that I have sent for my husband. I feel you know who I am. Are you here to blackmail me?"

Mira did not turn around. "No. I am not here to blackmail you. Is your husband, Joseph, going to bring the guards to arrest me? Are you so concerned that you would resort to such extreme matters? Do I look like a woman who needs money?"

"I don't know what you know or who you are or what we are going to do. What do you know about me?"

"I know that Kira is not your name, and I know that you are the daughter of Kadar of Kaspar. I know that you were exiled by your brother Shakir. I wonder why he would do that?"

Kira did not answer the question but asked one of her own. "How do you know so much about me, and why did you come here?"

Mira turned and faced Kira but did not uncover her face. "I came here to seek and visit a friend. I am on a journey, and I need a place to rest before returning to the mainland. I am on a mission of justice."

"Who is this friend, and why did you come to me?"

"My friend is a woman I thought had betrayed me. I have thought this for the last ten years. I have just recently returned from a long trip and found out she was the only friend I had in Kaspar."

"What is the name of this friend, and how can I help? Does she live in this castle?"

Mira turned to face Kira and removed the kufiya. "She does live in this castle, and her name is Shakira."

Kira was shocked to see Kasmira standing in front of her. She could not speak. She rushed to her and threw her arms around her. She was crying so hard she could not regain her voice. It was Kasmira who broke the silence. "My friend and sister, it is so good to see you. I am sorry about everything. I had to know that you were still my friend. When is that man coming? I want to meet him. I want to see your child, but like you, I need to stay incognito. Please refer to me as Mira. Mira and Kira, how could we be any closer? Tell me how you came to be wife of the prince."

"After you left, I started to question Shakir about my father's death and had some doubt about Davos and Ana being involved. I was sent away from Kaspar and did not know that upon arriving here I was to be murdered. Joseph saved me, and he and his father assumed that the same fate happened to you, but there was no one to save you. I thought you were dead. Where have you been?"

"That too is a long story. There was someone to save me. I was left in the desert to die. While I was in prison Davos and Ana told me that they were not my real parents. While I was in the desert I was saved by a woman in black. She was a witch and has power. She sent me away for a long time to protect me. When I returned, I discovered that this woman was my real mother. She is an enchantress and a good person. She has watched over me my entire life. You can tell Joseph everything about me except what I am going to tell you next. Promise me you will say nothing about what I am going to tell and show you."

Kira nodded her head yes.

"I need more; I need you to say it."

"I promise any secret you tell me will remain a secret."

"I have the same power as my mother. If I had known this and had developed my abilities when I lived at the castle at Kaspar, I could have saved everyone."

"How could this possibly be true? I grew up with you, and I saw no sign that you had or would ever have magic. I can't believe this."

The two women were facing each other about five feet apart. Mira suddenly disappeared right in front of Kira. Kira was in shock. *Where did she go?*

She could feel Mira's hands on both of her shoulders. Mira slid her hands to Kira's waist. "Breathe easy. This is why I had no fear about coming here. I have magic just like my mother. I am going to use this power to correct some injustices and return things to the way they were."

Kira was no longer in shock and turned and faced Mira. "I don't want things to be the way they were. I am happy here and I will never go back to Kaspar, and I don't care if I ever see that brother of mine again."

As Mira started to speak, there was a light knock on the door. It was Kira who called, "Come in Joseph, it is okay."

Joseph came into the room and looked at Kasmira. Without waiting for Kira to speak, he said, "I understand that you knew Kira before she came here."

Mira could tell that Joseph was upset. "I did. We grew up together."

Turning to Kira, Joseph said, "Is this true? Did you know this person back in Kaspar?"

Kira walked over and stood next to Kasmira. "This is my friend Kasmira, but we will call her Mira while she is here. I thought she was dead, but she survived the desert and has come to see us."

Joseph looked at his wife and then to Mira. "Where have you been? You were banished from Kaspar at least ten years ago. We thought you were dead."

"Where I have been, is not important. I am here now. I want to see your child and visit with your wife. I will only be here for a couple of days, and then I am going back to the mainland."

Joseph walked over and looked out the window and then turned around and said, "I am afraid that will not be possible. I cannot let you leave."

Kira spoke up. "We are not going to keep her prisoner. She is my friend. She is as close as a sister. I won't permit her to be a prisoner."

Joseph spoke as if Mira was not even there. "She was your friend; a friend you have not seen in ten years. For all we know, she may want revenge on your entire family. I will not chance our happiness on that gamble. She will be confined to a room with a guard outside her door, and she will only be allowed to move about the castle with an escort. There will be no further discussion."

Kira had never seen Joseph so forceful. She knew it was useless to argue with him. She turned to Mira and said, "I am so sorry that you are trapped here."

Mira smiled at her friend. "I am not trapped here. Let's go see your child."

Mira and Kira spent the day together and soon were laughing like the old friends they were. Everywhere they went there was a guard standing next to them. His name was Jon, and he was about the same age as Joseph. When Kira went to tend to her child, Jon and Mira were left alone.

"You must be a brave and powerful warrior to get such an assignment to watch me," she laughed.

Jon didn't find this funny and did not answer.

Mira could tell that Jon was irritated and continued to talk. "Have you ever had that sword out of your sheath? If I get up and leave, what are you going to do?"

Jon looked Mira straight in the eye. He did not like her mocking him. "I will subdue you and drag you back to your room. If you seem to be a threat to the princess, I will cut your throat. If you make another joke about me, I may cut your throat anyway."

Mira became serious. "I was only joking with you to help you pass the time. I am sorry that I was having fun at your expense. Please forgive me?"

Jon gave Mira a half smile. "You are forgiven. I know that you do not want a guard with you, and I understand that. I do not know who you are and why you need to be guarded. I am not sure if I am to protect you or to protect the princess from you. Joseph told me nothing."

Mira noticed that the guard did not refer to Joseph as prince or king.

He called him Joseph, which meant that they were friends. "What is your name?"

"My name is Jon."

"Well, Jon. I ask you honestly, how come you got this assignment? You look like an experienced soldier, and you seem overqualified?"

"Joseph loves his wife very much, and when it comes to her safety, he wants the very best for her. I am her personal bodyguard. Joseph and I grew up together. We trained together, and he knows I would lay down my life for Kira. I was close by when you made a statement to the princess which upset her. I find it strange that while you were in the courtyard she was upset with you, and now you seem like great old friends. I can only conclude that you are great old friends and you knew the princess before she came here. There is another reason I am assigned to you and the princess. If you know where Mira is from, you know she was attacked when she arrived. I was with Joseph when he saved the princess at the docks. She has been a part of the family ever since. Joseph does not want anyone knowing who she is or where she is from. He does this for her protection. I know the entire story, but I am not going to share it with you. The more you know the less likely you are to ever leave."

Barak and maybe Shakir planned to have Kira killed. No wonder Joseph wanted to hide her from the world. Mira now knew that Jon was a trusted friend of Joseph. He seemed a bit serious, but she liked him. She looked down the hall and saw Kira returning.

"Did you get bored sitting here with Jon? He does not talk very much."

Smiling at Jon, Mira said, "We got along fine. I feel we will get to be close friends before I leave."

Kira looked down toward the floor. "Joseph does not trust you. I feel that it may be some time before you can leave. Joseph said that you could never leave. I am so sorry. Once he gets to know you, he will change his mind."

Mira looked at Jon and then to Kira. "I told you, I can and will leave anytime I want."

Jon looked somewhat confused, but Kira knew that this was true. She decided to change the subject. "On the brighter side, there is a banquet tonight. You are invited. You can't be at the head table, but I will try to have you at a table nearby."

Mira turned to Jon. "You will have a problem. You won't be able to guard me and Kira at the same time."

Kira laughed out loud. "I will not need an escort tonight. I am going to be with Joseph. Jon will be your escort. You and I are about the same size. I will send you up a dress and some other things a little later."

Later in the day, Jon escorted Kira to her room. When they arrived, there was a second guard posted by her door. "I am going to leave you now. There will be a guard outside your door until I return to take you to the banquet. If you need anything just let them know. I will be here at six."

"Thank you, Jon. I'm looking forward to seeing you again."

As Jon walked away he thought, *that was sarcasm if I ever heard it.*

Just before six, Kasmira was standing in front of a full-length mirror and looking at herself. The dress was a pale blue and was low cut. *My, this may be a bit revealing.* She looked at her hair. It was long, coming down past her shoulders. *I am not sure this is the way an Arabic girl should look, but when in Rome.* Hearing a knock on the door, she turned away from the mirror. Opening the door, there stood Jon. He didn't say anything. He just stared.

"Well, what do you think? Am I presentable?"

"You are. The men will not be able to keep their eyes off you. I will be the envy of the night." He paused for a moment. "You are lovely."

Jon was right. Every man at the banquet could not take his eyes from her. Jon and Mira were seated at the end of a long table that was not far from Joseph and Kira.

After they finished their meal, Mira looked across the table at Jon. For the first time, she noticed how very handsome he was. His hair was short and medium brown in color. He was at least 6 feet tall and had a strong looking body. They had talked very little during the meal. The conversations going on in the room had blended in with the music, creating a peaceful level of noise.

"I am glad you came with me and sat with me. It would have been boring without anyone to talk to." When Mira spoke, she noticed that the noise level seems to drop as she concentrated on Jon.

"You are making fun of me," he said with a slight grin on his face.

She smiled. "I guess I am. You don't talk very much, do you?"

"I have no desire to be rude or to hurt you, but I was not assigned to you to make conversation. I will say this. It has been a very good assignment, and I like being with you. But."

"But what?" Mira was a bit angry, and she concentrated on Jon's face. The level of noise in the room was all but gone as they looked at each other.

"I am going to be honest with you. Joseph does not trust you. All he knows is that you are a friend of Kira. You two have not seen each other for many years, and he has no idea where you have been. He knows things about you that he has not shared with me. He thinks there is a possibility that you may do the princess harm, and he thinks you are going to try to leave. If you do, I will stop you. There can be no threat to the princess."

Mira looked Jon straight in the eyes. "I once lived in the castle at Kaspar. I was the daughter of the royal doctor. My life couldn't have been any better. Everything I had was taken away from me, and both Kira and I were banished. Both of us were to be killed. When I want to leave, I will. You can only stop me by killing me."

"Let us hope it does not come to that. I like you, but I will do what I have to do to protect this kingdom."

Mira knew she had said too much. "I told Kira where I was. I was with my mother. What else do you want to know?"

"Kira said you lived with your mother and father in Kaspar and that your mother and father were dead. So how could you be with your mother before you came here?"

Mira smiled to herself. "I see that I have been the topic of many conversations. Davos and Ana were my adopted parents. I was with my real mother."

Jon was confused. "Who is your father?"

"I don't know. My mother has told me very little about him. I only know his name and that he is dead."

Jon looked away when he heard a loud noise and turned back to Mira. "Where did you and your mother live during this time?"

"You would not believe me if I told you. There will be no more questions, except I need to know about you. Why are you really at this banquet with me? Any guard could fill the role you have. Don't you have a girl or wife that you could be spending time with?"

Jon's face changed to sadness. "I had a wife. She died."

Mira could see the hurt on Jon's face. *This was someone he loved very much.* "What happened?"

"She died in childbirth. I lost her and my child."

"I am so sorry; believe me, I do understand your pain."

Jon quickly tried to change the conversation away from his pain. "Is there someone in your life?"

Mira did not know how to answer. How could she tell him about a man who was from another time and another world? She decided the best answer was to be vague. "There was. We got separated, and I am not sure we can ever be together again. We met while I was in hiding and fell in love, but he had to go back to his family, and he forgot me."

Jon smiled. "I don't think anybody could forget you."

Mira smiled at Jon. *Is he flirting with me?*

Jon and Mira left the banquet and walked slowly back to her room. Mira looked over at Jon as they walked down the hallway. "Where do you live or stay?"

"I live here in the castle. My room is in the West Wing. Sometimes I live with the men, but most of the time I live here in the castle."

When they arrived back at Mira's room, a young guard was still sitting outside her door. Mira spoke to him. "I am sorry you will be in trouble in the morning, but there is nothing I can do to help you."

Jon scoffed. "What in the heck does that mean?"

Mira moved closer to Jon and kissed him on the cheek. "Thanks for such a wonderful evening. You are a good man." She turned and went inside her room and closed the door.

Jon could still smell her perfume after she went inside. Just for a moment he felt the attraction he had for her. It was not a feeling he had had since his wife died. He fought off the feeling and turned to the guard. "Lock the door and do not let her out until you are relieved in the morning."

Jon went to his room and was soon lying in his bed trying to go to sleep, but he could not get Mira out of his thoughts. It was well into the morning before he drifted off to sleep. He had not been asleep long until he was awoken by the smell of Mira's perfume and the feeling of cold steel pressed against his neck. He opened his eyes in the faint light and could see Mira straddled on top of him with her knife at his throat.

"Do not move if you want to live," she said as she pressed her knife to his neck. "Do not speak or cry out. I am here only to give you information. I have been to Kaspar and there are things that you and Joseph need to know."

He tried to get up, but her weight and the knife stopped him. "What are you talking about?"

"There is going to be a war, and it will appear to be provoked by Tranquillo."

"What do you mean provoked by Tranquillo?"

"Over the last several years, Barak has secretly been building a fleet of warships. He plans to take this island. In just a few weeks he will have men disguised as your soldiers attack his outpost in the west. You know where it is. He then will attack the island, catching Tranquillo off guard. He will justify his actions by saying he was just defending Kaspar."

Jon tried to shift his body under the weight of Mira but found he could not. "Why are you just now telling me this?"

"There is more. Shakir will be at this outpost and is going to be killed. The attack on the outpost and the death of Shakir will be enough reason for Barak to attack Tranquillo. I am telling you this now because you did not trust me when I came here; I am not sure you believe me now. But I had to take a chance. Time is running out. We must stop the attack on the outpost. If I take this knife from your throat, will you not try to arrest me?"

"Yes, I mean no, I really don't know. How do you know all this?"

Mira removed the knife from Jon's throat and stood up next to his bed. "I have been spying at Kaspar. I am very good at moving around castles without being detected, as you can see. There is more. We can buy time by stopping the attack on the western outpost. You need to meet with Joseph and tell him what I have told you. If you come to my room in the morning and arrest me, I will know that all is lost. When I get up in the morning and the guard is gone, I will come to the king and Joseph and tell them my story."

Jon turned to reach for his robe, and when he turned back, Mira was gone.

Dressing as quickly as possible, Jon went straight to Mira's room. As he approached he saw the young guard sitting next to the door. "Have you been asleep at your post?"

"No sir. I have not."

Examining the door, Jon found it still locked. "Unlock the door and you are dismissed."

Mira heard the door unlock and waited for Jon and the guards to come into her room and place her under arrest. This did not happen, and she knew that things were going to be okay.

The next morning, she quickly dressed and opened the door. Outside her room was a tray of food sitting in a chair with a note.

I have gone to talk to the king and Prince Joseph and the council. Do not go far because they will want to meet with you. I hope that I can convince them that what you told me last night is true.

It was not long before Mira was standing before the king, and Jon was standing by her side.

"Jon has told me what you told him last night. Why did you not come forth sooner?"

"I was not sure how my news would be received. I had to convince someone who would support me first. I chose Jon because he is wise, and I knew that this court held him in high esteem."

"Jon has told of what Barak plans to do. What you told Jon last night and the information from our spies matches. We have known that Kaspar has been building a larger fleet, but we don't know how large. I know they would like to take our place as the center of trade in this area. Do you know when the attack on the outpost will be?"

"I do not know the exact date, but I know it will be soon. I have a plan. I know the outpost has about ten men living there. I also know that Kaspar will send about twenty to twenty-five to attack it. If we have forty or so men waiting for that attack, we could save the outpost and expose Barak's plan."

"This is also the plan that we came up with. I have spies waiting to see movement of men toward the outpost. The problem is that if we don't know the exact time of the attack, we cannot arrive in time to save the outpost, and if we arrive too early we can't leave our men in the desert without water. We have to know when the attack will take place."

Mira thought to herself. *If I tell them I can find out the exact date they will know of my magic, and that I am a witch.* "Give me a day and let me think about what I saw and heard at Kaspar. I think I will be able to come up with a date that will get us there one day or two ahead of the attack."

The Battle at the Outpost

There were only two ways to get to the Northern Outpost. You could go by sea or you could take the Northern Trade Route. Not too many people took the Northern Trade Route because most of the people trading with Kaspar living in the north came by sea. Shakir and his companions would take the Northern Trade Route. The Northern Outpost was established during a time of unstable peace. It was feared that any attack coming from the east would come by way of land. To give ample warning, two outposts were set up, one in the north and one in the south. The one in the north at one time had about fifty to one hundred men stationed there. Since there had been many years of peace, the outposts were not needed anymore, but both were in use with only a few men stationed at each. The Southern Outpost was far more important than the one in the north. It sat where the Southern Trade Route split, with one road going on to Miamba and Lilly and the other turning north toward Kaspar.

After King Rhodes had agreed to protect the Northern Outpost, Joseph and Jon were told to select forty of their best men and to get them ready.

Mira, using her power, entered the dreams of Barak and was able to extract the date of the attack. When the date approached, Jon and Joseph led their men down to the docks to board the ships that would take them to a landing area near the outpost. It took two boats to hold the men and horses that were needed. Jon was loading his horse when Mira rode up, dismounted her horse, and told a soldier to load it.

Joseph came almost running up to Mira. "What do you think you are doing? You can't make this journey. It is far too dangerous."

Mira did not have a chance to answer. Jon had joined Joseph and said almost the same thing.

"You will let me go. I will stay out of the way. It will give me great satisfaction to see a plan of Barak's destroyed. Besides, I am not coming back. I want to visit my mother's village and see where she grew up. I never got to know her, and I want to."

Jon looked sadly at Mira. "You may not be safe when we attack the outpost, and you will not be safe looking for your mother's village by yourself. Go back to the castle and wait for us. I will help you find your mother's village when this is over. We need our space for fighting men."

Mira stared at Jon and then Joseph. *I don't think Mother would mind me using my magic to show off to gain something I need.* Mira reached down and pulled out her knife with her left hand by the handle. She flipped it in the air and caught it by the blade. Using her magic, she threw it some forty feet sticking it in one of the poles that supported the pier. "Could you use a fighting woman?"

At first, Jon did not say anything, and then he said, "I did not know you were left handed."

Mira smiled. "I am not."

Jon turned and called to one of his men. "Load her horse."

Even though the northern post was a small fortified garrison which could accommodate about fifty to one hundred men, now it had only about ten. It had barracks to house the men and a lookout in the center where you could view the eastern approach to Kaspar. The view to the west was not as good, so Joseph landed his ships about two miles west of the post. It was still dark when they approached the post.

Mira could feel that Shakir was inside. Joseph split his men into two groups, and they moved just south of the garrison on each side. There the two groups hid in the sand and waited until dark. They figured the attack of the mercenaries would come from the south after dark that night. Joseph, Jon, and Mira waited until just about sundown and approached from the north holding a white flag. Since there was not a war going on, they could enter the compound. Shakir took charge. "Greetings, and why have you come?"

The threesome wore nothing that would identify who they were, so Joseph identified himself only. "I am Joseph. I come from Tranquillo. I have come to warn you. We have reports that this outpost is going to be attacked by men disguised as men from our army."

"And why would they do that?" Shakir made this statement in a mocking manner.

"They would do this to provoke a war and to kill you."

Shakir scoffed, and said, "I am King of Kaspar, and I seek no war with Tranquillo." As he said this he made a gesture with his hand, and his men inside the outpost pulled their swords. Shakir did not pull his sword. "You are here from Tranquillo, and it looks like you are the ones who want a war."

Joseph stayed calm, while Jon and Mira said nothing. "I have fifty men with bows outside this camp. If I wanted I could have overrun this camp and killed or taken all of you prisoners. I have not. I am asking you to have faith in my words. All I am asking you to do is wait and see what happens. You will be attacked tonight."

Again, Shakir scoffed. "I think you may be right. We are going to be attacked tonight. But the attack will come from your men."

Mira, who was dressed like a man with her face still covered, stepped forward and said, "Shakir, I always knew you were naïve, but I didn't think you were stupid. Now I think you must be."

Shakir pulled his sword, and Jon and Joseph did the same, but Mira stepped between them.

Shakir held up his hand to stop his men. "You are a woman." He looked at Joseph. "Why have you brought a woman to this camp?"

Mira reached up and removed the wrap from around her head and revealed to Shakir who she was. "He brought me here because I asked him. I needed to see you."

Shakir was no longer calm. "Kasmira!" Shakir was in a state of shock. He tried to regain his composure. "Have you come to kill me? You want revenge."

"No, I want justice. Why would I want revenge against you?" Now it was Mira who did the mocking. "Didn't you do what you thought was right some ten years ago?" There was anger in her voice, and Shakir could sense that he was now in danger.

Joseph could see Mira's anger and spoke up. "We have not come to kill you. We have come to save you."

Shakir did not take his eyes from Mira. "When I banished you, I thought I was saving your life. It was later that Barak told me that you were probably sold into slavery."

Mira, who was still having trouble controlling her anger, said, "Barak never intended for me to be sold into slavery. I was taken to the middle of the desert and left there to die. As you can see, I did not."

Shakir was not sure what to say. "How were you saved? Where have you been all these years?"

"I will just leave you guessing about that. Right now, we need to save you and your men."

Shakir put his sword away and motioned for his men to do the same. "What is it that you want us to do?"

Joseph spoke softly and said, "Keep a small fire burning in the middle of the compound and just wait. Make sure your men have their weapons close." Joseph, Jon, Shakir, and Mira took a seat with their backs to the southern wall of the compound. The walls were low and not meant to withstand a siege. They all sat quietly while several of the men gathered around the fire and had a low conversation.

As they sat and waited, Shakir picked up a small piece of wood and threw it into the fire. "I notice that your companions call you Mira. What is that all about?"

"I need to keep who I am a secret. I don't want Barak to know I am back."

"If what you have told me is true, I will keep your secret and help as much as I can."

Suddenly Mira nudged Jon. "They are here."

"I don't hear anything. Are you sure?"

Mira reached into the small bag she was carrying and pulled out a small package. She motioned for one of the men with a bow to come to her. "Attach this to the end of an arrow and shoot it high into the air toward the southern sky."

Shakir told the man to do as commanded. Several of the men joined them looking toward the south. The arrow soared high into the sky. When it reached its zenith, Mira did her magic, and it burst into a bright white flame that lit up the sky and revealed the mercenaries crawling on the sand toward the compound. When they saw they had been discovered, they scrambled to their feet and with swords in hand charged the outpost. Shakir could see that they were vastly outnumbered, but suddenly a volley of arrows from left and right brought down most of the charging men. The four that remained stopped and fell to their knees, putting their hands behind their heads.

With four men captive and the others lying outside the outpost dead, Jon asked Joseph what they should do with the dead. "Drag them away from here and bury them in the sand and let the sand worms have them." Jon instructed the men to get rid of the bodies. Joseph started to question the remaining four. Just as he started, Shakir interrupted. "You men are dressed like you are from Tranquillo. Who gave you orders to attack this outpost?"

One of the men trying to salvage the attack said, "It was King Rhodes from Tranquillo."

Joseph spoke up. "I am from Tranquillo and King Rhodes is my father. I will offer you this. You can tell the truth and spend the rest of your life in prison, or you can continue to lie and have your throat cut right here and be buried with the rest of your men."

The man who had spoken look down at the ground and said, "We came here under the orders of Barak."

Joseph asked, "did Barak himself give you these orders?"

"No. Akeem gave us orders to kill King Shakir and make it look like the attack came from Tranquillo. He told us that the orders came from Barak. Have mercy on us?"

Shakir turned to Mira. "I have been a fool. How did you know about this attack?"

"I came to Kaspar several weeks ago and overheard Barak and another man talking and making their plans."

"Do you know who the other man was?"

"His name was Akeem. He is the man who made the poison that killed your father."

Shakir now had tears in his eyes. "Then what this man is saying is true. Barak ordered this attack. Barak has killed my father, he has killed my sister, and he tried to kill you. He is trying to take the kingdom. Is my wife involved in this?"

"Here is where you will have to trust me and her. She is not involved."

Shakir turned and walked to the edge of the fire. "I don't know what to do. I could go back and confront Barak, have him arrested and put on trial, but at this point he may have more power than me. I have just about signed over the throne to him. For all I know, he may have the council on his side."

Mira walked up and stood beside Shakir. "I don't know if he has the council on his side or not. I do know that there are others helping him."

Joseph, who had been listening to the conversation, spoke up. "Go back to the castle and tell him nothing. He will be confused. Tell the council that you have inspected the outpost and found that it may need more men, but it is serving its purpose. Barak will think that the mercenaries have taken his money and left the country. He will start making more plans, but we have bought some time. Meanwhile, you need to do everything possible to protect yourself and your wife and child. Remember, every day you live at the castle with Barak your life is in danger. In about a week, tell Barak that you want to take your wife on a trip and go visit Lilly. Do not let Barak choose your escorts. We must know who the real power in Kaspar is. We hope it is you, but if Barak is calling the shots, it will be dangerous for Tranquillo to get involved. Stay there until we have Barak under control."

Mira came over and gave Shakir a hug. Whispering so no one else could hear, she said, "Tell no one that you have seen me. Don't say anything or ask any questions, but I think you need to know that your sister is alive and safe."

As Mira started to leave, Shakir asked, "Did you come to my room several nights ago?"

Mira's smiled and said, "Did I?"

The Search

When Joseph, Jon, and Mira returned to Tranquillo, Mira immediately started questioning Joseph about taking her to a port that would be near Anemoi. It was agreed that he would arrange a boat to take her to Aquas Negras, a small port which was only about a day and a half from Anemoi. Joseph would only agree if Mira would agree to an escort of three soldiers. When she was waiting on the ship she looked across the dock and saw Jon walking toward the boat. When he came up the walkway, Mira smiled and spoke. "Have you come to see me off? How sweet."

"No. I have come to take you to Anemoi."

"I am honored to have such a person of your position accompanying me, but it is not necessary."

"I have seen how headstrong you are, and I have a feeling as soon as you land in Aquas Negras you will lose your escort. You will not lose me so easily." Jon came aboard and motioned to the crew to make way. "This was not my idea. Joseph and Kira insisted that I come."

Mira knew it was useless to argue, and when they were out to sea, she said, "How long is the trip to Aquas Negras going to take?"

"We will be there some time tomorrow morning. We will unload the horses, let them get their legs back, and after we have something to eat, we will be on our way. I would suggest we get some sleep if we can, but if you are like me, you won't sleep well on a rocking boat."

Mira saw some sacks of grain lined up in the middle of the ship and walked over and leaned back against one. "I am willing to share my bed, although it might not be all that comfortable."

Jon moved over and sat down next to Mira. "You are too kind."

Mira was not like Jon, and it wasn't long until she was sound asleep. Jon was watching her, and he began to wonder exactly what her purpose for this journey was. He began to think about what he knew about her. He really did not know who she was, so he would indulge her and hope she found what she was looking for. As he watched her sleep, he found his cold heart melting away little by little. He thought back to accompanying her to the banquet at Tranquillo and how she conducted herself at the raid on the outpost. She was not only one of the most beautiful women he had ever seen but maybe the most exciting, and he loved the mystery of her.

While Mira was in a deep sleep, she dreamed of David. In her dream, she was holding a baby and standing with him in front of a beautiful home. Her dream was ended by someone shaking her. It was Jon. "We are here. Time to get up. We will be at the dock in about ten minutes." The four travelers led their horses off the boat and walked them around for a few moments. They packed some supplies on the back of the horses, mounted them, and started away from the dock.

As they rode through the town of Aquas Negras Mira had the strangest feeling. It was like someone was calling to her. She stopped her horse and looked down a street that led to the sea. "Jon, what is out there, out there in the sea?"

"It is a place we don't want to go. There is a prison out there. It is called Isla de la Muerte."

Mira gave it no more thought, and they rode on. Jon shifted on his horse, so all could hear. "There is a tavern just outside of town on the road to Anemoi. We will stop there and eat before moving on. I have been to this tavern before. It never closes, and it is hardcore. Mira, you need to keep your head covered."

Mira scoffed. "How am I going to eat with my head covered?"

"We will try to keep you out of view once inside. Just keep your head down, and maybe we will get lucky."

The tavern was quiet, due to the time of day. There were about ten men scattered throughout the large room. Mira and Jon and the two other men took a table in a back corner with Mira taking a seat with her back to the wall. Jon went to the kitchen and came back carrying bread, cheese, and wine. Mira unwrapped her kufiya just enough to get food to her mouth and was just about through eating when a very large man came up and with a huge voice said, "Give me the woman and I will let you keep your life." Two other men came up and stood next to the man.

Jon didn't even look up. One of the other men spoke. "When we get through with her, we may give her back to you."

Again, Jon did not look up but said in a low voice to his two companions, "When I stand up, get Mira out of here. Wait for me about a mile down the road."

Rising out of his seat, Jon suddenly had a knife in his hand and plunged it into the first man. In the blink of an eye, his sword was drawn, and the second man was falling to the floor with a slash across his neck. The two soldiers took Mira by the arm and led her out to the horses. As Mira looked back, she could see about four more men coming to the support of the ruffians. The three galloped away as quickly as they could.

As the three waited for Jon, Mira was worried. She could have used magic and got them safely out of there. Now at least two men were dead, maybe more, and she did not know the fate of Jon. Using her magic, she concentrated on him and could feel him riding at a slow pace toward them. She felt relieved and looked forward to seeing him.

When Jon did arrive, he could tell that Mira was pleased to see him. She was now seeing him in a different light. He was a no-nonsense skilled warrior, but he also was kind and a good man. The foursome rode on during the day, stopping only to water their horses and to eat. Mira thought it was strange that they met no one on the journey. One of the soldiers said he had been in this area many times, and most people only travelled to the west to join the trade routes or to go to the city at Kaspar. Not many people had a reason to go to Aquas Negras.

As the sun set, they moved just a little off the road and spread their blankets on the sand. They also built a small fire. They were right on the beach and could see the waves crashing on the shoreline. There were several small trees to keep them covered and enough dry driftwood to keep the fire going during the night.

When they finished their meal, Mira surprised them all by saying she would take the first watch. They really hadn't expected her to take a watch at all. While the others got some sleep, Mira sat on the sand looking out at the ocean. Again, she had a feeling as if someone was calling to her. She did not understand these feelings, and again her thoughts turned to David. Was it him calling to her? She was relieved after midnight, and she took her place on her blanket next to the fire. Jon was awake, and he spoke softly to her as to not awaken the other soldier. "You asked me questions about my life back at the banquet the first night we met. I want to ask some questions of you. Why are you not married? Or like me, have you been married?"

"I have not been married. You know that I grew up in Kaspar. I was fifteen when I was banished. I was left to die in the desert but was saved. From that point on there is not much to tell. At the banquet, I told you I was in love and we got separated. His name is David. I am not sure we can ever get back together, but I do know that he will wait for me."

Jon started to ask another question, but Mira stopped him. "We need to get some sleep, or at least I do. Good night Jon."

The next day they arrived in Anemoi just before noon. Mira had very strong feelings and emotions she did not understand running through her mind and body. Asking directions, they found that Fadi was still the village leader, and they were directed to his tent which was in the heart of the village. The village had about one hundred to one hundred and fifty tents which were constructed in such a way that they were almost permanent structures. When they rode up to Fadi's tent, they found two men seated in front.

"We are here to see Fadi," Jon said.

The older man stood up and said, "I am Fadi. Why do you seek council with me?" The other man did not move but stared at the travelers.

Jon told the others to take the horses and find water and grain and a place for them to spend the night. Jon and Mira were invited inside the tent. The man who was seated with Fadi also moved inside. Mira noticed that he was wearing a sword. She was also surprised at how large the tent was inside, and the layout created more rooms. The four of them took a seat in a circle and Fadi said, "How can I be of service?"

Jon said nothing but left the rest of the conversation to Mira. "I have come far. I know that my mother was from this village. I would like to find out about her and get to know her better. She was also married here, and I would like to examine your records to confirm who she was married to."

"The way you talk, your mother and father are dead. Who was your mother?"

"My father is dead. My mother's name is Nyla. Can you help me?"

The man who had been seated with Fadi spoke up and said in an angry voice, "You are not who you claim to be. There has been only one Nyla from this village, and she died many years ago. Fadi, give them nothing. I will escort them out."

Once they were outside the tent, the man said, "You must be spies, and if I can't prove who you are, I will see that you are executed." Jon put his hand on his sword, but Mira spoke and motioned for him to remain calm. "Who are you? I don't understand why you are treating me and my friend this way. Why would anyone spy on this village?"

At first the man did not say anything. *Has Barak found out that I am still alive? Why would he be searching for records about Nyla and Jaul?* He looked at the two standing in front of him and decided to give them information to help find out why they were there. "My name is Raja. I was a friend of Nyla, and that is why I know you can't be who you say. As I said, she is dead and has been dead for twenty-five years."

Mira just stared at Raja, and tears came into her eyes. "You know, she thinks the same thing about you. She said you have been dead for twenty-five years. But I can see you are not dead."

Raja's voice became very calm. "Who are you?"

For some reason, it seemed now was the time for the truth. "My name is Kasmira. I am the daughter of Jabir and Nyla."

Raja remembered what Nyla had told him. *I am going to have a daughter, and if in the future she comes to you, her name will be Kasmira.* As Raja looked at Kasmira, he wondered what had happened. Why was he informed that Nyla had been killed? He also wondered why Nyla had told Kasmira that her father's name was Jabir and not Jaul. Why had she kept from Kasmira the fact that her father had been king of Kaspar? He decided to proceed with caution. "We need to talk alone. Come with me." When they were away from Jon, they walked to the edge of the village where there was a large oasis. They took a seat under a large tree and Raja started to question Kasmira. "What happened to Nyla? I left her at the castle and went to find what happened to your father. I was told that Nyla had been killed, and they tried to kill me. Thinking that Nyla was dead I assumed that there would be no baby, and there was no reason for me to come back to the castle."

"My mother was put in prison and told that you had been killed. Later the cell was set on fire. Somehow, she escaped and found Zanzura. That was where I was born. Mother was burned badly in the fire. She decided that I did not need to be raised in a cave in the desert, so she gave me to Davos and Ana who lived in the castle at Kaspar. For the past several years, Barak has slowly taken over Kaspar. Barak killed the king, blamed it on Davos, and had him put to death. Ana killed herself, and I was banished. The king's son, Shakir, became king but is weak. Barak will do anything to continue to rule at Kaspar."

"Where have you been all this time? Did you go back and live with Nyla?"

"I was banished and left to die in the desert. My mother saved me, but I have not been with her. My mother told me she trusted you, and you were her only friend. I must now trust you, and you must swear you will tell no one what I am about to tell and show you." She just stared at Raja and waited for him to respond.

"I will do what you ask. I will keep any secret you have."

"You may not believe what I am about to tell you, but I must trust you. Nyla was more than a healer. She has magic, strong magic. Some would call her a witch."

Raja leaned back against the tree. "That makes sense. When we brought your father to this village, everyone had given up hope. He spent one day in Nyla's care and was better the next day. In a few weeks, he was healed. She had to have some power to do that."

"Nyla had the power to save herself and change a lot of things, but she does not trust her power. She says to use the magic unwisely will cause her to turn dark and become an evil person. She will only use her power for good. She lives in the desert at Zanzura and does not leave very often, and even then, she does not go far. I think she wants revenge for all that has happened to her, but she calls it justice."

Leaning forward Raja said, "What do you want?"

"I want to kill Barak. At one time, I wanted to kill Shakir and Shakira, but I have found out they too were victims of Barak. I guess I want justice too."

"Is that why you came to me and Fadi?"

Mira looked at Raja with a caring smile. "I didn't even know you were alive. I want to know my father. You knew him. I want you to tell me as much as you can about him. You left Kaspar looking for him. Did you find out anything?"

"No. After Barak's men tried to kill me, I did go back to the site of our last battle and look for his body, but I could not find any sign of him. I questioned several men who fought alongside him, but they did not know anything. I came back to Anemoi and made it my home."

Mira seemed to drift away in thought. Raja did not say anything more but began to think. *Nyla has not told her daughter anything about her father. There must be a reason for that. She must believe or know that Kasmira has her same power and is scared that if she finds out the truth, she may seek revenge and become dark.*

"Kasmira, do you have your mother's power?"

For a moment Kasmira said nothing but thought to herself, *I must trust him.* "I do. I not only have her abilities, I have much more. Joseph of Tranquillo sent three men with me to protect me on this journey, but I don't need their protection. I can protect myself and much more. Tell me about my father."

"Your father had a birthmark. It was on his forearm. It was so perfect it looked almost like a tattoo. You had to look very closely to see that it wasn't. It looked like a crescent and a star together. Do you have any birthmarks?"

"Mother said I did, but she used her magic to hide it."

"Where is it?"

"It is on my back near my right shoulder."

"Do you have the power to bring it back, and can you show me?" Raja moved away from the tree and stood up.

Kasmira stood up and concentrated. She let her garment slide off her shoulder as she turned her back to Raja.

Raja moved closer and without thinking let his fingers slide over the birthmark. Pulling his hand back quickly, he said, "I am sorry, but I was amazed that your birthmark is so much like your father's."

Pulling her clothing back up over her shoulder, she said, "I have never seen the birthmark. It was only recent that I was told about it. My mother pointed it out. I think it only appeared when my powers came back to me. Would you draw what it looks like in the sand?"

Raja took a small stick and drew the crescent moon and star in the sand.

"I have seen this before. It is on the flag of Kaspar and on a tapestry in the council hall. This is strange."

Raja took Kasmira by the hands and looked into her eyes. "There is something I need for you to see, but I am afraid to show it to you. I know why your mother has told you nothing about your father. What I am about to show you will make you angry. You must promise me that you will keep your anger under control. If your mother is right, there will be enough anger to cause you to use your magic in such a way to seek revenge and maybe even kill. You must keep your anger in check. Can you do that?"

Raja and Kasmira said nothing as they walked back to the tent of Fadi. When they got back to the tent, Jon and Fadi were sitting outside talking. Raja looked at Jon and said, "I am sorry for keeping you in the dark. I have been with Kasmira and telling her about her mother. There is now something I must show her, and it needs to be done in private. She then can decide how much she wants to share with you. Would you give us some time to be alone?"

Jon was bewildered and said nothing. He quickly got up and left.

After Jon had left, Raja turned to Fadi. "Show her the book."

They followed Fadi inside to a small room in his tent. Fadi threw back a small rug to reveal the sand floor. He took a broom and began sweeping away the sand until it revealed a wooden box. Lifting the box to a table, he opened it and took out a very large book. He took his time turning the pages, and then he stopped. "Here is what you want to see. It is the record of your mother and father's marriage."

Kasmira walked up to the table and looked down. Looking at the page, she could not believe what she was seeing. She saw her mother's name, Nyla of Anemoi, and on the other line was not Jabir, but the name Jaul, King of Kaspar.

The room was silent as they waited for Kasmira to say something. Kasmira turned to Raja. "I don't understand. This says my mother was married to Jaul, King of Kaspar. Who was Jabir? Did Jabir marry my mother after my father was killed?"

"No. Your father Jaul came to this village and wanted to keep his identity a secret. He took the name Jabir to protect the village, and Nyla."

Mira took a second look at the book. "My father was the King of Kaspar. My mother should have been the queen. She has been living in the desert for twenty-five years and could have been living in the castle of Kaspar." Mira was not angry but confused. She was almost overcome with sadness about what could have been for her mother and her father. "I need to be alone and I need to clean up. I want to think. Is there a place where I could bathe and be alone?"

The Temptation

Mira was given a robe and drying cloths and directions to a secluded oasis in walking distance to the village. When she got there, she spread a blanket on the sand and lay back and looked at the cloudless sky. She started crying, and she could not control it. She cried herself to sleep, and when she woke up the sun was low in the sky. *My father was the king of Kaspar. That means that King Kadar was the brother of Jaul. That would make Shakir and Shakira my cousins. If my father had lived, I would be in line to be the queen of Kaspar.* She surprised herself by not becoming angry but thinking about her father.

Leaving her top garments on the blanket she moved slowly into the water. She had been given some soap. *I will have to take a chance that I am alone.* She took the under-garments off and let them drift in the water. The water felt good as she soaped herself. To her surprise, she had a feeling of contentment. She had found her past.

Suddenly the feeling of contentment left, and she started to become angry. She began to think of all the things that Barak had done. *He tried to kill Raja, Shakir, Nyla, Davos, and Ana, and no telling who else. He is evil. He started this evil plan many years ago and will sacrifice anything to attain power. He must be stopped. I am going to kill him. I will take Raja and go back to Kaspar and force him to take poison. I will kill him just like he killed the king.* She began to feel good.

The sun was just about to set when she started toward the bank. Finding her undergarments floating in the water, she struggled to get them on. When she got to the bank of the oasis, she stretched out on the blanket. *I told my mother I was taking this trip to find Shakira and my past. How can I go back and tell her that I killed Barak? Killing him will not solve the problems. Shakir would remain king, and still be a weak king. No one would know the evil that Barak has done, and there are others involved. Shakir would still be in danger. My mother would still be an outcast in the desert. Killing Barak would not solve anything. I am a lawyer. Everyone needs to have a fair trial. A public trial would show everyone the truth.*

Suddenly she heard someone walking toward her. It was Jon holding her robe. Her under-garments were almost transparent. and she let Jon put the robe around her. As he placed the robe around her, he put his arms around her and drew her close. "You know that I am falling in love with you?"

Mira looked up at him, and as she did he kissed her. She found herself kissing him back. When the kiss ended, she said, "I don't have time to fall in love." She found that her body tingled all over, and when he kissed her again she again found herself kissing him back.

When the kiss ended, they stood there not saying anything. Turning away from him and adjusting the robe she said, "I am sorry I let this go this far. Wait for me over by that gathering of trees. I will finish dressing and be there in a moment."

Mira quickly finished dressing and walked to Jon standing by the trees. Mira said, "I care for you, I care for you a lot, but once I have done what I came to do, I am leaving, and I don't think I can come back. If this were not the case, I would be tempted to stay with you."

Jon had a big smile on his face. "There is hope. You did kiss me back, twice."

Mira changed the subject. "You have been calling me Mira, and Raja has been calling me Kasmira. You know my name is Kasmira. You can use it. I am not going to disguise who I am anymore. I have found what I am looking for and now I must go to Kaspar to bring this story to an end. Sit back against that tree. I am going to tell you about my mother and what happened to her after my father was killed. I assure you there is going to be justice." Kasmira told Jon the story of how Barak had King Kadar killed and how he blamed it on Davos and had him executed. She told how her mother had killed herself. She told the story about being saved in the desert by the Woman in Black. But she did not tell him that the Woman in Black was her mother, and that she and her mother had magic and she was the daughter of King Jaul.

The Trip to Lilly

When Shakir returned to the castle at Kaspar, he was afraid that he could not fool Barak. He first went to Jada. Like always she was happy to see him, and he sent word to Barak and the council that he was back and would give a full report in the morning. Barak was in a state of shock, but soon, as was predicted, he thought he had been betrayed by the mercenaries and decided not to act until he heard Shakir's reports. Meanwhile he called for Akeem. "Do you have any idea what has happened? I want you to attend the council meeting in the morning and see if you can pick up on anything from Shakir. Something is not right."

The next day at the council meeting, Shakir kept his report short. He had made an inspection of the outpost before the attack so everything he reported was true. This kept Akeem from picking up on anything. Akeem did feel that something was off. He just could not put his finger on it. When he reported his feelings to Barak, Barak decided to come up with a new plan. He just did not know what it would be. Shakir avoided Barak for the next several days, and when they did finally meet, Shakir told him of his plans to take his family to Lilly. "I have told Jada that I want to spend some time with her and get away from the castle."

When Barak was alone, he thought to himself, *this is perfect*. Shakir would be gone for about two weeks. He would have his men attack the boat and kill Shakir. He would put off the attack on Tranquillo until after Jada became queen and he had absolute power.

When Shakir and Jada left the castle, they boarded one of the finest boats on the Viper River. Sailing up the river, Shakir told the crew to go slowly so he and Jada could enjoy the sights. Jada had never been on the river or to Lilly. While the trip didn't usually take that long, they were going to spend three days going to Lilly. The first two days of the trip were wonderful, and Shakir almost forgot why he had taken the trip.

On the last day of the trip, Shakir and Jada were lying in bed when Shakir said, "Jada, I need to tell you something."

Jada was caught off-guard by his tone. "You sound serious. Are you going to tell me you found someone else on one of your many inspection tours?"

"No. That would be easier than telling what I am going to tell you now." Shakir put his arm around Jada and pulled her close. "You know I love you more than my own life. I would never lie to you or do anything to hurt you. That is why this is so difficult. Your father tried to have me killed at the Northern Outpost."

Jada pulled away and sat up in the bed. "This can't be true. Why do you tell me this? Father loves me and you. He would never do anything to hurt us." Jada lay back down on the bed with her back turned to Shakir.

"Hear me out. Just listen and then you decide. I went to the Northern Outpost for the inspection just as planned. On the second night three strangers came to the compound with a white flag and warned us that we were going to be attacked. They told us that the attackers would be dressed like soldiers from Tranquillo. At first, I did not believe them, but later that night I found out it was true. We were vastly outnumbered, and had it not been for the strangers' army lying and waiting we would have been killed. All the attackers were killed but a couple. When they were questioned as to who ordered the attack, at first, they said it was King Rhodes, but when they found that King Rhodes's son was one of the three strangers who warned us, they admitted they were acting on orders from Barak. I also found out that Barak had given orders for me to be killed. The three strangers, or at least two of them, were from Tranquillo. This is why we're taking this trip. I am trying to keep us safe until we can come up with a plan to save our kingdom and my life."

Jada was in a state of shock. "Why would Father do this? This can't be true."

"Barak knows that I am going to take my authority to rule the kingdom back. With me dead and you as queen, he can continue to be regent and hold all the power. There is more. I now feel it was your father and not Davos who poisoned my father."

Jada turned over and faced Shakir. "We have to go back; I need to talk to Father. This is more than I can believe."

"Jada, listen to me. What I tell you is true. Remember, I told you that two of the strangers were from Tranquillo. I knew the third person. It was this person who told me they had found out that your father planned to have me killed."

Jada scoffed. "How could a person know of my father's plans?"

"This person was from Kaspar but was spying for Tranquillo. Barak is wanting a war with Tranquillo, and to make it look like men from Tranquillo killed me would be a perfect excuse. I took three men with me to the outpost for the inspection, and there were only ten more there. There were only thirteen of us total. The group from Tranquillo had fifty not counting themselves. If they had wanted, they could have put me to death on the spot."

Jada moved closer to Shakir and cuddled up next to him and started to cry. "For two days, I thought our lives could not be any better, and now I feel they could not get any worse. What makes you think that I have not been working with my father all this time? Isn't that a conclusion one might make?"

"I don't think you have been working against me with your father. I know this for two reasons. I couldn't love a person that didn't love me, and I know you love me. The second one is strange. When this is all over I will tell you the second reason, and it is the most important. Right now, I need you to trust me, and I will keep you and Kad safe."

Isla de la Muerte

That night, Kasmira avoided Jon. She had feelings for him, and the more they were together the stronger they became. After supper, she and Raja sat alone. "Tell me about my father. I want to get to know him."

Raja picked up a small stick and threw it in the fire. "It often gets cold here at night. Your father and I sat around many fires like this one and talked about many things. What would you like to know?"

"I don't know. What kind of man was he? Was he a good king?'

"He was a good king, but even a better man. He wanted good things for the people of Kaspar. While he was king, he made many laws that gave rights to the people of Kaspar. It was he who set up a council. Before he was killed, he wanted to end the war. We needed a victory to be able to negotiate a peace. As you already know, we did not get that victory, but we did get peace. He loved Nyla very much. After he was married and came back to our camp all he could do was talk about her."

That night as Kasmira slept in one of the guest tents, she had a dream. It was about her father. He was suffering inside a prison cell. She could feel his pain as he lay on a bare stone floor. When she awoke, she was covered in perspiration. The dream felt so real. She went outside and looked up at the crystal-clear night that was full of stars, and she had the same feeling she had on the boat when it was near Aquas Negras. Then it came to her. Her father could still be alive. Falling to her knees she concentrated on her father, and she could feel him. He was in a prison which she could tell was somewhere to the northeast.

Raja was awakened by someone shaking him. He opened his eyes and could make out that it was Kasmira. "Yesterday I told you I had more powerful magic than my mother. Tonight, I dreamed of Father. He is alive. He is in a prison somewhere northwest of here. Do you know of such a place?"

Raja struggled to get himself awake. "Don't you think that our conversation about your father has caused you to dream about him? Go back to bed. It was just a dream."

"Don't make the mistake of doubting my magic. I asked you a question and I demand an answer. Do you know of a prison northwest of here?"

"I do. There is a prison on the Island of Death. It is maintained by the Spanish. If your father was captured and put in prison, this is where he would be. But this is a long shot. It is most unlikely that anyone could survive twenty-five years in that place."

"He is there, and I am leaving today. I can be there this morning using my power."

Raja stood up and took Kasmira by the hand. "You might be able to get yourself there using magic, but can you get him back? If he is there, we don't know what kind of condition he will be in. Most likely he will be ill, perhaps too weak to walk. We can be at Aquas Negras in a day and a half, maybe a day if we ride hard. We can get a boat at the dock and find Jaul. Do this for me and my friend. We can't just march into prison and ask for Jaul. We would have to bribe the guards, and even then, they may want a large ransom."

"He is weak and very sick, and that is why we can't wait for the others. I am going to have to use magic to get him out of the prison, but we are to keep it from the others. If we tell the others, I know Jon will insist on coming. He has the strange notion that he is in love with me. If we are able to save my father, he is not to know who I am."

Raja scratched his head. "How are we going to tell him that you know your father is in the prison?"

"First we have to stop referring to him as my father. We will refer to him as Jaul. We may have to tell Jon and the others that he was the king of Kaspar, but we cannot tell them that he is my father. I know you will not agree to what I am now going to do. I am going to the island to make sure he is okay. I will be back as quickly as possible. I never have put my magic to a real test. This will be it. I don't know how long this will take. Jon will be looking for me this morning. Tell him I went for a morning ride or make up some other nonsense."

Standing in front of Raja, Kasmira covered her face and all the color went out of Kasmira's clothing. She was now dressed completely in black. Raja could not believe his eyes as Kasmira disappeared right in front of him.

Kasmira was right, because it was not long until Jon came looking for her. "Where is she this morning? She is one of the most unpredictable people I have ever met."

Raja tried to be casual. "I don't really know. She came by earlier and said she was going to take a ride. She said she wanted to be alone and do some thinking."

Jon scoffed. "She is going to be the death of us all. Which way did she go?"

You are righter than you could possibly know, Raja thought to himself. "She didn't say. She will be okay. It is safe around here."

Jon looked at the different directions that Kasmira could go and decided it would be useless to try to ride after her. He would just have to wait until she returned.

***

In an instant, Kasmira found herself on the island looking at a very imposing prison. It looked more like a castle than a prison. It was surrounded by a swamp, and the swamp was creating a heavy fog. The view was limited. You couldn't even see the top of the prison. The road to the front gate was made of stone, and the gate was made out of wood sitting on a wooden post to support it above the water of the swamp. There were no guards, but they were not needed. Using her magic, Kasmira moved all the way around the grey walls until on the back side she found some dry land that led deeper into the swamp. Next to that area was a small dock that had one small boat attached to it. *This is perfect,* she thought to herself. Standing on the dry ground and putting both hands on the wall, she could sense that Jaul was on the first floor and only about a hundred feet from where she stood. She could also sense that he was extremely weak and was dying. Quickly she

199

moved through the wall and found herself moving down the hall leading to her father's cell. The odor was almost unbearable. Suddenly, she heard voices coming down the hallway and getting closer. Looking ahead she saw the cell number 01-23. She could sense that this was her father's cell, and she quietly moved through the door to find her father lying on the stone floor. His clothes were extremely worn and full of holes. His hair and beard were about ten inches long. Looking at his worn clothing, she could see cockroaches moving about the holes in the pants. He had no shirt, and his body was pierced with sores and whip marks and bug bites.

Kasmira noticed that the voices had stopped just outside the cell, and she listened to what they were saying. One man spoke to the other in Spanish. "The word is that this man is going to die today. I suggest we throw him into the swamp and let the fishes have him."

The other man replied. "Juan says we must wait until they die before we dispose of them."

"What Juan does not know will not hurt him. I don't see why we should wait. He might hold on all day or several days. Let's get rid of him now."

Kasmira heard the key in the lock turn. She had no time to react. When the door opened, she reached down, pulled her knife, and threw it at the first man coming through the door, catching him in the neck. The second man was caught off guard. Kasmira used her power to pull him inside and flung him across the cell against the wall with such force that he was dead when he fell from the wall. Quickly she closed the cell door and went to her father. Kneeling next to him, she placed her hands on his head and concentrated on making him better. She could feel him starting to breathe better, and she continued until his eyes opened. He was looking up at her. Kasmira had never unwrapped her face, so all he could see were her eyes.

"What is happening? Who are you?"

"I am the person who is going to get you out of this place." She took her hand and closed his eyes. She placed him in a shallow sleep. She picked up the keys from the guard. Walking out into the hall, she sensed a prisoner in the next cell who was strong. She tossed the keys through the food opening on the door. *Use these the best way you see fit.*

Going back into the cell, she helped her father to his feet. They moved slowly up the corridor until they reached the outside wall. Jaul was in a dreamlike state and could barely walk. Quickly she moved them both through the wall. *If only I could transport us both to the mainland, but I cannot.* Helping her father into the small row boat, she sat in the back using her magic to guide the boat through the swamp until they reached the beach.

As she left the prison she could hear shouting inside. It appeared that the prisoner she gave the keys to was releasing other prisoners, and soon a bell was ringing to alert the guards of a prison break. *This will give us time to escape and not be discovered. They will think escaped prisoners killed the two guards.*

She continued to let her father sleep, and she knew he would have his strength back when they reached the mainland. *Well, here goes nothing.* She guided the boat on the waters that surrounded the island and into open water. She sensed that Anemoi was to the southeast. *I hope the weather is good,* she said to herself. It was way into the night when she pulled the boat ashore about a half day's ride from Anemoi. She continued to let Jaul sleep. She realized that she had used her power to kill. She left her father and ran down the beach, stopping to throw up. She thought of her mother's warning. As she walked back to her father she started to cry. At first, she was tempted to contact her mother in a dream and tell her what she had done. She decided to not tell her mother. *I have killed using magic, but I did it to save my father's life. I will have to live with that.*

Kasmira concentrated on Raja. He was asleep, and she entered his dream. *We are on the coast about a half day's ride from Anemoi. If you ride northwest, you will find us. Just before noon I am going to build a fire and cover it with seaweed to make lots of smoke. It will guide you on the last part of your trip. Meet us there at noon and bring two extra horses.*

As Jaul slept, Kasmira moved along the beach looking for something to eat. She was able to come up with some nuts and fruit that were growing just off the beach. As the sun came up, Jaul opened his eyes. He sat up looking up at Kasmira. He said, "You know I have lots of questions. The first one is, who are you?"

"I am the person who is going to make things right. I know who you are. I grew up in Kaspar. A lot has happened."

"I don't understand. Yesterday I could hear the guards saying I was going to die within a couple of days. I have a vague memory of you walking me down the hall that separates the cells. I saw a wall and things went blank, and I wake up here feeling better than I have felt in years."

"That is not important. What is, is we need to get you strong again, and we must get back to save Kaspar."

"I have been in prison for a very long time. I lost count of the years. Is my brother ruling the kingdom?"

"You are right. You have been in prison a long time. Kaspar is in trouble. Your brother had been ruling Kaspar for several years, but he has been killed. He was killed by an evil man by the name of Barak. Barak blamed the killing on a court doctor and had him killed. Kadar's son, Shakir has been ruling Kaspar but has let Barak take over the kingdom, and now Barak wants to kill Shakir, so he can rule. There has been a lot going on, and we have all morning to bring you up to speed."

"How did you get me out of that prison?"

"It was magic, just simple magic. You get no more questions. Go wash yourself in the ocean. You stink, really stink. When you get finished, we will have breakfast, and I will bring you up to date on what has been going on."

"I guess I do stink; the only bath I have had is a bucket of swamp water being thrown on me a couple of times a month. I will go in just a moment. When I get back, I am going to need a whole lot more information from you. I am not going to go anywhere with you until I get some answers."

"You go take your bath, I am going to try to convince a fish to commit suicide and make us something to eat. I will then tell you everything you need to know."

Jaul walked down to the edge of the water and watched the waves break right at his knees. The water was somewhat warm, and he had hoped it would be cooler. Leaving his clothes on, he waded into the water and started to use the sand to scrub his body. Looking back to the beach he saw Kasmira coming toward him. "Get those clothes off and really clean your body." She tossed him a cake of soap.

"Where did you get soap?"

"I travel a lot, and I keep soap nearby. Otherwise, I would stink just like you." She turned and walked back up the beach. It was not long until she had caught a fish just big enough to feed them.

When Jaul finished bathing, he put his ragged clothes back on and let the wind begin to dry both him and his clothing. Kasmira had built a fire, and the fish was well on its way to being cooked. After they finished the fish, fruit, and nuts, Kasmira looked at Jaul. He didn't stink anymore, but his body was full of lesions. His full beard and his hair were a tangled mess.

Jaul lay back in the sand to rest and said, "I didn't know that food could taste so good. Now, I need to know how you knew I was in that prison, how you got me out and who you really are."

Kasmira had once read an article on Joseph Goebbels, and he was quoted as saying that people would not believe a little lie, but they would believe a big lie. So, she decided she would tell a big lie. "I told you I was from Kaspar. When I left I traveled about. I supported myself by stealing or any way I could. I didn't stay in any one place very long for fear I might get caught. I was on the southern part of the peninsula when I overheard a rumor that you might be in a prison off the coast of Aquas Negras. My mother and father had been accused of killing your brother, so I decided to see if the rumor about you being alive might be true. I found out that King Lucas had died shortly after the war and that he might have put you in prison. I traveled to Aquas Negras and came across a guard of the prison. A little flirting and a lot of whiskey got me the information that a man of your description was in the prison. I also found out you were near death. I found a healer from whom I was able to purchase an elixir from that she told me would keep you alive. I was able to bribe the guard and hire four men to help get you out. We came to the prison in two different boats. The guard I bribed let them in and they brought you to my boat. I gave you the elixir, and you immediately started getting better. The old lady must have been a witch because by the time we got to this beach, you were much better."

"King Lucas had me put in this prison, and I was told that a bribe was paid, but not to let me go but to kill me. It was paid by the same Barak you mentioned killed my brother. Now tell me again, who are you?"

"I am the daughter of Davos and Ana. Davos and Ana are both dead because of Barak. I was exiled. Now you know everything." Kasmira could tell that Jaul believed everything she had told him.

"You seem to know everything. I was married; do you know what happened to my wife?"

"She is alive and lives west of Kaspar. She thinks you are dead."

Jaul wanted to ask more questions about Nyla. Kasmira put him off. "I know you want to know about your wife, but you can't expect me to know everything. You tell me about her."

"We met in Anemoi. We fell in love, got married, and we only got one night together. I think that it may have been the worst thing that could have happened to her. I think about her every day. She was going to be my queen. I wonder if she remarried. Does she have children? You know, I have been so caught up with my own problems, I have not even asked you your name."

"My name is Kasmira."

"What is your connection to all of this?"

"As I told you, Barak killed my mother and father. You know I said that Barak blamed the death of your brother on the doctor. I am on a mission of justice. We have friends coming to meet us. They will be here around noon. We will use that time to give you information about Kaspar."

Jaul got up and started to put sand on the fire, but Kasmira stopped him. "We need the fire. Let it burn. We will put wet seaweed on it after a while to mark where we are."

***

That morning, Raja informed Jon that Kasmira had gone to the coast. "She wants us to meet her there around noon. You and your men do not have to go, but I am leaving right away."

Jon didn't know what to think, "Why in the hell did Kasmira go to the coast?"

As the four men left Anemoi, Jon had even more questions. *Why are we taking two extra horses? How come she told Raja where she was going and not me? Why did Raja act like he did not know where she was the day before? Something is just not right.*

Just before noon they were in sight of the coast. When they rode out onto the beach, they could see smoke about a mile up. As they rode up to the source of the fire and smoke, they could see Kasmira and a man in rags. All the men stayed on their horses except for Raja. Walking up to the man in rags, his heart was pounding. When he saw that it was Jaul, the two men hugged each other, and both fell to their knees and wept. Jon did not get off his horse but only stared at Kasmira. *Who is this woman? She is no ordinary person.* Kasmira walked over next to Jon's horse. "Thanks for coming. Did you bring food and drink?"

They both smiled, and he said, "Is that all you got to say to me? I did bring food and drink."

"I am very glad to see you."

A few minutes later, after Raja and Jaul had regained their composure, they were seated around the small fire on the beach when Raja spoke to Kasmira. "Did you tell Jaul who you are?"

Kasmira looked at Jaul. He was waiting for her answer. "As I have told you, I am Kasmira. I am a spy. I can get in and out of most places. It is a gift."

Raja knew he had said too much. For some reason Kasmira did not want Jaul to know that she was his daughter. He would just wait and keep who she was a secret.

Jaul said, "I don't know how you got me out of the prison. It does not seem possible. But it seems like a good bribe will go a long way."

Kasmira had a big smile on her face. "Like I told you, I bribed the guards, and the men I hired helped to load you into the boat. They were glad to help."

Jaul was amused at Kasmira's story but knew she was not going to give him any more information. Then Jon spoke. "Jaul, I am surprised that other than being so ugly you seem to be in very good health."

"I don't understand this either. Two days ago, I was dying. The last thing I remember is hearing someone say, 'He won't make it through the week,' and now I wake up on a beach and feel fine."

Kasmira was getting uncomfortable with all the questions. "Let's get started back. I am looking forward to seeing what this old man looks like cleaned up."

Raja spoke up. "Wait, I brought some clean clothes for Jaul to wear. I don't think those clothes would make it back to Anemoi."

Lilly

Barak was not sure what to do next. He and Akeem were walking in the courtyard when Akeem said, "You know, if Shakir is onto us and he can get back before the council, they will restore his full power, and we will be put to death."

"The council may or may not restore his power. They would need a reason not to. What do you suggest?" Barak knew that there were members of the council who would not want Shakir to be the king if he held full power.

"I think we should convince him to give up the throne and make his son king. You could rule until the young boy comes of age. You and I both know that he has never really wanted to be king."

Barak was becoming aggravated with what to do about Shakir. "Why don't we just kill Shakir? We could blame it on river bandits. How many men did he take with him?"

"Not very many. This is a sign that he does not trust anyone. For some reason I believe he knows of our plans to have him killed at the outpost. He was acting strange when he got back." Akeem picked up a stone and tossed it into the water of a nearby fountain. "Here is what we need to do. We don't want to kill Shakir. I could go to Lilly and kidnap the boy and his mother. I know how much Shakir loves the young prince, and he also is very much in love with your daughter. They will not be harmed in any way. We can't just kill Shakir. I am sure he has told his wife about what happened and that you tried to have him killed. If we have him killed, she will know it was us and turn on us. I think this way she will not speak against us, and Shakir will resign and give you the power. Once you have the power, you can explain to your daughter if she wants to protect Shakir, she must keep everything a secret. This will work because Shakir has never wanted to be king and will be content to continue to let you run the government, and Jada's life will not change."

Barak thought for a moment and then said, "Good plan, good plan. When can you leave for Lilly?"

"I need about fifteen men we can trust."

"Don't get men like you sent to the outpost. We don't want them to run off with our gold."

"We really don't know if they did."

Akeem walked over to the fountain and took a seat, "We need to find out what happened there. Something is just not right that they would leave."

Barak walked over to the fountain and dipped his hand into the water. "I am not so sure they did. I am going to send a couple of men to the outpost, so we will know. This will take a couple of days. Meanwhile, I will have men waiting for you in the morning, and you should be on your way to Lilly. Do not go by boat, take horses. Just before you get there, exit the main road and come in the back way. We don't want to alarm Shakir. Once you have Jada and her son, take them to Miamba. I will give you a letter with the royal seal to explain that you represent the court. Do not let Jada have any contact with anybody in the castle. Keep her comfortable and isolated. Let her know that if she does not help us, Shakir will be killed, she will have to mourn several years at Miamba, and her son will be brought back here."

Akeem got up from his seat, walked a few steps away, and turned back to face Barak. "There is something else. I feel something has happened, and I am not sure what it is. I think it might be Jaul. We both know that Lucas did not kill Jaul. He kelp him alive and put him in prison. I feel he is still alive and is no longer at the island. Is there any possibility that he has escaped from Isla de la Muerte?"

Barak scoffed. "If he has escaped, he will be the first. No one has ever escaped from the Island of Death. Besides, he would have died many years ago. When did you start getting this feeling?"

"Just a couple of days ago, and it is getting stronger."

"Well, you are a warlock, and I pay you well for your power. I am worried. If Jaul has escaped, he would have had to have help. Someone would have had to have known he was there and bribed the prison master. But who? Let us assume that Jaul has escaped. What would he do? He would want to establish who he is and raise an army. The only place he could do this would be Miamba. There are about one hundred men there. This could be a problem. If we are going to take Jada there, we can't have Jaul there at the same time."

Akeem laid his hand on Barak's shoulder. "If Jaul has escaped and wants to go to Miamba, it will take several days. He has been in prison for many years and will be too weak to travel very far. Most likely he will make his way to Anemoi and rest and get stronger. It may be months before he can make his way to Miamba. To be safe, I will send eight men to Lilly and see if they can find him. If Jaul is going to Miamba, he will have to pass through Lilly. If we are lucky they can intercept him. This man is like a cat. How many lives can he have?"

Barak scoffed. "If Jaul has escaped from the prison and is recovering at Anemoi, he will not be at Lilly. Tell your men after they have Jada and the boy to look for Jaul, but if they can't find him go ahead with the plans to take Jada to Miamba."

Kidnapped

Shakir and Jada took up residence just outside of Lilly in the family's vacation house. It sat in front of a large blue lake. It was just off the road to Anemoi and Aquas Negras. It was good that it was private, but it was not very well protected and had just a small staff.

During the next couple of days things seemed to go well. Shakir and Jada loved the home. It was so quiet and clean. There was very little noise, and they almost forgot their troubles. They often said this would be a great place to raise their son, and maybe they should just let Barak continue to manage the country's affairs. Shakir really knew he could not let this happen. Barak wanted a war with Tranquillo. He had to be checked or many innocent lives were going to be lost on both sides. Shakir knew as long as he was alive Barak would not attack Tranquillo.

On the fifth day of their visit to Lilly, Shakir took a morning walk around the lake. He was so content watching the birds, and he could see goldfish swimming in the lake. He took a few pieces of bread out of the bag he was carrying and tossed them into the water. Several fish began to compete for the bread. Shakir watched for a few moments and then made his way back to the house. In the courtyard, he saw one of his guards lying on the pathway with his throat cut. Rushing inside, he found two more of his guards killed. Calling for his wife, he got no answer. Rushing up the stairs he met a servant crying. "They have taken them. They have taken them. They are both gone. They gave me this note to give to you."

Shakir took the note from the servant's trembling hand. *Your wife and son are not going to be harmed if you will cooperate. There is a large grove of trees up the road. The trees are not on the road, but you will see them. Meet us there in the morning, and we will discuss terms of how you can save your wife and child.*

Shakir did not know what to do. *Was this the work of Barak, or was it bandits? It must be bandits. Surely Barak would not harm his own daughter and grandson.* All he could do was wait.

Jaul and Kasmira

Raja and Jaul rode side by side and carried on conversation as they rode back to Anemoi. Kasmira was behind riding next to Jon. She had given Jaul his strength back, but she had not taken away his scars from the many years of torture while living inside Isla de la Muerte. Most of the sores on his body would heal on their own, and she was content to let that happen. She knew that this is what her mother would do.

Jon was thinking about Kasmira. *There is no way she could have gotten into the prison and got Jaul out in the short time she was gone. She would have had to have help, but this doesn't explain how quickly she did it.* Jon turned to the side on his horse to face Kasmira. "You are special, aren't you?"

"I would like to think so. I think you are special too."

"You know that is not what I mean. When we get back to Anemoi, we need to talk."

Kasmira gave Jon a sly grin. "We are talking now."

Jon straightened himself on his horse. *This girl is impossible.*

Kasmira slowed the gait of her horse, and when she did so, Jon did the same. *I need to send Jon away. He is suspecting that I have magic.* "When we get back to Anemoi, you and your two soldiers need to go back to Tranquillo. You are not needed anymore."

Jon felt somewhat hurt. "Joseph and Kira said I was to stay with you and give you protection. I will obey his orders until we get back to Tranquillo."

"I am not going back to Tranquillo. When I am sure that Jaul's sores and scars have healed, I am going with him to Kaspar. I know you know that he is king, and the fact that he has been in prison does not change that."

Jon still had the hurt look on his face. "What if I told you that I just enjoy your company and want to spend more time with you?"

Kasmira brought her horse to a stop and let the others ride ahead. Jon stayed with her. Looking at Jon she said, "I know what you want, and probably given time, I could fall in love with you. You have been wonderful to me. The truth is I don't have time. As soon as Jaul is reestablished as King of Kaspar, I am leaving, and I am not coming back. You staying with me is only making the leaving harder. But I am leaving. I am not going to tell you that you have to leave, but if you stay, things will start to become clearer. When we get back to Anemoi, I will tell you something that will help you understand."

Kasmira and Jon brought their horses up to a gallop and caught up with the rest of the group. When they arrived in Anemoi, they were greeted by Fadi. The two men hugged each other. Fadi was so happy and could not stop laughing with joy as he greeted Jaul. "I know you have been traveling all afternoon. It is time for the evening meal. Everyone, come inside, and we will eat."

Jaul gave a laugh. "Can that wait a few minutes? I doubt that anyone will enjoy eating looking at me in my condition. Can you give me some clean clothing and cloths to wash and dry myself? I remember there is a sort of private oasis nearby."

"Of course, I will get you something right now." Fadi was gone only a few minutes and returned with what Jaul needed.

As Jaul started walking away from the tent and toward the oasis, Kasmira yelled out. "Wait, I want to walk with you."

Jaul smiled. "I think I can find it, and I do want to bathe in private."

"Relax old man, I will give you your privacy, but I need to talk to you alone."

They decided to ride horses to the oasis, because the afternoon was hot, and Jaul wanted to stay fresh. When they got to the oasis, Kasmira took a seat behind some bushes and Jaul took off his clothes and began to bathe. "This water really feels good. It is not like salt water. You never feel clean bathing in salt water. You just relax. I may stay in here for a while. If you get tired of waiting, you can go on back to Fadi's tent."

Kasmira, who was close enough to hear, responded, "This is true, you don't feel clean taking a bath in the ocean. Back at the beach you asked me about Nyla. I want to give you some more information. I felt we needed to be alone for this."

Jaul was eager to hear about his wife. "You said she was still alive but thought I was dead. How do you know this?"

"I told you that my father was accused of killing Kadar. Afterwards, he was found guilty, and I was banished and left in the desert to die. I was lucky. I was left not far from where Nyla lives, and she found me and saved me. She lives at an oasis called Zanzura."

Jaul finished his bath and came to the bank and started drying himself. "I have heard of this place. Most say it does not exist."

"It does, and Nyla lives there alone. To my knowledge, she never leaves unless she needs supplies. During my stay with her, she told me about you, but she does not know you are alive."

Jaul finished dressing and sat down next to Kasmira. He looked much better. The birthmark on his forearm stood out. "I see you have a tattoo," she said to gain information.

He looked down at his forearm. "It is not a tattoo. It is a birthmark. It is foretold that this birthmark marks the one who will become the true leader of Kaspar. I have this mark, but my brother Kadar did not. I don't know if it is true or not, but my father had the mark."

Kasmira thought for a moment. "What if a person is born with this birthmark but does not want to be the king, or for that matter, queen?"

"I don't know. To my knowledge that has not happened, and there has been no female to ever bear the mark. Kaspar has had nothing but kings."

"Strange." Kasmira moved closer to Jaul and reached into her bag and pulled out scissors and a razor. "Let's really make you look better." She first took the scissors and cut his hair to a shorter length. She removed as much of the hairy growth from his face as she could. Making a lather, she removed the rest with the razor.

He rubbed his hands over his face. "This sure feels better. I wish I had a mirror. I have not seen what I look like for many years."

Kasmira moved to face Jaul. "Trust me. You no longer look like an old man. I believe that even I could fall in love with you," she said with a smile.

He knew she was only kidding with him, but it made him feel good.

"Thank you for everything that you have done for me. If we can get to Kaspar, and I can get my throne back, I am going to reward you greatly."

Kasmira said nothing as they mounted their horses. Looking at Jaul she thought, *when should I tell him that he is my father, and what should I do about Mother?*

Suddenly Jaul broke the silence; it was almost like he was reading her mind. "I need you to tell me how to find Nyla."

For a moment, she stopped her horse and Jaul did the same. "I told you where she was. She is at Zanzura. When this is over I will take you there."

"No. That is not good enough. What if something happens to you, or we get separated? I need to know how to find her. She is all I have left."

You have me. At first Kasmira said nothing. "You have a nephew and niece, Shakir and Shakira. They both have children." Kasmira looked at her father, and he seemed somewhat surprised. "Did you not think that Kadar would have children? They have done nothing wrong. At one time, I would have killed Shakir, but now I know he has done nothing wrong except show how weak he is. Shakir is the king of Kaspar, but he has let Barak take advantage of that."

"What about Shakira? Does she live at Kaspar Castle?"

"No. She was banished from Kaspar, and there was an attempt on her life like mine. She is safe, but right now I am not going to tell you where she is. I will give this information to you when you become king, and I know she will be safe."

Jaul did not know what to say. *How can this young lady know all this information?* "How do I get to Zanzura?"

"Take the trade route east. You will need lots of water. You will need enough for ten days. On the route east, you will come to a dried-up oasis. That is going to take at least five days. There you will head due north. You are well over two thirds there, but crossing the desert is going to be slow and hot. It will take you at least another three days to get there. You must travel slowly because of the heat. If I am not with you, take a small tent. Use it during the day to block the sun. Travel only at night, and rest during the heat of the day. If you miss Zanzura, you will die in the desert."

They had supper with Fadi, and all took a seat around a fire just outside Fadi's tent. As they sat around the fire, Jaul started to show the leader he was. He did not know of Kasmira's magic, so his plans did not include it.

"We are going to start tomorrow toward Lilly. There we will spend the night. It is a two-day trip to Miamba from there. Miamba is a castle in the mountain pass. It was built many years ago to protect our southern border and to protect the traders going to Lilly. It wasn't needed. There weren't any enemies using the southern route, and most traders did not want to come through the rocky pass. There should be a few fighting men stationed there and a small staff to maintain the castle. Here comes the tricky part. I must convince those men who I am, or we might find ourselves in a dungeon. If we can get a few men to join us, we might be able to come back to Lilly and get even more and then march on to Kaspar castle."

Kasmira watched as her father took charge and was so proud. She liked this plan. If it worked, her father could reestablish himself as king, and she would not have to use magic.

The next day as they started to Lilly, Shakir was meeting with Jada's kidnappers. He was told to do nothing but to go back to his quarters and wait for instructions. He was told that Jada and his son would not be harmed in any way if he would just do as he was told. As the kidnappers started to leave, Shakir pulled his sword. As he started to step forward, Akeem stepped out of the shadows.

"Don't do anything foolish. Barak has a plan. If you do anything to upset this plan, there is a backup plan. You and Jada will both be killed, and your son will become king, and Barak will continue to be the real power of Kaspar."

Shakir dropped his sword and fell to his knees. "Take care of them. I will do everything that you ask."

eyes and concentrated on little Kad. It was just a moment when she looked up at Raja and said, "Jada and Kad are at Miamba, and for the moment they are safe. Now we must kill some time. We can't make this look too easy."

They both leaned back against the trees. Raja, showing concern, said, "When are you going to tell Jaul who you are?"

"I don't think I am going to. He has a hard road ahead of him. He can't be thinking of me as his daughter and do his job." She paused and looked Raja in the face. "I don't think words can express how important you have been on this quest. Have you really been in Anemoi all these years? You were an important man in a great army. I can't believe you could really be happy living in a village?"

"My life seemed to come to an end with the death of your father and your mother. You coming to the village with the news that they are both alive brought me back to life. Besides, I have not been lonely. There is a woman who lives in the village, and she slips into my tent occasionally. Her husband was killed, and she has a daughter about your age. When this is over, I think I will take her as my wife. What about you? You said you are not staying. Where will you go? It is obvious to anyone with a brain that you have supernatural power. Are you going to hide yourself from the world, so you are not looked upon as a freak?"

Kasmira thought for a moment. "That is a good question. I am going to a land that is truly magical. It is a place that has machines that fly. Weapons that can kill thousands at once. Machines that allow people who are thousands of miles apart to talk to each other. It is a place where women are almost equal to men in opportunity. It is a place where I feel important because I speak seven different languages, and it is the place where the man I love lives. It is a place where my magic is not needed."

Raja tried not to look shocked, but he didn't believe a word. "Good luck on getting there, and I might want to go with you. Let's try to get some rest."

They had not intended to go to sleep but they were exhausted, and both did. When they awoke, they could tell it was late in the night. Raja looked at the moon. "It is past midnight. I am going to let you lie us out of this one."

When they got back to the camp, questions were coming from all directions. "Hold on," Kasmira said. "We got the information, and I only had to sleep with three men to get it. The princess and her son are being held at Miamba." All the men were standing with their mouths open, apart from Raja, who was about to break into a laugh.

Jon was the first to speak. "How did you get the information?"

"Don't worry about it. I got it, and I didn't kill anyone or break any laws, legal or moral. It seems that a drunk man will give a pretty woman information if he thinks he has a chance of getting her into bed. Jaul, have you come up with a plan to get us inside the castle?"

"I have been thinking about it, and it's my guess that Akeem has no more than twenty men with him. There may be as many as one hundred other men stationed there. I don't think that Akeem will stay at Miamba. He will leave Jada and her son there, and he will go back to Kaspar Castle. We will have to convince the men that are in Miamba to join us. No one is going to know who we are. Kaspar is not at war, so I suggest we go right up to the main gate and ask them to let us in. Who knows? This may work."

Raja knew what Jaul was thinking. "I believe it is worth taking a shot."

To Jon this was shocking. "I can't believe you believe that this will work. I am not going to commit suicide. They will let you in, but once you are inside they will question you, and if they don't like your answers, you will end up in a dungeon or worse."

"You are right Jon; Raja and I will enter the gate. We know that this is a gamble. The rest will stay out of sight, and if we fail, you can come up with a different plan."

Later that night Kasmira was awakened by Jon. "I want to help you, but Jaul is going to get us all killed."

"There is another way. If Jaul fails, I will use it. Just have some faith."

"You are one weird woman." He lay down beside her. "Go to sleep, and I will watch over you tonight."

She looked up and smiled. "You are one good man, and thank you." She closed her eyes and was soon asleep. Jon put his arm around her. *I have heard about women like you, but I was always led to believe that they were evil. You are a witch, but you are also a very good person, and I love you very much. I will keep any secret for you. You just have to trust me.*

When Kasmira awoke the next day, Jon was already gone. She could sense that he had held her close during the night. *He is a good man, and I must learn that I can trust him.*

As they sat around eating breakfast, Shakir looked worried. "I know that you are going to try to save Jada and my son. What am I to do? I want to go with you, but if they see me, I am afraid that they will kill Jada and my child."

Kasmira started to speak, but before she could Jaul spoke first. "Your wife and child are in no danger. They are a part of a plan that requires that they both stay alive. Give us a one-day head start and then go down to the river and catch a boat north. Keep your face covered. Don't let anyone know who you are until you get to Kaspar Castle. Then meet with the council and tell them you wish to resign, but don't. Tell them the only way you will resign is with your wife, the queen, by your side. This will force Barak to send for her. This should give us a month to save your wife and get some support from Miamba. I hope we are lucky. I would look at it this way. If this does not work, you will be killed and if Jada tries to protect you, she will be killed, and it is your life that is in the most danger. He needs your son alive, and he needs Jada to take care of him. She is safe until little Kad gets a little older."

Shakir lowered his head and looked at the floor. He knew what Jaul was saying was true.

Saying goodbye to Shakir, the small band left Lilly and headed to Miamba. It would take two days to make the trip. The latter part of the trip required that they go up in the mountains. As they went up in elevation, the air got cooler and cooler, almost colder than they could bear. Kasmira had not paid any attention to the pack horse that Jaul was pulling behind him. Then he stopped. "Everyone get off your horses and come here. If you have not been here before, you did not know how cold it can get. I have some warmer clothes on the pack animal. This will make the trip more bearable until you get used to the temperature. Then you will be fine."

Jaul was right. It wasn't long until they were getting used to the air and did not seem to need the extra clothing.

After a short ride, there it was: Miamba, a castle made of rocks and built into the side of a cliff. As they got closer, they saw that the bridge was down, but the gate was closed.

Jon rode his horse next to Jaul. "Are you sure this is what you want to do? I don't have a stake in this, but you are a good man, and I don't want to see you killed."

Jaul smiled at Jon. "Thank you for your concern. I don't see this as a gamble. They don't know who I am. At the very worst, I can gain us some important information. If I fail, we can turn over the spy work to Little Miss 'I am very good at spying' and let her do her magic. She got me out of the prison at Isla de la Muerte. That was impossible. We will see if she can do the impossible again if I fail. Trust me, I will be safe."

Jaul and Raja rode on ahead. As they approached the bridge, Raja said, "I agree with you, we are not taking a big chance here, but we are taking a chance. We are not going to know anybody inside this castle, and if you tried to tell them who you are, I think they would kill both of us. So, don't tell them for a while."

Still looking straight ahead, Jaul laughed. "You and Jon are like two worrisome old women. No, I don't think we have anything to fear. We are not at war; these soldiers do not know us. They will let us in, question us about the purpose of our visit, and that will be it. I am not going to tell them who we are unless I can sense we have someone who will believe us."

"It is your hope that there will be somebody who knows who you are? It has been twenty-five years. The odds are against us, my old friend."

Jaul looked at Raja and smiled. "I guess they are, but the odds were against us a long time ago. It is about time our luck changed."

Jaul was right. They crossed the bridge, and after just a slight inquiry the gate went up, and they were inside. To Jaul and Raja's surprise, the men were barely men at all. They were mostly young with the average age about twenty. *These men were not even born when I was captured. I don't think my plan is going to work.* "Who oversees this castle?" Jaul asked one of the young soldiers.

A tall man in his late forties stepped forward. "I am, and what do you want? The King of Kaspar never sends or comes here or checks on us, and now in less than a week two official visits from the castle. I assume you are from Kaspar?"

Jaul turned to see who was talking, and he immediately recognized his face. It was Faas, one of the men who had helped Raja bring Jaul to Anemoi. They were fighting side by side when Jaul had been captured. "Yes, I am from Kaspar, but the Kaspar of long ago. Right now, I am seeking an old friend to ask for help."

A glassy-eyed Faas said, "This can't be possible. I saw you pulled from your horse before I was knocked unconscious. Later I was told you were dead." The two men embraced.

Jaul whispered into Faas's ear, "Do not identify me yet. We need to talk in private. I have other friends waiting outside. Raja will fetch them while you and I talk."

Faas came to Raja and gave him a hug. "It is good to see you, my old friend. I was told you survived the war only to be killed later. Go get your companions and join us." Raja mounted his horse, rode out the gate, and motioned for Kasmira and the others to come inside.

Jaul and Faas went inside the great hall, and soon Jaul was telling him his incredible story. "You see Kaspar is in a mess." Just then the door opened and Kasmira, Raja, and Jon came in. Jaul introduced Jon and said, "This is Kasmira. She saved my life and is helping me reclaim the kingdom. If we can ever straighten this mess out, I am going to adopt her as my daughter." He gave Kasmira a big smile and winked at her.

Raja walked over to Kasmira and said just loud enough for her to hear, "You are going to be in line to be the queen of Kaspar. You can never leave now."

Kasmira did not smile but answered lowly, "I have that anyway without an adoption." She gave Raja a big smile.

Jaul saw that Kasmira and Raja were smiling. "You two know something I don't. I am not too old to have a daughter."

Jaul turned back to Faas. "This is where you can help. Shakir's wife has been taken prisoner, and she is being held here. How many guards were left here to watch her?"

Faas was surprised that Jaul knew about Jada and her son. "Eighteen, but only two are with her at a time, and the guard changes every four hours. We were told that her life was in danger and that she is being protected."

Jaul could see some distrust come into Faas's eyes. "I can sense that you fear we may be a threat to the queen. We can settle that quickly enough. We need to go talk to her."

Faas ordered five men to join him, and Jaul, Raja, Kasmira, and Jon were escorted to Jada's room. As they approached the two guards, Faas said, "Stand aside and open the door."

Both guards pulled their swords, and one said, "This is not allowed."

Faas motioned to his men to hold fast. He could tell the two young guards were scared. "Are you two willing to die right here and now? We are going to talk to the queen. You can stand aside, or we can step over your dead bodies, but we are going to talk to her."

The two guards put their swords away and stepped away from the door. Looking at his men, Faas said, "See that they stay here." The door was opened and Faas, Jaul, Jon, and Kasmira went inside. Jada was sitting on the edge of the bed holding her son. She had been crying. Jaul started to speak, but Faas stopped him. "My dear Queen, why are you here?"

Looking at Faas through teary eyes, he only appeared as a blur, to Jada. "I was kidnapped. I was kidnapped by my own father! I believe he has a plan to take over the entire kingdom. He is going to force Shakir to resign, and then I know he will have him killed. This is what you are a part of."

Faas didn't need to hear any more. He walked over to the door. "Arrest these two and get enough men to arrest the others. Put them in the dungeon." Coming back inside he approached Jada. "My dear Queen. I know you are telling me the truth, and at this point you and Shakir are in danger. We are here to help you." He turned to Jaul. "You can talk to her now."

Jaul walked over to the edge of the bed and kneeled in front of the young boy. Looking only at the boy he said, "Hello, my name is Jaul. I thought I had no family, and in just a short time I have found I have a nephew, a niece, and now I am greeting my great-nephew." He looked up at Jada. "I can't express how sorry I am for what has happened to you. I was once king of Kaspar, and I intend to be king again. When this happens, I want you to know that you are part of my family and will be treated as such."

Jada's eyes had cleared, and she looked at Jaul's kind face. "I have been told of you. They said you were killed in the great war. Everyone says you were a great king. How can you be here? How can this be true?"

"I was not killed in the great war. I was captured and have been in prison. My life has been stolen from me by your father. He knew I was in prison and paid to keep me there."

Jada's eyes again began to fill with tears. "I have learned so much in the past several days about him. I have just recently found out that he had two wonderful people put to death. I think your niece and her friend Kasmira were both killed. What is going to happen to my father?"

"Your father died a long time ago when he put his plans to take the kingdom in place. Right now, my concern is for Shakir. I must make sure he is safe."

"Thank you." She got up and gave Jaul a hug. "Who do you have with you?"

"This is Raja, my best friend and advisor. Jon is from Tranquillo. He is a friend of Kasmira, who saved my life and will soon become my adopted daughter."

When Jada saw Kasmira, she fell to her knees in front of her with her hands spread on the floor. Between sobs she said, "I am so sorry for what has happened. You have every right to kill me, but I beg that you do not for the sake of my son. I know what you have been robbed of. You lost your mother and father. I also know that had they not been killed, you might have been queen instead of me."

Jaul was watching all this and getting a better understanding of Kasmira. Her life had also been stolen. *Was he part of some revenge she was planning? Was he going to have to protect Jada from Kasmira?*

Kasmira kneeled, took Jada by the hands, and pulled her from the floor to a standing position. She gave Jada a hug. "I don't blame you for what your father has done. I am still alive and have had a good life. Shakira is married and a very happy woman, and like you has a child. I did not come here to kill you or Shakir. I did come here for justice, and that is not revenge. Your father and only your father has to answer for the crimes that he has committed, not you or Shakir or your son."

Jada released the hug. "What has happened to Shakir?"

Jon, who was watching all this thought: *Kasmira could have been queen of Kaspar, and yet she just said she has had a good life. Where has she been? Who is the person who she says she is going back to?*

Jaul was also watching Kasmira and Jada and had a better understanding of Kasmira as she spoke. "Shakir is well. He is on his way back to Kaspar Castle. He is a part of this plan. He will be okay. He knows that we have come here to save you from these men. He is becoming more like the man everyone thought he could be. We have found out that you and your son are the most important things in his life. Unlike your father, he is willing to give up his kingdom to save you."

Jon spoke for the first time. "My queen, I want you to know that had it not been for Kasmira, your husband would already be dead. She saved his life back at the Northern Outpost and located you when you were captured. She has a gift, and she is good. You will be safe with her."

224

Jada now knew Shakir's second reason for knowing she was not involved in this conspiracy.

Kasmira looked at Jon and gave him a smile. For the first time, David seemed far away.

The next morning Faas, called out all the troops to meet Jaul. They were told his story and that by right he was still king. When they were told that King Shakir was going to give up the throne, there was much rumbling among the men.

Jada stepped forward. "My name is Queen Jada. Some of you have been to Kaspar Castle and know me. I can assure you that King Shakir is going to give up his throne in favor of King Jaul. My father, Barak, is trying to take the throne. This will not be good for Kaspar. He has plans to try to take Tranquillo and destroy their trade. Standing next to me is Jon from Tranquillo. Tranquillo is not weak and has increased its military strength. If Kaspar tries to take Tranquillo, the losses will be a disaster on both sides."

After King Jaul had addressed the soldiers and told them he wanted only peace with Tranquillo, he now had an army of just over one hundred men. A young soldier came running up to Faas and said something. Faas turned quickly and came to Jaul. "About five soldiers have left Miamba, and I fear they are going to warn Barak."

Jaul at first said nothing and then calmly said, "We will just have to deal with it."

When they all went back inside and were sitting around a large round table trying to decide what to do next, Jaul spoke. "I figure that the men that left are about six hours or more ahead of us, and that is okay. Barak will have to know we are coming sometime, but what he does not know is which direction we are coming from. They can only name Barak to power if Shakir gives up the throne before we get there. If we can prove that Jada and Kad are safe, we still can pull this off. Even if the men get to Barak, what can they tell him? They can say that Faas discovered they were holding the queen and her child, and he freed her and arrested most of the men left to guard her. He will know that Faas saved the queen, and he will know that the queen will tell of his deceit. He will think that Faas will keep the queen here for safety. We must move quickly because when Shakir demands that Jada be present when he gives up the throne, all hell is going to break loose if she is not there. At that point, Barak is going to kill Shakir and make it look like some type of accident or blame it on someone else. Once Barak knows the queen is safe, he will do everything he can to keep that news from reaching the council. We don't know how many men support him on the council, and they too may be corrupt. We must get moving. Jon, you and Kasmira and five men take Jada and her son to Lilly and catch a boat to Kaspar Castle. Faas, Raja, and I will take about seventy-five men and head east following the mountains north until we hit the Northern Trade Route. We will ride hard, and we should be just outside Kaspar Castle in about five days. You and Jada should also reach the castle in about the same time. We will all start tomorrow morning."

Raja scratched his head. "There is a problem. If Barak figures we are coming and the direction, he is going to send his army to meet us. If we can't convince his army who you are, we are going to be destroyed."

Jaul nodded in agreement. "Let's hope he does not guess which direction we will be coming from."

For the rest of the day, Kasmira tried to relax. Something did not feel right, but she could not put her finger on it. That afternoon she sat on a bench inside the square courtyard of the castle and watched the water cascade down about eight layers of waterfalls. It was amazing that the castle had been built around the natural waterfalls of the mountain. The steady roar of the falling water almost put her to sleep. Suddenly she was thrust out of her peaceful moment by the sound of Jon's voice.

"If I were not already in love with you, I think I could fall in love with the image of you sitting here." He walked over to her and sat down beside her. She said nothing. "I know you have power and have used it to save Jaul, Shakir, and Jada. What I don't know, is why? You tell me you can't love me because there is someone else and you are leaving. You have told me that Barak killed your parents. This has to be more than justice. Let me help you take your revenge, and then come back with me to Tranquillo and be my wife. I will love you regardless of who or what you are."

Kasmira lowered her head and began to cry. Jon put his arm around her and held her close but said nothing. After several minutes, Kasmira stopped crying and looked up at Jon. Putting her hand to the back of his head she pulled him close and kissed him, a long and loving kiss. "I told you the longer you stayed with me the more difficult this was going to be for both of us. I am falling in love with you, but the thing you have never seemed to understand is that I don't want to stay here."

Jon returned her kiss. "If you don't want to stay here or in Tranquillo, I will go with you any place you want to live."

Kasmira stood up. "You don't understand and can't understand. When this is over I am going to explain things to you, and you still won't understand." She left him standing there and walked back into the castle. *I don't know what I can do to make him understand that I am not going to ever be with him, but I must try. From this point on I am going to give him no encouragement.*

***

Jada heard a knock on her door. She knew she was safe but opened the door only slightly to see who it was. Peeping through the crack, she saw a young woman about her age. She opened the door wider and said, "What do you want?"

"My name is Amal. Faas sent me here to tell you that you are leaving in the morning to go back to Kaspar Castle. I am also to help you with your child. Faas has asked me to accompany you to Kaspar Castle to help with the prince. Is that okay?"

Jada did not answer. She just looked at the young woman. She was tall, about five seven and had a wonderful figure, and her skin was perfectly smooth and tan. She asked, "Is this something that you want to do?"

"Yes, I am excited to go. I see it as a grand adventure."

"Are you not married? Wouldn't there be someone you would be leaving behind?"

"No. The opportunity has never presented itself."

"I can't understand why not. Most women your age would have been married long ago."

"I have met Kasmira. She is about my age, and she has never married. I guess there are some of us that must wait until the perfect man comes along. That is one reason I want to go to Kaspar. I want to improve my chances."

"Have you never been before?"

"I have not. Father keeps telling me that he is going to take me, but here I am."

"I would be glad to have your help on the way back to Kaspar. You do know that there could be some danger."

Back to Kaspar

That afternoon, Kasmira came into the great hall. Sitting next to the fireplace on the floor with his back against the wall was Jaul. "Could you not find a comfortable chair?"

"They did not provide a chair at Isla de la Muerte. This is the way I have rested for the past twenty some years. I will finally get used to the chairs again."

Kasmira walked over to Jaul and sat down beside him. She leaned up against him. He instantly put his arm around her. "You know, something does not seem right about what we are about to do. It bothers me, and I don't know why."

Kasmira turned her head toward him. "That is why I am here. It is not right. If we go to war to gain your kingdom, many innocent men are going to die. It does not matter if some support Barak or you, many are going to die. I think that there might be a better and different way."

Jaul gave her a tender squeeze. "Tell me."

"If we send the army north on the Eastern Trade Route and somehow let Barak know they are coming, he will send an army to meet them. When the two armies meet, ours will be vastly outnumbered, and we will back down and move back toward Miamba. Barak's army may or may not pursue. If they pursue, our army could move into the desert. We will make sure that our army has an ample supply of water. Barak's army will not expect a retreat into the desert and will not be able to pursue for the lack of water.

When our army leaves the castle, we will send word that you are coming to Kaspar to meet with the council. You and a small band of men will leave and travel the mountain trail. I understand it is rough, but passable. Jada and I will travel to Lilly to catch a boat north to Kaspar Castle."

Jaul smiled. "I think your trip is much easier than mine. What you are saying is that we just need to present our case to the council and charge Barak with treason. I know we can make a case for me being king, but can we make a case for treason against Barak and get justice for your parents? It is a good plan. It may put our lives in more danger, but it also saves a lot of lives if it works. I will meet with everyone else tonight and set things in motion."

Kasmira did not get up and was content to sit leaning up against her father. *How much I have missed. If I stayed in Kaspar, I could make up what I have lost. I want to get to know my father and mother, and I want to have a real family, but I don't want to be queen. I want to be Marie.*

As they sat there Jon came walking up and saw the two sitting together. He did not understand and at first didn't say anything. *What is going on? What is her connection to Jaul? Is she in love with this man? He is old enough to be her father. Does she have some plan to make herself queen?* He looked at them and walked away.

The next morning with all plans made, the three groups moved out. The army under Faas moved east, Kasmira, Jada, Jon and Amal along with six men moved west, and Jaul, Raja and five others moved north on the Old Mountain road.

Jada, Amal, and the young prince were traveling in a covered wagon, and Kasmira and Jon were riding horses. After about a half day Kasmira rode up to the back of the wagon and called for Jada. "I am going to ride ahead and might not be back until you reach Lilly. If I don't get back, I will meet you at the boat. Make sure you don't let anybody recognize you. Keep covered. I will be back when I can." She rode ahead to catch up with Jon. "I am leaving the caravan for a while. Please make sure the queen is safe. I will be back soon."

Normally Jon would have protested, but he did not. He was still angry about seeing her all wrapped up with Jaul. He just let her ride off, and as soon as she was gone, he regretted that he had let her go.

As soon as Kasmira let the caravan get out of sight, she used her power to disappear and was soon standing in the trading area of Kaspar. There she searched until she found the tent of Omar. When he was alone, she went inside and closed the flap, so they would not be disturbed. He looked at her, smiled and said, "Your face is covered, but I can see that you must be a good looking one and looking for a man."

Kasmira uncovered her face and he smiled even more.

"I see you don't recognize me."

"Have we met before? I don't think I would forget such a pretty face."

"You don't remember me but let me remind you about our meeting before. Many years ago, you dropped me off in the desert and gave me only a bag of water to make me die slowly. You can see I did not die at all."

Omar remembered the young girl and how he had been paid by Barak to leave her in the desert. He pulled his sword. "How is this possible? Why are you here?"

"It is possible, and since I did not die, I am here for justice."

Omar came forward and drew back his sword to strike Kasmira. Kasmira waved her hand, and in an instant the sword was no longer in his hand but hers. "How is this possible?" he asked, falling to his knees in front of her.

"I have the power to find and kill you or even worse. I don't plan to kill you, but I might. King Jaul is alive and coming back to Kaspar. He will have to go before the council. I want you to testify before that council that you were ordered by Barak to kill me. Do that, and you can live."

"If I do that, Barak will kill me and my family."

"If you do this you are right, Barak may kill you. Don't do this and it is sure you will die. You must choose between might be killed and will be killed. Besides, with your testimony Barak may lose all his power and may be put to death for treason. Be at the next council meeting. If you are not there, I will hunt you down and kill you, but it will be a slow death. I will take you into the Great Desert and leave you with only one bag of water." Kasmira walked over to Omar and placed the sword to his throat. "No, I don't think I will leave you with any water."

***

Soon Kasmira was inside Isla de la Muerte. The old prison warden had been there a long time. She could see that the prison had been taken back over, and the men were back in their cells. She hid in his office and waited until he was by himself. Coming out of hiding she bolted the door to his office. He looked up just in time to see all this happen. He reached for a knife, but Kasmira had used her magic, and he found he could not move his arms.

"Hello, I have come to check on prisoner number 01-23."

"You are too late. He died and was thrown into the swamp. Just after that we had a riot, and the guards who did this were killed." The warden tried to free his arms but found he could not. "Who are you and what do you want?"

"It does not matter who I am. I know that prisoner number 01-23 is not here, but that is not why I came. Do you know who he was?"

The warden did not answer, and suddenly not only was he unable to move his arms or get up from the chair, but he also found he was now in pain.

Kasmira walked over to the chair and sat on his table. "This is only the beginning of your pain if you don't answer my questions. The pain is going to end in your death. So, answer the question I just asked."

"It was Jaul. The king of Kaspar."

"If you knew he was the king of Kaspar, why did you keep him here? You know they would have paid a ransom for his return."

"He was offered for ransom, and it was refused. I was offered gold to keep him here. I was paid about ten years ago to kill him. I chose not to and let him live."

"Why didn't you kill him?"

"I thought that I might be able to blackmail my benefactor for even more money. It worked, and the last several years I have received gold from Kaspar."

Kasmira stood up, and when she did the pain in the warden's arms increased. "You say Kaspar, but who in Kaspar would do this? Was it Jaul's brother?"

"No. It was Barak. He has been the only one I have ever dealt with."

Kasmira lessened the pain in the warden's arms. "Can you prove this?"

"I can. I have all the correspondence still in my possession."

Kasmira separated herself by about twenty feet from the table so she would have time to react if the warden betrayed her. She released his arms. "Show me, and I will let you live a few days, or even weeks longer."

Rushing over to a large wooden box, he grabbed several rolls of paper and spread them on the table. "You can see that Barak has signed them, but some of them were brought to me by a man named Akeem."

Walking over to the scrolls, Kasmira picked them up and quickly disappeared.

***

She decided to spend the night at Anemoi. When she arrived, she quickly found Fadi and asked if she could spend the night. He was delighted to see her and asked if they could have supper together. He wanted to know about everyone, and she told him what she could. Later he showed her to a tent, and she went inside and lay down to get some sleep. *This is nice. I am away from Jon. I am not sure about how I feel about him. Surely, he doesn't think I am in love with Jaul. He sure has been acting funny since he saw us. How could he love me so much the way I have treated him? Am I giving him too much encouragement? Am I fooling myself? I do have feelings for him, and they are getting stronger every day. I must do something to set him free of this love he has for me.*

That night, Jon was sitting by a fire. He felt it was safe because they had met no one on the road, and they could quickly cover up who they were if they did meet someone. He was looking into the fire when he began to think about his wife. *What would my life be like if she had not died and my child had lived? Life sure makes some strange twists.* He started putting together what he knew about Kasmira. *She was raised in Kaspar Castle. She grew up with Shakir and Kira. Her parents were killed when she was only about fifteen. She was condemned to death by Barak. Somehow, she was saved. The next ten years are a blank. No idea where she was or why she chose to come back at this time. She has magical power. What has she bartered to get it? Is this all just her revenge? After ten years, she comes to see Kira, saves Shakir, gets Jaul out of a prison, saves Jada and her son. How are all these people connected?*

His peaceful gaze into the fire was broken when Amal emerged from the back of the covered wagon. Jon looked at her and for the first time noticed her beauty. "Can I join you for a while? Jada and the little prince are asleep, and I am restless. I am excited about going to the castle. Lilly is the furthest west I have been, and I have never been on a large boat."

He did not know why, but it was not long until he told of his life in Tranquillo, his wife, his loss of a child. He did not tell her of his love for Kasmira. "I have talked a lot about me, what about you? Why are you living at Miamba?"

"My father is stationed there."

Jon picked up a small piece of wood and threw it into the fire. "Just about everyone I have met at Miamba is young and not old enough to have a daughter your age. So Faas has to be your father."

She smiled. "You are smart, aren't you? My father has been stationed at Miamba for a long time. My mother died about seven years ago, and I thought we would leave, but we did not."

He looked at her and saw how striking she was. She had long black hair and smooth skin. Her eyes were as dark as her hair. "You are not married?"

"No. I was in love once, and I have always felt that no one could ever take his place. We were going to get married, but just a few days before the wedding he was killed in the mountains on a useless patrol. I just had no interest in any of the other men, or in most cases, boys, at the castle. I have seen the way you look at Kasmira. She has returned the love back to your heart, but has she given you her love?"

"You are right. I have fallen in love with her, but she does not love me enough to be with me. She has feelings for me, and I feel they are getting stronger, but she will not give in to them. I think she does not know what she wants. There is someone or something that is pulling her away from this land. She will not tell me anything."

Amal went over to the wagon and got a couple of blankets. "I am going to sleep by the fire tonight. Here's a blanket for you."

They spread the blankets on the ground just a few feet apart and soon were asleep.

***

Kasmira was sound asleep inside the tent when she awoke. Someone was coming toward the caravan. Jada and the young prince were in danger. Concentrating, she entered the dreams of Jon. *Wake up, strangers are coming. Wake up, strangers are coming.*

Jon was jolted from his sleep and quickly got to his feet. He shook Amal. "Return to the wagon, quickly."

He woke his men and had them hide on either side of the road. Soon seven men came riding up. They were not in uniform, and Jon suspected they might be bandits.

The first bandit hollered. "Hello, my friend. We saw your fire and thought we might want to share it with you."

Jon answered back. "I am not sure I invited you to share my fire. I think you should just move on."

The seven bandits came closer to the fire, and again the first bandit spoke. "Who are you traveling with, my friend?'

"You use that term 'friend' very loosely." Jon put his hand on his sword. He thought he might tell them something that would encourage them to move on. "I am with my wife and son and her sister. We are going to Lilly to meet my sister's husband. Please move on."

"But my friend, we want to share your fire, and your wife and her sister. Are they pretty or are they fat and ugly? No matter, we share anyway."

Jon pulled his sword, and when he did, six arrows came from the brush and darkness. Five of the seven bandits were on the ground dead, or soon to be dead. A half second later arrows cut down the remaining two bandits, and the soldiers emerged from the brush. "Good job men. Help me get these rogues away from the camp. Take all the gear off the horses and let them go."

After the camp had been cleared, Jon told the ladies it was safe to go back to sleep.

Amal came out of the wagon. "You have got to be fooling. How could we go back to sleep? How did you know they were coming?"

"I didn't know. We were warned. I am now going to post a guard. I should have done it before. I will take the first watch." As Jon walked toward the road he thought, *Now I am on the list that owes Kasmira their life, and I have let her so distract me that I am not doing my job. This comes to an end now.*

Kasmira could feel that the camp was safe. She was glad she chose to warn Jon and not return to the camp herself. She had used a lot of magic the last couple of days. She knew her mother was afraid to use too much magic, and the warning through a dream seemed the lesser of the two choices.

The next morning after breakfast, Jon and his companions started their trek toward Lilly. Not much was said about the attack. Jon was glad it was bandits and not soldiers from Kaspar. Jada and Amal stayed in the back of the wagon and were glad when they were out of the high country.

About midmorning, Amal moved to the front seat of the wagon to enjoy the view. The attack of the previous night had taken some of the excitement from the trip, but seeing the valley that led to Lilly helped it return. She enjoyed seeing Jon riding ahead. Overnight he had changed. He seemed more confident in himself and was more like a military leader than before. As she watched him slowly leading the caravan, she saw him stop. Looking ahead of him she saw Kasmira sitting on her horse waiting for the caravan to catch up. *Where had she been, and why would Jon trust her to go off unescorted into the night? This does not make sense.*

At noon, they stopped to rest and to eat. They prepared the meal on the back of the wagon and ate standing up. Jon motioned for Kasmira, and they walked away to stand under the branch of a large tree. "How successful have you been on your little journey?"

"Very, I have all we need to bring Barak down. One witness and several documents will do the trick. Now all we have to do is get everybody there before the council."

"Good, do you have any idea where Jaul is?"

"Yes, he is making good time, and if he continues at the same pace he will arrive at Kaspar just a little ahead of us. I don't know where Faas and the army are."

***

Over the last several days, bad news could not seem to stop coming to Barak. He had found out that Jaul had escaped from prison. Jada was nowhere to be found and might be coming back to Kaspar Castle. Now he had received word that an army was coming up the Eastern Trade Route. He sent for Akeem. When he arrived, he said, "You have some magical power. What do you think we can do? You know that if I go down we both go down."

Akeem thought for a minute. "Let's look at what we have going for us. Jaul was not able to rule the country. Yes, he was in prison, but everyone thought he was dead. As we know, there is no link to you and his being in prison. Kadar was declared king. This was legal because Jaul was unable to rule. We don't know where Jada is, and if we can keep her from getting here, we still can control Shakir. I would assume that Jaul is at the head of the army coming up the Eastern Trade Route. It can't be large. There were only about one hundred men stationed in the south that he could get to join him. An army of two hundred and fifty men could block him from getting here, and you could have everything in control. If Jaul is not at the council meeting, you can still convince Shakir to resign and name you as ruler until his son comes of age."

Barak thought for a moment. "If he or someone he is working with rescued Jada, they could be with him coming up the Eastern Trade Route. There are members on the council who don't want to make any changes." He looked at Akeem. "There are six members of the council who want our trade interest increased and will not want Shakir or Jaul as king. A vote could be six to six, and I control the deciding vote. We are okay."

***

Kasmira and Jon and their party reached Lilly that night but were unable to get passage north until the next day. They decided to let the soldiers ride north on the trail to Kaspar, and they would take the boat. The boat was somewhat large for a river boat and was overloaded. They found a place against the inner wall. The women all kept their faces covered, and it was lucky that the prince wanted to sleep most of the time. The first day of the trip seemed to take forever. As they approached the bridge at the old mountain trail crossing, the boat started slowing down and was soon brought to a halt. Word quickly spread throughout the boat that it was being searched for the queen because she might have been kidnapped by bandits.

Jada was scared. "What are we going to do? There is no way off this ship, and I am going to be discovered." She began to panic.

Kasmira was sharp with her. "Stop and stop now. We are not going to be caught. All you must do is listen to me and do exactly what I say, and you will be okay. Hand the baby to me. Jada, sit next to me. Jon, you and Amal sit next to each other away from us. Pretend you are husband and wife, and you just got married. They don't know you. When they come to this area of the boat, you two act like newlyweds."

Jada calmed down and everyone did as they were told. Soon soldiers came down to the lower deck questioning the travelers. When Jon noticed that the soldiers were coming his way, he took Amal in his arms and they began to kiss. One of the soldiers pointed toward Jon and Amal. Soon the soldiers were standing in front of Jon. "Why are you on this boat?"

"I am from Tranquillo. I came here to get married. Amal and I got married yesterday in Lilly, and I am taking her back to Tranquillo."

One of the guards looked at Amal. "You are one lucky man. I understand that there were others in your party."

"You mean the other women. They are not with us. They were here, but they must have moved." Jon looked toward the wall where they were sitting, and no one was there.

Amal was not thinking about Jada and Kasmira. She was thinking about the kiss. For a moment, it seemed so real.

Kasmira had moved Jada and her son beyond the wall, but she could hear the soldiers questioning Jon. Soon she could tell they were gone. She waited until no one was looking, and the next time Jon looked to where they had been seated they had returned. Jon said nothing. Soon the boat was moving toward Kaspar.

When they arrived at Kaspar they quickly left the boat. Kasmira concentrated and knew that Jaul and his group were hiding just outside the castle wall. "Jaul is waiting for us. Let's grab something to eat and keep moving." Kasmira pointed to a market just ahead.

As they walked beyond the market, Amal came up to Kasmira. "How can you do what you do? You calmly get us through every situation. Nothing seems to faze you. You even have the love of a wonderful man, and you just seem to let it pass you by. Are you not human?"

Kasmira looked at Amal and thought of David. *I do have the love of a wonderful man, and I am human.* "Once we are inside this castle a lot is going to come out. I assumed you came along to help Jada with her child. Just a thought. Are you here for the Queen or for Jon?"

Amal looked at Kasmira, and without a smile said, "Yes."

A few minutes later they met up with Jaul and his party. "Where are your men?" he asked.

Jon quickly answered. "We didn't need them, and they would have called attention to us on the boat. They rode by horse and may already be here. I told them to be at the council meeting."

"Our timing is good. The council meeting is this afternoon. It has been moved up. I think Barak thought we might get here and has moved up everything by a couple of days, so we would miss it. It is working in our favor." He turned to Kasmira. "Got any plan to get us inside the castle?"

"Yes, we are going to walk right through the front gate. The only person who could be recognized is Jada. They will be looking for a young woman with a young child. Jon and Amal will take the child and go through first. Jaul, Jada and I will be about twenty feet behind. There will be a slight disruption when they stop Amal and Jon, but they will soon see she is not the queen. They will not suspect a man and his two daughters."

Jon scoffed and was somewhat annoyed that Kasmira was talking to Jaul and not him. "You think this plan will work?"

Kasmira had sensed a change in Jon. "I do, unless you've got a better one."

Jon looked at Jaul. "I don't, but I hope you are right, because if you are wrong we are all going to be killed." He quickly pulled Kasmira aside. "Why don't you use some of your magic and get us safely inside?"

Kasmira was getting angry. "What in the hell is wrong with you?"

"You are taking too many chances. There are seven bandits' dead on the side of a mountain because you chose to ride off. You could have used your magic, and my men would not have had to kill those men."

Kasmira looked at Jon and said, "I could use my magic and turn you into a eunuch, and if you keep pushing me, I just might. I have been learning to use this magic on this trip, but I was taught by my mother to only use it if there were no other options. Yes, you are right. I could have come here, released Jaul from prison, killed Barak and left. There is more than that I want. I want to restore a family, a good family. We are going to do this my way, and if you don't like it get the hell away." She left him and walked over to Jaul. "I am not sure Jon is up to his role in our ruse to get into the castle. You might have to be a grandfather escorting your daughter and grandson into the castle."

Jon stopped Kasmira before she could say anything else. "I have reconsidered. I would love for Amal to be my wife, and I will escort her into this castle." Kasmira could still feel his anger.

Barak had given very little notice about the council meeting, and not many people were going to be present. This was both good and bad. If they could get past the guards, it would be easier to get inside the council meeting, but it might be harder to get past the sentries.

Barak was inside his room waiting for the meeting to start when Akeem came rushing in. Before he could speak, Barak called out. "Have you heard anything? Is there any sign of Jaul?"

"Our army stopped their army coming from the south. They were greatly outnumbered, and they fled into the desert. We could not pursue because we didn't have enough water to go very far into the hot sand. We don't know if Jaul was with them or not. I would guess not, and I think that the army coming from the south was just a decoy. Every road and every boat from Lilly has been blocked or searched. There is no sign of the queen or her child. I think we should be prepared because they both may be here. There something else of significance. I feel the presence of a witch on our grounds or maybe inside the castle. It is my feeling that Jaul has secured the help of a sorceress. This person is powerful, much more powerful than me. I have some power, but the power I feel is great. We cannot win against such power. If this witch gets Jaul into the council meeting, it is going to make it difficult. But we still have the law on our side, and we don't know if Jada is here or not."

Barak thought for a moment. "Can you hide yourself from this witch?"

"I don't think she can feel my presence. She will be distracted, and I think she will have no idea that a warlock is here."

"You mingle among the gallery. Find her and stay close. If things turn against us, kill her, and I will have my man send an arrow through Jaul's heart. I will then have this man arrested and killed on the spot and make it look like he acted on his own. We have a chance."

As Amal and Jon crossed the bridge leading into the great castle, they knew and trusted that Jaul, Jada, and Kasmira were not too far behind. Kasmira had been right. Once they were in the courtyard, Amal and Jon were stopped. They watched as Amal was forced to remove the cover over her face. They were able to walk right by, and soon they were making their way up to where the council was going to hold the meeting. At the top of the steps, Jada pointed to a room were Amal could take the young prince, and she continued to mingle with the crowd.

Inside the large room where the council meeting was taking place, the noise level was high. Suddenly it went quiet as the council members came into the room and took their seats on one side of the hall. Barak came in and took a seat to the right of the king's throne. There were a few whispers while the crowd waited for the king. After about a minute, the door opened from the back. Shakir came through the door, walked the full length of the room, and took his seat next to Barak.

Akeem was with the crowd waiting for the meeting to start. He could feel the presence of a powerful enchantress. As he walked, he looked for a person who could be the witch. He knew she was close. Then he saw her. He could tell she could not feel his presence. He stayed close and waited for Barak's signal.

Kasmira was watching Barak and waiting for the meeting to start. She had no idea that a warlock was standing not too far behind her. Her mind was focused on Barak, and what she had to do.

Barak moved over and whispered to Shakir. "Are you ready to resign your throne today?"

"I am. When the meeting is called to order, I am stepping down."

Jaul looked over at Jada, who still had her face covered, and gave her a wink. Barak stood up and was just about to call the meeting to order when Jada stepped out of the crowd. She uncovered her face and walked up and took her place next to her husband.

Barak almost choked and could hardly speak, but did manage to say, "The council is called to order. The first order of business is that King Shakir wants to address the council." Everything went quiet and Shakir stood up. "I have not been a very good king; I have turned most of my duties as king over to Barak. I have been more interested in minor duties, but one thing I have done a good job of is being a husband and father. I would like the council to know how much I have treasured their support. Today I am resigning my position as king."

There came a rumbling through the crowd. Barak suddenly felt he had won. Shakir raised his arms to quiet this rumbling. "I know that giving up a throne is a complicated process, but there are two reasons that I am doing this. I have already told you the first reason. I am not a very good king. The people of Kaspar deserve better. The second is that I really have never been king. I recently found out that King Jaul was alive and living in the prison on Isla de la Muerte." This time the chatter in the hall was extremely loud. The entire council stood up and raised their arms to gain control. The ranking member of the council spoke up over the rumbling which had gotten quieter but still loud. "King Shakir, how can this be? We all know King Jaul was killed over twenty-five years ago."

Again, Shakir raised his arms. He looked at Barak, who was trying to maintain his composure. "Many of these council members are old enough to remember King Jaul. Let me present him to you. King Jaul. You may address this council."

Jaul walked to the center of the floor and uncovered his face. Again, the crowd noise grew to a new level. While this was going on, Akeem who had located Kasmira and was standing just behind her with his hand on his knife waiting for a signal from Barak. Jaul walked up and faced Barak, then turned away to face the council. Many of the council members were talking among themselves saying, "This is King Jaul." Jaul walked down the full length of the council so all could see him, and then he walked up and faced Shakir. "I have come here for two reasons. The first is that I am here to reclaim my throne." Looking at Shakir he said, "Since you resigned, I don't think you have any objections. The second reason is that I want to charge Barak with treason." Again, the noise level in the meeting hall rose. When it was quiet, King Jaul continued. "Here are the charges I am placing against Barak. First, he conspired to murder my brother, King Kadar." The meeting hall was in a state of shock and now extremely quiet. "Second, I am charging Barak with blaming the murder of King Kadar on Davos and Ana who worked in this castle and were put to death for his crimes. Third, I am charging Barak with conspiring to kill Davos and Ana's daughter by leaving her in the desert to die. Fourth, I am charging Barak with an attempt to kill my niece, Shakira, by having her banished and then trying to have her kidnapped and killed. Fifth, I am charging Barak with an attempt to have King Shakir killed while trying to start a war with Tranquillo. Sixth, I charge Barak with kidnapping his own daughter and threatening to kill her if Shakir did not resign. These are the first six charges. There will be more coming."

Barak stood up and faced the council members. "Some of what Jaul, or whoever he is, has said is true. As for most of the charges, they are just the ranting of a mad man. There is no proof that I killed King Kadar, but there was evidence at the time that the crime was committed by Davos. It is true that I sent their daughter Kasmira away, but I did not plan her death. We don't know what happened to Shakira, and as far as planning a war and trying to kill Shakir, this is something he made up to cover how weak he has been as a king. I did have my daughter kidnapped to protect her."

Marco, head of the council, stood up. "Jaul, can you offer any proof of any of these charges?"

"I can." He turned to Kasmira. "This is Kasmira, daughter of Davos and Ana. She survived the desert and is here with her story and with proof of the other charges."

Kasmira stepped out of the crowd of onlookers. "With the council's permission, I will address each of the charges."

Marco nodded, and Kasmira continued. "Charges one and two. I can offer no proof that Barak committed these crimes, but there was no compelling evidence presented at the trial of Davos and Ana that they did either. Those two charges will be supported by proof of the other charges against Barak. On the third charge, Omar please come forward. Your name is Omar; do you know me?"

"Yes."

"How do you know me?"

"I left you in the desert to die. I gave you only enough water to make you suffer a longer death."

"Why did you do this?"

"I was paid by Barak. For some reason, he wanted you dead. I didn't want to do this, but if I didn't, he was going to kill me."

Barak scoffed. "How do we know this is true? You could have paid this man to support this charge against me."

Kasmira was looking at the council while Omar was giving his testimony, and she noticed some had no facial expressions at all, while others seemed to be in shock. "On the fourth charge, Jon, please step forward. Do you know what happened to Shakira?"

Jon stepped out of the crowd. "I do. She was banished to Tranquillo. When she arrived, there was an attempt of several men to kidnap her. Prince Joseph, who was on the boat coming from Kaspar, had his soldiers meet Shakira and saved her. She was placed in protective custody, and her name was changed to protect her. She has been in hiding ever since."

Kasmira walked over and stood beside Jon. "Did you find out from the kidnappers who was behind this?"

"We did. Most of the kidnappers were captured and persuaded to give us information. We were told that Barak of Kaspar had paid them to kidnap Shakira and kill her. We also found out that they intended to rape her before she was killed."

Barak again scoffed. "Tranquillo wants better trade agreements with us. I have not given in to their demands. Perhaps they think they will get a better agreement with Jaul, or whatever his name is."

One of the council members stood up. "I was on the council when Jaul was king. I want the records to show that this is King Jaul."

Kasmira again noticed that several of the council members again showed no facial expressions. *This is not good.*

"On the fifth charge, I offer this evidence." She reached in her small bag and pulled out some documents. "These documents show that the warden of Isla de La Muerte was being paid to keep King Jaul there, and that he later was being paid blackmail money from Akeem and Barak not to release him." Kasmira walked forward and placed the documents in the hands of the council. When she came back, she walked up to Jaul and whispered in his ear. "We have a problem. I can tell that several of the council members are on Barak's side. They will not change."

Jaul glanced over at the council. "Go ahead and continue. We will see where this goes."

"On the last charges, I will simply ask two questions to Shakir and Jada. Jada, did your father have you kidnapped and threaten to kill Shakir if you did not cooperate?"

"He didn't, but Akeem did, and he is Father's right-hand man."

Everyone looked around but did not see Akeem. He was still hiding in the crowd not too far from Kasmira.

"Shakir, how did you know that Barak planned to have you killed at the Northern Outpost?"

"I was saved by Prince Joseph and soldiers from Tranquillo. When the attackers were questioned, they told us that it was Barak who ordered the attack."

Kasmira turned toward the council. "I have presented evidence that four of the charges are true. If they are true, it stands to reason that the other two charges are true and show a pattern of Barak's plans to take the power to rule Kaspar."

Kasmira took her place beside Jaul to hear what the council was going to do. Marco stood up and began to speak. "These are strong charges, but these charges have all been countered by Barak. Barak has served our council, as well as Kaspar, well. I am sure he has had to take strong measures to protect us from our weak king. I am going to call for a vote from the council on each of the measures before us. First, do we accept the resignation of King Shakir as king of Kaspar?"

Ten of the twelve council members stood up. "Let the records show that the council has accepted the resignation by a vote of ten to two." The council members again took their seats. Barak has been charged with six counts of treason. How does the council stand on charge one?" Six members stood up signifying that they found Barak not guilty. On charge two, again six members stood and voted, and the count remained six to six.

Marco turned to Barak. "This is most unusual. The council is deadlocked, and our law says that you as chief regent get to break the tie." A heavy rumbling went through the gallery. Jaul whispered to Kasmira, "We are beat."

"Not yet." She addressed Marco as the noise stopped. "That is not what the law says. What it does say is that in matters addressing legal leadership of the kingdom, the council will have sole authority. It goes on to say that if the council cannot decide, members of the royal family will cast the final vote. We have enough members of the royal family here to decide if the council cannot. I suggest the council go into a private meeting and come to some consensus about the treason charge. The treason charge is a leadership issue."

One of the council members who was not standing said, "What the young woman says is true. The conspiracy charges do affect leadership. As a council, we must decide or let the family break the tie."

Barak was seated, watching the reaction of the gallery. It was now time to throw some confusion into the mix. He gave the signal to Akeem.

Kasmira was looking at Marco trying to get a read on what he was going to do. The crowd was shouting, mostly against Barak. Then she felt it. A knife being plunged deep into her back. There was great pain followed by a feeling that she was going to faint. She knew what had happened to her. Jaul saw Kasmira fall forward onto the floor with the knife in her back. He started toward her. Akeem could have escaped into the shouting crowd, but suddenly a large flash and the sound of a large clap of thunder came into the meeting hall. And there standing a few feet from Kasmira, was the Woman in Black. Her face was covered, but there was a fierce anger in her eyes. Jaul was stopped in his tracks. She pointed toward Akeem, and a lighting flash struck him down. She turned to the council, and the six standing council members were dropped down the same way.

She rushed to Kasmira, held her in her arms, and pulled the knife from her back. Jaul was now kneeling next to Kasmira, and the Woman in Black looked into his eyes and handed him the knife. "Kill that man." Jaul stood and without thinking threw the knife straight into Barak's heart. He turned back and looked down at Kasmira and the Woman in Black. He heard her say, "Kasmira, I need your magic. I need your help. I cannot do this alone." Kasmira opened her eyes and the two women disappeared, leaving a stunned and confused crowd.

Jaul quickly moved to the front and joined Shakir and Jada. After he got the crowd under control, he addressed the six remaining members of the council. "I am going to assume control of this kingdom until the council can be brought back to full strength. During this time, I am going to investigate the unlawful acts of Barak. There are many here who would have reason to want revenge against Barak and his men. This was not revenge, but it was justice. I would suggest that any person who has been supporting Barak leave before my justice catches up with you." He then saw Omar. He pointed to him. "Bring that man to me." Jon and two guards brought Omar and threw him down in front of Jaul.

Omar raised to his knees. "King Jaul, Kasmira promised me she would let me go if I gave testimony to help convict Barak. I have done this. She said she would let me go."

King Jaul stood up and placed his foot in the middle of Omar's chest and pushed him onto his back. "I made no such promise. Arrest him and place him in the dungeon until we can have a trial."

Jaul and the six remaining members of the council, along with Shakir, held a brief meeting. All the guard captains were brought in and informed that King Jaul would oversee Kaspar until order could be restored. Things seemed to go well.

The Search for Nyla

That night, King Jaul had a meeting with his family and friends. Looking toward the window, he felt a tear run down his face as he thought of Kasmira. Raising a glass of wine, he said, "I want to thank everyone who helped me. In just a few short days I was taken from a prison where I had less than a week to live to this moment where our future seems bright. I want to thank Shakir and Jada for their support at this time, Jon and his companions from Tranquillo, and all who had some part large or small who helped save Kaspar. My first act as king is to name my chief advisors. I want these men to be my nephew Shakir and my friend Raja. I would like Jon of Tranquillo to become an ambassador and help with relations between our two great kingdoms. I also want Jon to find Shakira and tell her I want her to come home. During the next week, I am going to leave and search for my wife. Kasmira told me she is still alive and how to find her. I am leaving in the morning, leaving Shakir and Raja in charge until I get back. Meanwhile, enjoy yourselves."

Jon watched as King Jaul walked over and sat down near a fireplace which had not been used for a long time. He walked up and sat down next to him. "I don't need to go back to Tranquillo to find Shakira. I know where she is."

Jaul shifted toward Jon. "Will you tell me?"

"I will if you will let me go with you to find your wife."

"I agree; it is a small price to pay for what you have done for me. Besides,

I may need your help getting there. I believe we are going to have to carry lots of water."

"I don't understand the water, but your niece is married and has a child. She changed her name and is now Kira. She is married to the son of the king and queen of Tranquillo. I don't think she will come home, but we are only a day away from going to see her."

"I see I owe you even more."

"Not really. It was Joseph who saved her from the men on the dock. He is a good man, and you would be proud of your niece."

"I am glad you want to help me find my wife, but I don't understand why you want to go."

"I was with Kasmira ever since we left Tranquillo to protect the Northern Outpost. She didn't tell me a lot, but I know that one of her goals was to reunite you and your wife. I fell in love with Kasmira, but I don't think that Kasmira and I were ever meant to be, and this will give me some closure."

Jaul gave Jon a smile. "Her name is Nyla, my wife, her name is Nyla." He stood up, extended his hand to Jon and pulled him to a standing position. "You are a good man. I hope things go well for you."

Jon got up and walked back over to Shakir.

Raja was watching Jaul. He could see the last several days had taken their toll. Jaul looked tired. *I should go over and let him know that Kasmira was really his daughter, but I am not going to. If she is dead, he does not need any more pain.*

Jada and Amal were standing near a large open widow which faced out over the sea. Jada handed her son over to Amal. "Take him back to our room. There is a nurse there. She will stay with him, and you can return here and spend more time visiting. I understand your father may be here at any time. You know, this is only half of a celebration for us. My father is dead, and a hated man. I have not talked to my mother. Shakir and I are going to do that now."

Jada, Shakir, and two soldiers walked to Barak's quarters. They opened the door and walked in to see Jada's mother crying. She looked up at Jada. "This is terrible; they have killed my husband."

Jada did not call her Mother. "Maren, did you know that Barak was such an evil man? Did you know he killed Davos and Ana, killed King

Kadar, tried to have Shakir killed, tried to kill both Shakira and Kasmira, and now has had Kasmira killed? Did you know all this?"

"He did all this for you. He wanted to make you queen."

"He did nothing for me. He did all this for himself." Jada turned to her husband and with tears rolling down her cheeks said, "Arrest her, she is guilty of conspiracy."

***

Amal returned to the gathering and noticed there were now more people than before. Jada and Shakir were not there. Faas, her father, had arrived from the east and was talking to King Jaul. As she walked around, she noticed Jon was no longer there. Asking for him, she was told he had gone to the garden, and she quickly followed and saw him next to one of the fountains. "Need some company?"

Looking up, he smiled and said, "I am not sure how good my company would be right now. Things sure have moved quickly this week. I thought Kasmira was going to fall in love with me, and in the end, she turned on me, and now she may be dead."

"I don't think she turned on you. I think she was just telling you to move on. I did not know Kasmira very well, but if she couldn't fall in love with you, there must have been someone else that she loved very much."

Jon shifted so he could face Amal. "At one time, I thought she might have feelings for Jaul, but now I know that this is foolish. We just don't know the entire story."

"I did not see what happened when she was attacked. My view was blocked by the crowd. Did you see what happened?"

"It was fast. Akeem came out of nowhere and stabbed her with his knife. Suddenly, a woman who was dressed in black came out of nowhere and killed Akeem and half the council, and I saw the woman take Kasmira in her arms and disappear. I don't know where she came from or why, but she helped us. She killed Akeem first and then six members of the council with some type of magic. She pulled the knife from Kasmira's back and gave it to King Jaul, and he threw it into Barak. Then it was all over. The Woman in Black and Kasmira were gone."

Jon put his arm around Amal and said, "At one time I thought that Kasmira was seeking revenge for the death of her mother and father and I could not see any way she could pull it off. She told me once that she was not seeking revenge but justice."

"Kasmira was a witch, and another witch came to her aid. What are you going to do now? I heard that you are going to be our new ambassador to Tranquillo. Is this correct?"

"Yes and no. I have agreed to this position, but Tranquillo will have to approve. I think they will. I do know people in high places there." Jon stood up. "In the next few days I will be with King Jaul, to help him locate his wife. He knows where she is, and I am going along for the ride. I have a feeling that going with Jaul and finding his wife will let all the pieces fall into place, and I can get some closure to all this. Let me walk you back to the castle. Do you have your own room?"

"I do. It is right next to Shakir and Jada's room. They want me close. I am glad you are going to be here at the castle." They started walking back inside. Amal took Jon by the hand and said, "When you get back, come and see me. I hope we can become good friends." *Maybe even more.*

***

The next day, Jaul, Jon, and ten others started south on the Eastern Trade Route. The first part of the trip was alongside the mountains with the desert to the east. It was easy to find water on this part of the route. Once they turned east, they stopped at the Southern Outpost. The outpost already had the news that Jaul was now king. They loaded up with water and moved on toward the Dry Oasis. The Dry Oasis would sometimes have water, and sometimes it would be dry. It was very hot, and the trip seemed to take forever. When they reached the Dry Oasis, luck was with them. It had an abundance of water for this time of year. They spent the afternoon filling their water bags and resting for the trip across the desert. With the sun low in the sky, Jaul met with his men. "Jon and I are going north into the desert. I want you to wait here. If we are not back in eight days, or if the water starts to dry up, leave and go back to the castle. Bury four bags of water next to the rock I am standing next to."

Jon walked over to Jaul. "Are you ready? I figure if Zanzura is halfway to the sea, we can be there in about a day and a half. If we can't find Zanzura then we are going to die. If your wife is not there but there is water, we might be best to continue north. We should be close to the Northern Outpost. We could get supplies there and head east back to the castle."

"Let's hope we find water. If we don't, we might be in a lot of trouble."

The two companions rode north into the desert. At times, the horses had trouble with the loose sand, but they had luck in that the moon was full and seeing was no problem. They were consuming more water than they expected, and they had not faced the daylight heat yet. They rode until midmorning when the heat became almost unbearable. They made a makeshift tent at the base of a sand dune and covered themselves and their horses the best they could. The heat of the day passed very slowly, and water consumption was great. Not only did they have to have water, but so did the horses. With the sun low in the sky, they continued north. Jon, who was just behind Jaul, called for him to wait until he was alongside. "How do you know we are going the right direction? If we are off just a little, we will miss Zanzura. If we don't find Zanzura, I feel we might find our graves. I hate to think of my bones bleaching in the desert sun."

"I am just guessing. I think we are going north, but for all I know we may be heading west or east. You had better hope I am a good guesser," he laughed. "There is a star in the lower part of the sky. It does not move, and it is due north. I just keep going straight at it. I could see it from my prison window, and I know it well."

Jon felt better. "If Zanzura is halfway across this desert we should get there sometime tomorrow. We could gamble and ride some during the heat in the morning."

Jaul agreed with Jon, and the next morning as the sun came up Jon said, "This may be a problem. Riding north now will really be a guess."

They rode a few miles further and Jaul stopped his horse. "This is really too much of a gamble. We need to stop for the day and hope we can adjust our course at night."

Jon stood up and stretched himself on his horse. "What do you think happened to Kasmira?"

Jaul patted his horse on the neck. "I really don't know. She was an enigma. I tried not to think too much about it, but there is no way she could do what all she did."

"You and I both know she had power, but I don't want to call her a witch."

Jaul scratched his head. "The Woman in Black who took her must have been a witch, and she took her away."

"Do you think she could still be alive? She kept telling me she was not coming back. There must be a place where people who have her power live."

Jaul got down from his horse. "Kasmira was going to be my adopted daughter. I really have no idea what happened to her. We all owe her so much, and I can only hope she still lives. I could care less if she is a witch."

"Do you feel it, and can you smell it? The air seems a little cooler, and I smell fruit."

The two rode to the top of the next sand dune and looked down into a valley. They could see a small lake surrounded by trees and grass. When they got to the lake, they got off their horses and fell into the water, drank their fill, and washed off the dirty sand from the trip. Jaul walked over to the large rocks where the water seemed to bubble up from, kneeled, and looked into the water. "Jon, there seems to be a cave entrance under the water line. The water is very cold here. This must be the underground source of the water."

Jon was already picking some fruit. "If your wife is here, I am going to greet her on a full stomach."

As Jaul walked back toward Jon, he suddenly felt that someone was behind him. Instantly, he put his hand on his sword as he turned. There she was. Dressed in blue, her head was uncovered with her dark hair blowing in the warm breeze. He just stared and said nothing, looking at her until she almost disappeared in his tears. Wiping his eyes, he ran to her and took her in his arms. "I have no words to tell you how I feel at this very moment."

After a long hug and several kisses, she said, "You seem taller and more handsome than I remember."

"You are just as lovely as I remember. There is so much I have to tell you. First, I am again king of Kaspar. That makes you a queen. How long have you lived here?"

"More than twenty-five years."

"How is that even possible? Living here by yourself." As they continued to talk they walked back to where Jon was eating. "Jon, this is my wife, Nyla."

Jon motioned for her to sit. "You were easier to find than I thought."

The three sat and talked for what seemed like a long time. Then Jaul said, "Nyla, it seems strange that we have been talking for a long time, and you have not asked how we found you here."

"I know how you found me. Kasmira told you how to get here."

Both Jon and Jaul were surprised by her answer, and Jaul said, "You know Kasmira."

"I do." Looking at Jaul she said, "You asked me how I could live here so long. I don't live alone. There is another here. She is only referred to as the Woman in Black. She is able to come and go at will. We have all we need, and while I thought you were dead, I had no desire to leave this oasis. I know the next question you will ask me. Is Kasmira here, and is she alive? She is here, and she is alive. The Woman in Black found her and brought her to me. As you know, I am a healer."

Jaul stood up. "Where is she? I owe her more than I can ever pay. She saved me from the prison; she helped me regain my throne. She has magic. Is she the daughter of the Woman in Black?"

"She is."

"Where is she? Is she going to be okay? I must see her."

"If you want to see her, you will have to get wet. She is in the cave, and the only way in is underwater."

Both men followed Nyla to the large rocks which hung over the underwater cave entrance. "The opening is just below the waterline. It is only a few feet until you are inside the cave."

Jaul jumped into the water and looked up at Nyla. "Are you coming?"

"Not just yet. You go ahead."

Jon joined Jaul in the water. The two plunged down into the water and were soon inside the cave. As they emerged from the water, they were amazed how much light was reflected from the white sandy bottom of the lake into the cave. It was a neon blue in color, but you could see everything clearly. They climbed the rock, and at the top they saw Kasmira lying in a large bed facedown. She was naked but covered with a sheet from her waist down. Jaul walked over and looked at her bare back. The knife wound was not dressed but was healing. It was about two inches wide and surrounded by a deep red.

Jaul, looking at the wound, said, "Her wound has some infection, but she is healing? I wonder how deep her wound is?"

Jon, who was also looking at the wound, said, "I don't know. I would guess several inches. I would say that the Woman in Black saved her life. There are no healers that could save a person from a wound like that."

"I know of one, and I think that is the reason she is here. Nyla is a wonderful healer and saved me from a wound much deeper than this one."

Jaul reached over and touched the skin and with his finger traced from the wound upward. There he saw it, and it dropped him to his knees. There on Kasmira's shoulder was the birthmark. The moon and the star. He now knew Kasmira was his daughter. He sobbed openly. Jon put his hand on Jaul's shoulder not knowing what was happening. Jaul could not regain control and continued to cry for a few moments. Then he said. "Kasmira is my daughter. I never knew."

Jon was confused. "I just heard Nyla say outside that Kasmira was the daughter of the Woman in Black. That would explain her power. How can she be your daughter?"

Turning toward Jon, Jaul showed his birthmark and pointed to the birthmark on Kasmira's back. "There is no Woman in Black. There is only Nyla." As Jaul turned back to his daughter, standing across the bed from him was Nyla.

"Now you know. I am more than a healer. I am a witch. I have power, power I don't like to use."

"You used that power to save me back in Anemoi. It was the only way I could be saved."

Nyla brushed Kasmira's hair away from her face with her hand. "I am doing the same thing with Kasmira that I did with you. I have saved her from dying, but now I am letting the wound heal naturally."

Jaul touched Kasmira's hair and let his hand take Nyla's. "Is she in a coma?"

"No. I gave her something to make her sleep. She will sleep for a couple of hours and then you can talk to her. In a few minutes, I will cover her wound and make her presentable."

"You know that I was going to adopt her and put her in line to be the next ruler of Kaspar, but now I won't have to."

Nyla walked around the bed and put her arms around Jaul and lay her head on his chest. "You can talk to her, but I don't think Kasmira will stay in Kaspar. When she is healed, she will leave, and I am not sure if she will ever come back."

Jon, who had been watching all this, scoffed. "She can't go anywhere. She is a princess. What reason could she have to leave that would be greater than becoming queen? I know that King Jaul is going to do great things, and she can, no, she will, continue them."

Nyla pulled the sheet up to completely cover Kasmira's back. "When I took her from the desert, she was just a child. The two people she knew as parents had just been killed, and she had been left in the desert to die. I knew she had power, and if she stayed with me, she would have developed that power and used it for revenge. There is no telling how many people she might have killed. I didn't give her a choice. I knew there was a portal that would take her to another world, and I took a chance that that world would make her a better person. After a while and when I felt she was ready, I brought her back to this world. She came back, but her heart did not. Someone is pulling her back to that world. She will go."

Jon did not say anything because he already knew that he had lost her, and there was no way that Kasmira would ever return his love. He turned to Nyla and Jaul. "I am going back outside. You two stay. I am going to spend the night under the big trees. I will see you tomorrow?"

Jaul hugged his wife. "It does not seem fair. I am finding out that I have a daughter and losing that daughter the same day. When will she be ready to leave?"

"She is about two weeks away if she chooses to let her wound heal on its own. She has the power to heal herself, and if she does, she will be gone quickly. Since we got back, we have talked. She knows how I feel about magic. I don't use it unless I must. I think good things come from going slowly. If I had healed you quickly, you would see me as just a witch. We would never have fallen in love. What is going to happen now? I mean with us."

"I am going to spend every minute I can with my family. I am not going back until Kasmira leaves or changes her mind and stays with us. Either way, we will go back to the castle, and you will be my queen. I will never mention that you have magic, and I will never ask you to use it. I think there are people you will want to see. Raja is now one of my advisors. My nephew, Shakir, is going to help me rule the kingdom. His wife is the daughter of Barak, and they have a little boy." Suddenly Jaul stopped talking. "Am I telling you anything you don't already know?"

"No," she smiled. "Kasmira has told me a lot, and I can feel other things. I guess some of my magic is always working. I can't control that."

Kasmira was in a shallow sleep. She began to think of David, and she located him and entered into his dream. In the dream, she walked to the edge of his bed and let her blanket fall to the floor. Raising the bed covering, she slipped into his bed. He took her into his arms and said, "Where have you been? I have missed you so much." He kissed her on the lips. It was a deep, passionate kiss. Holding her tight he said again, "Where have you been?"

"I have been home. I have saved my mother and father, and I am now ready to join you. If you can get to France in the next couple of days, do so. Stop and get Luce and Oliver, and come to the cabin. I will be there very soon."

David continued to kiss Marie, and they made love. He could feel her softness and the wonderful scent of her body. It was a deep love and full of passion. It was like they blended into one person. Their love lasted the night, and when he awoke, he was alone, but he could still smell her sweet scent. This wasn't a dream, this was real. He reached for the phone next to his bed. In a few moments he was talking to the airlines. "I want a ticket to Paris, France, and I want the next available flight."

***

About supper time Kasmira began to stir, and in a few moments, she opened her eyes to see Jaul. She felt good. "Hello, Father. What took you so long to get here?"

"You didn't tell me how hot that sand was in this area of the desert. How are you feeling? Why did you not tell me that you were my daughter?"

"I didn't want to burden you until our mission was complete. Now I don't want the pressure of being your daughter. You are king, and I don't ever want to be queen."

Jaul placed his fingers on Kasmira's lips. "We will discuss that when you are well."

"I am hungry. Where is Mother?"

Nyla had dressed Kasmira knowing that when she woke, she would want to sit up and talk to her father and Jon.

"Jon is with me. You know, the only reason he has helped us, is that he is in love with you."

"Are you trying to put me on some sort of guilt trip?" She paused for a moment. "I guess in a way I love him too. I am glad he came. I treated him very badly the day we slipped into the castle. I need to set the record straight. The problem is that I am too weak to get outside to see him."

She really wasn't weak at all. She just needed time to formulate what she was going to say to Jon. "I am glad he came with you, but I feel his love for me is passed, and he is ready to move on. He really is a good man."

Jaul looked at his daughter and gave her a wink. "Nyla says you have the power to heal yourself. If you want to heal yourself, I won't tell."

Kasmira gave her father a smile. "Who says I have not healed myself already? When I heal myself, she will know. The problem here is that she is a mother first and a witch second. I would rather face the witch than the mother. I am feeling much better. I assume everything is alright back at the castle. Has justice been served?"

"Justice has been served. Barak is dead, Akeem is dead, the corrupt council members are dead, and Barak's wife Maren is in prison. The new government is just about set and ready to function."

"Do me a favor when you get back to the castle. Pardon Jada's mother. I think that she is a victim of Barak, and he brought her down this road. Can you do this?"

"I can, and I understand."

"Where is Mother? You know, it feels so strange calling her Mother and you Father. I like it, but it is so strange. In a way, I have been lucky. Most people only have one mother and father. I have had three mothers and three fathers. Davos and Ana were great parents. When I leave, I am going to a place where there are two other people I call Mother and Father, and now I have you and Nyla."

Jaul leaned over and kissed her on the forehead. "I like calling you daughter, and I don't mind sharing you with the other people who have been important in your life. When you feel better, I want you to tell me all about your other parents."

"We have all been so unlucky. You and Nyla, I mean Mother, have lost so many years. You spent all that time in prison. Mother has been in a prison of her own here. I have had some good things in my life. Davos and Ana were like real parents to me. Has mother told you about the other world?"

"She has."

"In that world, I have two people who are like real parents. His name is Oliver, and she is Luce. They are wonderful. They had lost their daughter in a war, and they let me take her place. Now I come back here, and I have you and Mother. Where is Mother?"

"She went outside. For a woman who does not like to use her magic, she sure comes and goes a lot through that cave wall." They both laughed.

About that time, Nyla came through the wall. Jaul looked at her and saw she was carrying several things. "What do you have?"

"I have been to the market. I have wine, meat, bread and a few other things to make tonight's meal special. I think we shall eat next to the lake tonight."

That night, the meal was prepared by Nyla outside. Once she went back inside, she and Jaul took Kasmira by the arm, and they walked through the wall. Soon all were seated around the blanket and eating the food and drinking the wine. When the meal was over, Jon said to Kasmira, "How are you feeling?"

"Much better now that I am outside. Jon, I want to thank you for all you have done for Father and me. I know that I was short with you back at the castle, and I want you to know why, and I want Mother and Father to know. You are a wonderful man. I have fought with every ounce of my strength not to fall in love with you." She looked at her mother and father and then back to Jon. "The Kasmira that you love is no longer here, she is gone. I became angry with you at the castle because I was scared, and you made me doubt myself. You were right to question what we were doing. You have been such a great friend, and this venture would not have been the same without you. Your future is here; mine is not. I am sorry that I led you on."

"You did not lead me on. I led myself on. You have been nothing but honest with me. I am going to be okay. Thank you for letting me be a part of your life, if only for a short while."

Kasmira looked back to her mother and father. "I am not sure what the future holds for me. I just know it is not here. Just know that I love you very much, and if I can come back to see you in the future I will."

Jaul and Nyla looked somewhat confused. Nyla, with a trembling voice, said, "Kasmira, you are scaring us."

Standing up, Kasmira said, "My name is Marie." She looked at her mother and said, "I am sorry, Mother, I healed myself." She smiled at her father and then Jon and disappeared.